ACES ARE HIGH—
BUT MURDER IS A WILD CARD

SIDNEY KENYON—This ambitious and unorthodox cop knew it wasn't a square deal when Scotland Yard pulled him off the case.

TONY VALLENTA—He was the most powerful mobster in London, controlling gambling, prostitution, and extortion. He often talked about retiring—but crime isn't like most professions. You can't just quit.

LEN MALORY—He was Kenyon's partner, until Kenyon was suspended. A straight, by-the-book cop, he was more interested in pleasing his superiors than in solving crime.

ANGELA CURZON—When she married a dangerous underworld figure, she gave up her position as London's most exclusive call girl . . . but some habits die hard.

THE LONDON DEAL

n.j. crisp

AVON
PUBLISHERS OF BARD, CAMELOT AND DISCUS BOOKS

AVON BOOKS
A division of
The Hearst Corporation
959 Eighth Avenue
New York, New York 10019

Copyright © 1978 by N. J. Crisp
Published by arrangement with St. Martin's Press, Inc.
Library of Congress Catalog Card Number: 78-3987
ISBN: 0-380-50740-4

First Avon Printing, January, 1981

AVON TRADEMARK REG. U.S. PAT. OFF. AND IN
OTHER COUNTRIES, MARCA REGISTRADA,
HECHO EN U.S.A.

Printed in the U.S.A.

THE LONDON DEAL

CHAPTER ONE

To get to the men's lavatory, you went through the Public Bar, across a small yard, and pushed open a grubby, green wooden door which bore the legend GENTS.

Detective Inspector Sidney Kenyon thought it was odds on that precious few "gentlemen" were in the habit of passing through those peeling portals. Inside, the stink in the urinal was only excelled by the smell of something else in the WC.

"Don't the bloody Health people ever stick their noses into this hole?" Kenyon inquired rhetorically.

One of the men there grimaced, but otherwise the little group silently carried on with their various jobs. Kenyon coughed, and lit a cigarette, hoping to achieve some small degree of personal fumigation. The only individual who was completely unaffected by the stench was the one lying in the WC, who was limp and still, and whose head was jammed into the filthy, overflowing bowl.

"Hullo, Arthur," Kenyon said, nodding at the man from Forensic. He studied the dead body, and noted the rosy tinge of the water in which the head was immersed.

"Cause of death might be of academic interest, in due course," he said.

"Could de drowning," Arthur said. "Too early to be certain yet. We'll let you know."

"Someone altered his face first though," Kenyon said. "Hammered it against the wall, by the look of it." He pointed his cigarette at the aging, dirty whitewash above the urinal, where congealing blood was beginning to seal some of the flakes into place.

"Could be," Arthur agreed.

"Must have got a bit carried away," Kenyon said. "I think I'll see how Len's getting on." One day, he thought, perhaps he might come across a body in circumstances where death had arrived with some degree of dignity, but so far he had only seen that in films. Even his mother, who had died of a stroke in a hospital bed when he was twenty-one years old, had altered when the moment came. Until they tidied her up, her gaping mouth and blindly staring eyes had given her features a cold, awful cast which bore no resemblance to the warmhearted, kindly face he had taken for granted, and which now only existed in fading photographs.

He went back into the pub, and leaned on the bar. The landlord, whose name was Denver, was gulping down a whisky. He seemed to need it rather badly.

"I wouldn't mind one of those," Kenyon said. He fumbled for some change.

"On the house, Inspector," the landlord said. He was justifiably drawn and nervous. Drunks he was accustomed to, violent death he was not.

Kenyon sipped his scotch and listened as Detective Sergeant Len Malory asked his questions in a quiet voice. He studied the uneasy group of men, as withdrawn and apprehensive as though they were in some fiendish dentist's waiting room. They were failing to provide any satisfactory answers.

The pub was in a seedy side street, just north of the elevated motorway, and not far from a decaying, disused branch of the Regents Canal. The customers were the kind of morning drinkers Kenyon would have expected to find in such a place, layabouts, scroungers, a couple of out of work Paddys, and three who had passed through Kenyon's hands at some time or another; a small time ponce, a pickpocket, and a half-witted youth whose idea of supporting his favorite football team was to throw opposing fans through shop windows. But there were also a few ordinary citizens such as factory shift workers and London Transport staff, local men from neighboring streets, who regularly called in for their morning refreshment before starting work. Kenyon wondered if Doctor Gallup had ever come across one hundred per cent "don't knows."

A few yards away, a man had been beaten up, had his face smashed against a wall, and finally, it seemed, been forcibly held face down in a blocked-up lavatory basin.

It seemed doubtful if all this had happened in a few moments, or in dead silence, and yet no one had heard anything, or noticed who might have joined the dead man in the lavatory some minutes before he finally expired. Bloody marvelous, Kenyon thought. He tapped his empty glass delicately on the bar. The landlord took the hint and refilled it.

"You seem to be running a pub for the blind and deaf," Kenyon remarked. The landlord chose to treat this as a jest, and offered a shaky smile, but no opinion, one way or the other.

"But you can't be afflicted, Mr. Denver," Kenyon said softly. "Or you wouldn't be able to run a pub, would you?"

"They had the juke box playing," the landlord explained. "And I'm single-handed in the mornings, so I was a bit busy."

"Yes. Sure," Kenyon said.

He took his glass to a table, sat down, lit another cigarette, and waited. Mr. Denver was straight, at least as far as he knew. It was just possible that the cacophony of the Top Ten might have out-yelled the screams the man out there would have uttered. But once the body had been discovered, by the bespectacled commercial traveler with the overfull bladder who had come in, ordered a lager, gone straight out for a pee, and stumbled back in, horrified and shaking (which he still was as he explained all this again to Malory), why could no one remember who else might have visited the lavatory in the preceding half an hour or so?

Kenyon drew on his cigarette, contemplated in his mind's eye the dead, swollen face, the blood-stained water, the flashy, tight-fitting Italian suit, once the victim's pride and joy, now torn and stained, and thought of the possibilities. Was there anything which might induce a common bond between the petty villains and the honest citizens who used this pub as their local?

Eventually, Detective Sergeant Malory finished his patient questioning, walked across the bar, and sat beside Kenyon.

"I reckon we could let this lot go," he said.

"No likely witnesses?" Kenyon asked, making sure, knowing the answer.

"They might remember once we've got something to prod their memories with," Malory said. "But for the time being, collective amnesia's set in."

"No one you fancy as a suspect? None of them good for it?" Malory shook his head. "No," he said definitely.

"OK," Kenyon said. "But let's have a quiet chat with the landlord."

Malory might not be Kenyon's ideal copper in some respects, but he was a methodical and able detective, and Kenyon, who subscribed to the axiom that there was no point in keeping a dog and barking yourself, was prepared to rely on his judgment. Moreover, it would have been surprising if whoever had murdered the man out there in the lavatory had then chosen to linger over a glass of beer until the police arrived. Not impossible, of course, if he needed the attention of men in white coats. Kenyon eyed the half-witted youth as he turned to go, but the dead man was no football fan, as far as Kenyon knew.

The landlord crossed unhappily to the table, and sat down. Malory followed, having first selected a full bottle of whisky, and three glasses.

"A good idea," Kenyon said. "But no more Freeman's. We've got nothing to celebrate and nor have you, Mr. Denver." The landlord blinked unhappily. "Off-license price suit you?" Kenyon asked.

"No, no," the landlord said. "Nothing, really. My pleasure."

"You can stick it on *your* expenses," Kenyon told Malory, who sighed and carefully counted out notes from his wallet.

"You see," Kenyon said to the landlord, carefully filling the three glasses, "I don't like it when someone gets knocked off like this, and no bugger knows anything. Especially when one of them is a publican who needs to keep his good character along with his license. I'm not happy, Mr. Denver."

"Well, I'm not delirious about it either," the landlord said, trying to be defiant.

"Cheers," Kenyon said.

"Down the hatch," Malory said.

The landlord swallowed a mouthful of whisky, and said nothing.

"Do you know the identity of the dead man?" Kenyon asked.

"I think I may have seen him before," the landlord said cautiously.

"I think you may have," Kenyon agreed. "Do you happen to know his name?"

"I'm not sure," the landlord said. "Mac something, perhaps."

"Macintyre," Kenyon said. "Otherwise known as Flash Mac."

"Because of his taste in clothes," Malory said. "Not because of what he kept under his raincoat."

Kenyon stifled a yawn. Malory's jokes bored him. "In his small way, something of a local celebrity," he said.

"I never read the papers," the landlord said.

"You don't have to read the papers," Kenyon snapped. "Just listen to your own bloody bar gossip."

"Christ," the landlord said. "You don't know much about my job, do you? I have to nod and look as though I'm paying attention. That's not the same. If I had to actually listen to it all, I'd go potty."

Privately, Kenyon was prepared to concede that one to him. Perhaps. He glanced at his watch. "They'll be a while out there yet," he said. "But you should be able to open again for business this evening."

"I'm in no hurry," the landlord said. "Not after this little lot."

"You'll be busy," Malory said. "Everyone'll be coming in for a look see."

"So I suggest you get that filthy bog cleaned up," Kenyon said. "When we've finished with it."

"There's a fellow supposed to come in regularly," the landlord said plaintively. "But like everyone else, these days, he turns up when he feels like it."

"It's your pub, not his," Kenyon said, unsympathetically.

"I've been meaning to see to it," the landlord said. "But the wife's been ill, and what with visiting her in hospital, and seeing to deliveries, and working half the night because I can't get staff . . . Still, I suppose you don't want to know about my problems."

"That's right," Kenyon said. "Just what you know about ours."

"I've already explained to the sergeant . . ." the landlord began.

"You have," Malory said. "But anything else that might occur to you . . . ?" He tilted the whisky bottle, and topped up the three glasses. Nothing appeared to occur to the landlord, except relief at the prospect of further refreshment.

"So you didn't know Archie Macintyre," Kenyon said. "You didn't know that he was wicked with a knife, or so he liked to say." The landlord was shaking his head. "But you do know that withholding information is an offense," Kenyon went on. "You do realize that if I'm not satisfied, you might have a bit of trouble getting your license renewed."

"I swear to God . . ." the landlord began.

"Don't give me that crap," Kenyon snarled. "Unless you want me to stick perjury on you as well. You're in enough trouble already, sunshine. This is a murder you're trying to cover up."

The landlord flinched, and perspiration oozed on his pale forehead. He said, weakly, "But I don't know anything."

"You'll bloody know something before I've finished with you," Kenyon said, harshly. "You'll know what the inside of the nick looks like, for starters."

It was Malory's turn to look mildly bored. He occasionally got fed up with being the friendly, kindly, helpful one. Sometimes, they varied the routine when the circumstances called for this kind of play acting, and it was Malory who did the shouting. He preferred that. He liked being the hard man for a change.

"I can solve all your problems about visiting your wife and keeping this place going," Kenyon told the landlord, bleakly. "I can make sure you lose your license, no trouble at all. Then your missus'd have no home to go to when she comes out of hospital, would she? You'll find out what it means to obstruct the police. In fact, I've got a bloody good mind to arrest you here and now, and you can try to explain to the brewers why you won't be open tonight."

Malory knew his lines. "I think you're being a bit hard, sir," he said.

"It's up to him," Kenyon said, flatly.

Malory leaned forward, the soul of concern, and gripped the landlord's arm sympathetically. *"I'm* sure you weren't involved, Mr. Denver," he said, emphasizing the personal pronoun. "But let's face it, you're the one with a lot to lose. Just tell the complete truth, that's my advice. I'm afraid that's the only way you can help yourself, Mr. Denver . . . by helping us."

The landlord began to speak volubly, urgently and fearfully. He had been busy. A lot of people had come and gone whom he did not know. The juke box had been deafening. A glass had been smashed accidentally, and he had had to clear up the pieces. A disagreement had broken out over a darts match, which the landlord had been obliged to sort out.

"Was Macintyre involved?" Kenyon inquired.

"No. He was just sitting quietly on his own."

"When he first came in," Kenyon asked, "did the other people in the bar seem to know him?" The landlord thought about that one. "Did they?" Kenyon insisted.

"I think there was a kind of . . . pause," the landlord said, at last. "And some of them sort of looked at him . . . just for a few seconds, before they started talking again . . . you know the way it happens."

"Did you hear if they were saying anything about him?"

"I told you, I don't listen unless I have to," the landlord said. "I'm here to pull pints, not have my ear bent."

"Don't go in for the Landlord of the Year competition," Malory advised him. "You wouldn't win."

"The wife always does the social bit," the landlord said. "Or she did, until she got ill . . . she's very good at it . . ." He looked at the pub clock unhappily. "Christ knows what she'll have to say about all this."

"Are you supposed to go and see her today?" Kenyon asked.

"Four o'clock," the landlord said, cautiously.

"You'll make it," Kenyon said, reassuringly, relaxing the pressure. "Now, try and remember what happened when you saw Macintyre get up and go to the lavatory."

"I didn't see him go anywhere," the landlord said, sharply. "I told your sergeant, I remember serving him, but after that . . ."

Oh, well, Kenyon thought, most times the old dodges

were only useful when someone was lying. You can't trap an honest man, as W. C. Fields might have remarked, and conceivably did.

They went over it, and round it, backwards, forwards, sideways, and upside down, but in the end Kenyon knew no more than when they had started. He thanked the landlord, and supposed that he had things to do. The landlord went behind the bar, with relief, and started washing up.

"He could be telling the truth," Kenyon said, quietly. "Which is annoying. And leaves us with the ones we've let go."

"How do you want to play it?" Malory asked. "Wheel them in one at a time, or go and see them at work? Those who've got a job," he added.

"Neither," Kenyon said. "Not yet." He thought about Archie Macintyre. "Nick Vardin handled that case, didn't he?"

"Or cocked it up," Malory said. "Matter of opinion."

"I don't know enough about it to have one," Kenyon said. It was common knowledge that Malory loathed Detective Sergeant Nick Vardin, far more than he disliked any villain, in which he was not alone among the CID officers working in Bayswater Division. "But I think I'd like to have a chat with Nick about it."

"The file's back at the nick," Malory said.

"If I wanted to read the file," Kenyon said dangerously, "I'd go and bloody read it. So separate your ass from that chair, and go and find Nick."

Malory stood up. "All right," he said. "I'll try. But no one ever knows where that bastard is."

"You're supposed to be a detective," Kenyon said. "So go and detect his whereabouts. I'll give you an hour."

"Where will you be?"

"Here," Kenyon said. "We'll have a working lunch, Lionel."

Malory walked out, irritably. He preferred to be known as Len, rather than by the name on his birth certificate, although Kenyon had a private bet with himself that the day Malory made Chief Inspector he would become Lionel again overnight. Chief Inspector Lionel Malory had the sort of ring to it which went down well in the press, and on the TV newsreels. "And the way things are going," Kenyon thought, reminded, "he'll make it before I will."

"How about something to eat for three in an hour's time, Mr. Denver?" he called, finally making peace.

"There's nothing hot," the landlord said. "The wife used to do the cooking."

"Whatever you've got," Kenyon said.

"Well, there's cold chicken, salad, and French bread."

"Fine," Kenyon said.

"The bread's a bit stale," the landlord admitted.

"You surprise me," Kenyon said. "I thought you were trying to get into *The Good Food Guide*."

He lit a fresh cigarette, and wandered out to the GENTS. The man from Forensic had finished. So had the photographers, who were packing their equipment away. The dead body had been removed from the WC, and was lying on the floor. A uniformed Sergeant was carefully placing his possessions inside a plastic bag.

"Did he have a flick knife on him?" Kenyon inquired.

"No," the sergeant said. "Just what's here."

Kenyon peered at the contents of the plastic bag. A gold cigarette lighter, a packet of Gaulloise cigarettes, a chunky, gold plated watch, a pocket diary, a pen, some keys, and a wallet, which appeared to be well stuffed.

"Can't think why the money wasn't taken at least," the sergeant said.

"No," Kenyon said. He handed the plastic bag back to the sergeant. "I'll examine that lot later."

That could have been a mistake. On the other hand, it might not have made any difference at all.

Kenyon was due to give evidence the following day at the Central Criminal Court, more commonly known to the public as the Old Bailey, and to the police as "The Big House." It would be a day out of his life, and he regarded it as a waste of time. The man concerned had frightened several young couples in Hyde Park, and seriously injured two girls, and one elderly passerby who had gallantly if unwisely intervened, but everyone knew he was a raving nut case who would be committed during Her Majesty's pleasure. Still, Kenyon had been the arresting officer, and he used the time while he waited for Malory

15

to return, carefully going over again the evidence he would give the next day.

". . . and when cautioned," he rehearsed, "the accused said nothing." The accused, he reflected, remembering that white, drawn face, had gone like the proverbial lamb. It was Kenyon's belief that the poor devil was relieved that he had been caught, that in truth, he actually wanted to be put away. He only hoped that some psychiatrist with more ego than commonsense would not decide he was cured in two or three years' time, and recommend his release. Otherwise, Kenyon thought, some other police officer would be rehearsing similar evidence, and there would be more girls in hospital. Or possibly the mortuary.

Malory and Nick Vardin walked in, interrupting his thoughts. He put the file back in his briefcase.

"That was quick," Kenyon said.

"Against all the odds," Malory said, "he was actually sitting at his desk."

Nick grinned. "I go in once a week," he said. "To fill in my football coupon. Hullo, Inspector Kenyon, sir," he said, with exaggerated respect. Nick was a cheeky bastard.

"Sit down," Kenyon said. "And pour yourself a drink."

"The invitation, I like," Nick said. "The place I don't. This must be the worst pub in the manor."

"It's in the running," Kenyon agreed. "Blame Flash Mac's lack of taste."

"I'll drink to that bastard's end," Nick said. "Here's to whoever did it, God bless him."

"The landlord was using that glass," Malory said.

"Well, I don't suppose he's got bloody foot and mouth disease," Nick said. "Still, if you insist, I'll have a clean one." He handed Malory the glass. Malory's normal good humor seemed on the verge of deserting him, but he went to the bar and fetched a clean glass.

"And we'll have our food now," Kenyon said. He pretended not to see Nick's cheerful wink. He wished he did not like Nick Vardin more than he liked Len Malory, who was, after all, the Detective Sergeant he had worked with for a long time. There was no justice, not in this world anyway, and he very much doubted if there was another. If there was, he thought that Nick might have even more explaining to do than he would.

The landlord bustled about bringing the food, which proved to be surprisingly palatable. They were probably eating Mr. Denver's supper.

"We're going to need another bottle though," Nick said. "This one's more than half empty."

"Are you buying?" Malory inquired.

"I was bloody invited," Nick said.

"All right," Kenyon said. "I'll see to it."

In many ways, Nick was his kind of copper. He probably knew even more villains than Kenyon did, mixed with them socially, was on easy first name terms with them, and put them away, when he could, any way he could, with a fine disregard for such niceties as the Judge's Rules. But . . . Yes, there were altogether too many "buts" about Nick Vardin.

"I hear you've found a good way of sucking up to the brass on the fifth floor at Scotland Yard," Nick was saying to Malory, with smiling affability.

"Whoever formed that opinion," Malory said, tightly, "is due to have his teeth pushed down his throat. So you can tell your snout just that, Nichol-arse."

"Can't remember who it was," Nick said mildly. "Perhaps I got it wrong."

"You did," Malory said.

Nick Vardin had been a regular soldier in the SAS. He had bought himself out, for reasons about which he was vague, joined the Metropolitan Police Force and rapidly gained a transfer to the CID.

He was six feet tall and, although over forty years old, still a hard, strong man, with no paunch, despite the fact that he drank like a fish. His face usually wore a humorous expression, negated, if one looked closely, by ice blue cynical eyes. He had joined the force late, and he would never get to be more than a Detective Sergeant, but this worried him not in the least.

If half the gossip about Nick were true, promotion would be the last thing he wanted, since it would spoil certain extramural business activities he was rumored to have. Kenyon kept a quasi-open mind about these rumors. He did not know if they were true or not, to the extent that it was not his business to find out. It was also possible that some of the do-gooders, and no-hopers, in the job, envied Nick's success rate, and spread malicious tales about him. Just remotely possible.

Kenyon thought it more than likely that Nick would never draw his pension. He might not end up at Ford open prison either, as some senior officers Kenyon knew had done, but the time might well arrive when a problem would be resolved all round by his resignation from the force.

That time would arrive when the Complaints Investigation Branch focused on Nick for some reason, accidental or otherwise. The name might have been changed from the Complaints Department, or A.10—as the press still persisted in calling it—but it was still staffed by the same ruthless, flinty-hearted bastards, Kenyon thought. The CIB might well be necessary for the good of the force, but Kenyon was not the only detective who regarded them as the natural enemy. They went rigidly by the book, and drew little distinction between corruption for personal gain, and the kind of sailing close to the wind which Kenyon believed was often necessary in order to secure a conviction. There was, admittedly, a fine line between the two, but Kenyon believed that he was capable of drawing that line for himself, and had no desire for the CIB to mark his card.

The ferocious enthusiasm with which Nick Vardin put villains away might not impress the CIB, when and if the time came, but Kenyon approved of it. There was a war going on in the streets of London, and no man in the front line of any war could keep his hands completely clean. Especially a war which was prolonged, and waged with growing intensity year by year, and if the under-manned Metropolitan Police Force were not actually losing that war, they sure as hell were not winning it either. They were doing well these days if they could hold their own.

"Tell me about Archie Macintyre and that kid," Kenyon said to Nick. "I was on leave at the time."

"I heard you were living it up," Nick said. "The flesh-pots of Paris must come expensive now."

"I only went to see some friends," Kenyon said. "I didn't stay. I went on to Brittany."

When it came to the point, he had not called on the person he had intended to see. In London, he had wanted to believe that the brief note saying she was now in Paris was an invitation. But in the small but still expensive hotel near the Military Academy, as he unfolded the note to check her phone number, it suddenly seemed much more like the sort of polite letter she might have fired off out of courtesy to a whole list of people whose addresses had once appeared in her diary. What kind of invitation was it that began "Dear Sid," and ended "sincerely, Sarah"? Kenyon had suddenly felt foolsh. The whole notion was silly and juvenile. What the hell, she was married now, she was happy, and those few months were in the past, time out, best forgotten. They meant nothing. Kenyon had not made any phone call. He had checked out of the hotel the following morning, and pointed his car west.

"Any good crumpet in Brittany?" Nick inquired.

"No," Kenyon said. The schoolteacher he had met on the beach, as bored and solitary as himself, did not qualify under that heading. "And I haven't got all day, even if you have."

"OK," Nick said. "A little girl was sent to the corner shop for a bottle of milk. Her name was Katie Martin. She was seven years old. Didn't come home. Father phoned the nick. He's a caretaker in a crummy block of bed-sitters. A PC found her in the recreation ground, late that night. She was lying on the grass, eyes wide open, wouldn't move, wouldn't say anything. Shock. She hadn't been raped, but she was badly bruised, and she had some cuts round her private parts, inflicted by a knife. I saw her in hospital later. Got her to talk a bit. Do you want the details of what the evil bastard had made her do for him?"

"No," Kenyon said. He hated crimes against children. From the look on Nick's face, he took it pretty personally too.

"So I wheeled in Archie Macintyre," Nick said. "Unfortunately, I never had the chance to get the sod alone for five minutes."

"What made you think it was Archie?" Kenyon asked.

"I didn't think," Nick said. "I knew." He ticked off his reasons on his fingers. "The girl's description. None too clear, admittedly, but for Christ's sake, she's not much more than a baby. She said the man spoke funny. Archie had a thick Glasgow accent. Also, he had that kind of form. Served three years for a precisely similar offense in Glasgow, down to every perverted detail. He was known to carry a knife, been done for it last year. He had the usual phoney alibi, of course, but he couldn't account for his movements before Katie disappeared. Archie was good for it, all right."

"And yet," Malory said, softly, "the charge was dropped for lack of evidence."

Nick sighed. "Katie failed to pick him out at an identification parade," he said. "Poor little soul, she was still so terrified, she couldn't look at their faces. Even that wouldn't have mattered, if I'd had more time, but some smart brief turned up before I could lean on the bastard."

"You let Archie send for a mouthpiece?" Kenyon asked, surprised.

"Don't be stupid, Inspector Kenyon, sir," Nick said, tartly. "The day I let vermin like Archie Macintyre exercise their legal rights, I'll be senile, and you can have me put away. No, the smooth shit turned up out of the blue. Said he'd heard his client had been arrested. He pulled every trick in the book. Real high-powered stuff. I didn't stand a chance."

"What the hell was a small time nothing like Archie Macintyre doing with a high-powered lawyer?" Kenyon wondered.

"God knows," Nick said. "Or the devil, more likely. Anyway, that's what happened." He swallowed some whisky, and brooded for a while. "Archie didn't even have his knife on him when I nailed him," he said, mournfully. "I couldn't even do him for carrying an offensive weapon. Nothing but a few quid in his wallet. I did try and hold him on suspicion of having knocked off his wristwatch, but the old man wouldn't have it. Said it wasn't worth the aggro. The bloody mouthpiece practically had squatter's rights on the nick by then."

"I suppose most of the people concerned still thought it was Archie Macintyre, even though he was released," Kenyon said.

"They bloody knew it was," Nick said. "Like me."

"Including her father, I suppose," Kenyon suggested. Nick shrugged, and gave himself more whisky. The second bottle had nearly gone. "And other male relatives?" Kenyon inquired. "Grown up brothers, anything like that?"

Nick glanced over his shoulder. The body of Archie Macintyre, on its way to the mortuary for the post mortem, was being maneuvered across the bar. "Whoever killed that evil sod deserves a medal, in my book," he said. "I wouldn't lift a finger to get him fined, much less set him up for life imprisonment."

"You can keep your personal vendettas for your own cases," Kenyon said. "This one's mine."

Nick lifted his glass. "May your never solve it," he said.

"Don't push me, Nick," Kenyon said, levelly, "or I might decide to start inquiries into a few things I hear."

"Like the ownership of certain greyhounds and whether the races they won were fixed," Malory said, coming to life in support of his guv'nor.

"You're another pair of evil bastards," Nick said. "Happily, it's all lies. A chum of mine owned some dogs once, but he's sold the greedy beasts."

"I can think of other possibilities to look into," Kenyon remarked.

"All right," Nick said. "Straight up. As it happens, I can't help you, and I can say that with what people tell me is a clear conscience. Katie's got no brothers, and I'd be amazed if it was her father. On the other hand, it could be half Paddington, including me, except I've got the best alibi in the world." He slapped Malory cheerfully on the shoulder. "Ask my old mate here." Malory winced.

"Katie's address," Kenyon said. Nick was beginning to bore him too.

"Basement flat, 26 Everard Street," Nick said.

"OK, Nick," Kenyon said. "Sorry to have dragged you away from your football coupon."

"Any time," Nick said. "Though you're on a wild goose chase. Still, you'll find that out for yourself." He stood up. "I reckon you're onto a good thing, snuggling up to the fifth floor," he said to Malory.

Malory ignored him. "Do you want me to come with you?" he asked Kenyon.

"Cheerio, squire," Nick called to the landlord, as he left the pub.

"No," Kenyon said. "Nick's probably right. You take the

car, and see if you can get one of those bloody amnesiacs to remember something. I can walk from here."

He strolled the few hundred yards, which was all it was. Everard Street was in an area which might have seen better days, but was now steadily heading for worse. It was Autumn, but the day was warm and sunny and, apart from the rotting smell emanating from a dustcart mechanically mashing up its refuse, the air was mostly pleasantly fresh.

The front door of number twenty-six was festooned with bells, most of which seemed in imminent danger of coming adrift. None of them referred to anyone called Martin, or a basement flat. Most simply had numbers roughly inked on bits of card tucked behind plastic.

Kenyon backtracked, went down the steps into the area, and hammered on the door adjoining a window, between the grimy curtains of which he could see a brass tap, and an old-fashioned sink.

A man opened the door. A little girl held his hand.

"Mr. Martin?" Kenyon said. "I'm Detective Inspector Kenyon. We think you may be able to help us with some inquiries . . ."

The fresh air vanished as he followed Martin through the kitchen into the living room, and was replaced by stale cooking and dankness. Inside was a kind of permanent dusk. Kenyon lived in a basement flat himself, in Gloucester Terrace, and he knew the problems, which he solved as best he could by opening windows and having the lights on, even when it was broad daylight outside. But electricity cost money, the possession of which was not much in evidence in this place, and the windows looked as though they had never been opened this century.

Nick was right, Kenyon knew that. Martin was only in his middle thirties, but he was small and slight, moved awkwardly, and dragged one foot as he walked. There was no way he could have done Archie Macintyre the kind of damage he had suffered.

"Do you mind if I ask what the problem is?" Kenyon inquired. "What happened? An accident?"

"Oh . . . no . . . polio, when I was a kid," Martin said. "I suppose I'm lucky it wasn't worse."

Katie had not relinquished her father's hand for a

second, nor had she made a sound. Martin lifted her onto his knee. "I made sure this one had all the shots though."

"You must be Katie," Kenyon said.

The child turned her head, and shrank away from him. She would have been a pretty little thing, except that her large eyes were withdrawn behind some veil of wariness, and there were unnatural hollows in her cheeks. Her legs and arms were thin too.

"She could do with a bit more flesh on her," Kenyon said, more abruptly than he intended.

"She won't eat enough," Martin said, simply. "Can't seem to fancy it."

Kenyon was experiencing the kind of helpless rage which Nick must have felt. "What the hell am I doing here?" he wondered. "Who cares who killed Archie Macintyre?" But he was a copper, and he was paid for it, and it was his job to enforce the law. That was what he was doing there.

"Is Mrs. Martin at home?" Kenyon asked.

"She's out at work," Martin said. "Cleaning."

"Is there anywhere Katie could play for a few minutes?" Kenyon asked.

"She won't," Martin said. "She's all right when she's near me, but otherwise . . . well, I expect you know."

"It's concerning that matter," Kenyon said, hoping the child would not comprehend. Impossible to mention Macintyre's name in front of Katie.

"I expect you'd like a cup of tea," Martin said. "Katie, go and put the kettle on for me, will you? There's a love."

Katie slipped off Martin's knee, gave Kenyon a wide berth, and went into the kitchen.

"Macintyre's been found dead," Kenyon said, softly.

Martin lifted his head like a man who could not believe the news that he had won a fortune. "Thank God," he breathed. "Thank God." There was the sound of running water from the kitchen. "Perhaps it'll be all right now," he said, quickly. "You don't know what it's been like . . . knowing that if I took her out, she might see him at any time . . ."

Katie came back, and climbed onto Martin's knee. Much of lined sadness in the man's face had been replaced by relief. "Did you put it on the gas?" he asked. Katie nodded. "There's a good girl," he said.

They talked for a few minutes in a seemingly aimless fashion, although in reality Kenyon was using obliquely casual questions designed to pass over Katie's head, establishing what he wanted to know. By the time Martin took Katie into the kitchen to make the tea, he was satisfied that Martin had no knowledge of Macintyre's death, or any idea who might have caused it. Not that he would have volunteered any information, Kenyon knew, but he was equally certain that Martin had nothing to conceal. He wondered how Malory was getting on.

Katie was deputed to pour the milk into the cups, which she silently and solemnly did. Martin said, "I've been thinking . . . if it's fine tomorrow, we might go to the zoo, you and me . . ." Katie looked at him. Martin smiled at her tenderly. "How about that?"

Kenyon thought that Katie was a nice kid, and her father was a good sort. Perhaps she would be all right after all, in time. Although Kenyon did not really believe that any girl child ever completely recovered from, or forgot, the kind of experience Katie had been through. He sipped the strong tea, and looked at his watch.

"I'll check your list of tenants before I go," he said.

"I don't do the lettings," Martin said. "The owners see to that, and collect the rents."

"You must know who lives here," Kenyon said. He gave Martin the kind of warm smile which his clients never saw, and very few others in his life either. His father, sometimes, when the old chap was not being irritating, and Sarah, perhaps, before it all went wrong. The smile of an ordinary man with normal emotions, rather than the calculated facial expressions of a copper always on guard. "Just going through the motions, that's all," he said. "Something for my report, apart from drinking your tea."

Martin dug out a dog-eared notebook, and leaned over Kenyon's shoulder as he cursorily scanned the list of names. "Oh, she's gone," he said, "moved out last week. A couple of students have taken it."

Kenyon nodded, and went back to the name which had attracted his attention. "I know this one," he said. "How long's he been here?"

"Close on a year," Martin said.

Kenyon considered what he knew about the man in question. "Is he any trouble?" he asked.

"Trouble?" Martin was surprised. "No. He sometimes comes and sits with Katie, if I've got to go out somewhere. He's the only man she'll have near her, now, apart from me. She calls him Uncle Bill."

Katie looked up at her father's face.

"Do you like your Uncle Bill?" Kenyon asked, gently. Katie gave him a sideways glance. The fractional movement of her head might have been a small nod.

"They kind of took a shine to each other," Martin said. "He used to take her out now and then . . . of course, that was before . . . well, you know."

"Yes," Kenyon said. "I'd like to see his room, if that's all right with you."

"Why?" Martin asked, worried.

"Perhaps no reason," Kenyon said. "But if you wouldn't mind . . ."

He followed Martin and Katie up four long flights of gloomy stairs. He lost count of the number of shabby doors he passed, each one opening into a cramped room with its gas ring, its curtained off sink, its minimal battered furniture, its tattered carpet on frayed lino, its metered gas fire. The equipment with which countless people lived, or at least existed, in this great city of London.

Martin finally stopped in front of a door at the end of a narrow corridor. He sorted out the right key from the bunch he carried, and inserted it into the Yale lock.

"Who's that?" a gruff voice inquired.

"Oh," Martin said, taken aback. "I thought he'd be out."

"All right, Mr. Martin," Kenyon said. "I won't trouble you any more." He pushed open the door.

"That you, Katie?" the gruff voice asked.

"No, Bill," Kenyon said. "It's me."

"Hullo, Mr. Kenyon," Bill said. "Haven't seen you for a few years."

He was sitting at a rickety table smoking a cigarette, with a ball-point pen in his right hand, and a marked copy of the racing edition of the *Evening Standard* in front of him.

"Found any winners?" Kenyon asked.

"A dead cert in the four o'clock," Bill said. "I was just off to the betting shop."

"Plenty of time," Kenyon said.

"What can I do for you, Mr. Kenyon?" Bill inquired. The voice was not only gruff, but just a trifle slurred as well, Kenyon noted.

"I thought I'd come and have a drink with you," Kenyon said.

"Haven't got none in," Bill said. "Sorry."

"Not to worry," Kenyon said. "I'm making some inquiries . . . usual thing . . . so tell me where you've been today."

"Nowhere," Bill said, promptly. "Woke up late, and I haven't been outside this room."

Kenyon could smell the whisky on his breath. There was no empty bottle in sight. He doubted if any newsboy could be persuaded to deliver the *Evening Standard* four flights up, with no lift. And before Bill belatedly remembered, and shoved his left hand into his pocket, Kenyon had seen the stained handkerchief which was wrapped round it.

Kenyon sat down opposite him. There was another dead cert in this tiny, congested room, apart from the winner of the four o'clock, and that was the identity of the man who had killed Archie Macintyre.

The thought that he had found him gave Kenyon no particular pleasure.

CHAPTER TWO

Bill Jarvis somewhat resembled a patriarchal ape. Gray hairs bristled from his nose and his ears, thatched his head, and stubbled his chin. His face was lined and baggy, and his eyes were sunken. He was sixty-two years old, and looked it, but he was still a massively powerful man, with huge hands, long arms, and great shoulders which bulged under his ill fitting jacket.

An unlikely companion for the delicate, tiny Katie, Kenyon thought.

Years before, as a newly promoted Detective Sergeant, Kenyon had put Bill Jarvis away for murder. There was no ill feeling about this transaction on either side.

Bill, who was amiable enough when he had not been drinking, despite his potentially murderous build, accepted it with resignation as one of the hazards of his trade. At the time, he was a strong arm for an ambitious East End team which was moving into the West End, and incurred the displeasure of the incumbent mob in so doing.

It was a private fight, mostly conducted in private. The rival teams clubbed and battered it out between themselves, and if the police knew what was going on, they saw no reason to intervene. Then it got vicious, and a hostess whom Bill was much enamored of in those days collected a face full of acid.

"How's Millie?" Kenyon asked.

"Don't know," Bill said. "She went back north, I think. I did write a couple of times, but she never answered."

Only a dumb gorilla like Bill would have fallen for that one, Kenyon thought. Millie pretended to be twenty-nine, was forty-three, and as hard as they came. She took Bill's presents, keep him on a string, and laughed at him behind his back. That was before she was found in her car, her hands clutched to her face, screaming.

Bill drank a bottle of whisky, and went berserk. He found the acid thrower in a restaurant, dragged him into the kitchen, and dispatched him with a meat cleaver.

It was the kind of murder which Kenyon was decidedly relaxed about. After all, they were only killing each other; that was his attitude. Privately, he had some sympathy with Bill Jarvis. There were far worse than him amassing huge sums of money, untouched by the law. Still, murder was murder, and Bill duly got life imprisonment, which usually, given good conduct, amounted to ten years.

Once in prison, denied access to the booze which did something to him, Bill became gentle and co-operative, a model prisoner, who eventually impressed the Parole Board by his probably genuine contrition, and he was released after eight years.

"I hear you're on parole," Kenyon said.

"I been a good boy," Bill assured him. "Clocking in regular."

"What did you do to your hand?" Kenyon asked. Bill gazed at his undamaged right hand blankly. "The other one," Kenyon said.

"Oh . . . cut it on some broken glass," Bill said.

"Let's have a look," Kenyon said.

"It's nothing," Bill said.

"Do as you're bloody told," Kenyon said. Bill unhappily produced his left hand from his pocket. Kenyon unwrapped the handkerchief. "Looks more like cuts from a knife to me," he said.

"Broken glass," Bill mumbled.

"I suppose you've sobered up a bit," Kenyon said.

"Since when?"

"Since you killed Archie Macintyre," Kenyon said.

"I don't know what you're talking about," Bill said.

"Is the knife here, or have you thrown it away?"

"What knife?"

"It wasn't in the bog anywhere."

"What bog?"

"All right, Bill," Kenyon said wearily. There were times when he seemed to have been listening to replies like that all his life. "I've got better things to do than look for myself. Once you're inside, we'll come back. My lads'll find it, if it's here."

"You mean you're taking me in?" Bill sounded somewhat aggrieved, but none too surprised.

"You're on for Archie's murder," Kenyon said. "You can regard that as a caution."

"I didn't even know the bastard was dead," Bill said.

"I can put you there," Kenyon said, lying. "You were seen. You didn't think they'd all keep quiet, did you?"

From the skeptical expression on Bill's face, he evidently thought, with good reason, that they would. "You can't con me that way, Mr. Kenyon," he said.

"Are you trying to tell me you weren't there?" Kenyon demanded.

"I haven't been near that pub for weeks," Bill asserted firmly.

"What pub?" Kenyon inquired softly. "I didn't say anything about any pub."

"You were talking about a bog," Bill floundered. "Bogs and pubs . . . I took it for granted . . ."

"You've got some stains on your jacket," Kenyon said, pointing. "Looks like blood."

"That'll be from my hand," Bill said.

"Well, we'll get Forensic to check it out," Kenyon said cheerfully. "See if any of those stains match Archie Macintyre's blood group."

"Oh, what's the fucking use?" Bill said.

"Where's the knife?"

"Under the mattress," Bill said.

Kenyon found the knife, took a plastic bag from his briefcase, and slipped it carefully inside.

"What'll it be this time?" Bill asked. "Life again?"

"Plus the unexpired portion of your previous sentence," Kenyon said.

Bill developed a coughing fit. His chest rattled. He stumbled across to the bed, fished out a chamber pot, spat out a gob of phlegm, and breathed more easily.

"Sorry, bronchitis," he apologized. "Life plus . . . what does that make? . . . oh, it doesn't matter . . . I'll never come out this time."

"They'll look after you, inside," Kenyon said.

"Fancy dying in prison," Bill said glumly. "What a way to go."

"I suppose you'd gone out searching for Archie," Kenyon said. There were various kinds of facts. It was a fact that he felt compassion for this aging bulk of a man, now harmless, yet but a few hours earlier a brutal killer. But his job called for other facts, like how it happened and the degree of intent, and they came first.

Bill was shaking his head. "No," he said. "I swear to God . . . I wanted to do him . . . by Christ I did . . . but I didn't want to go back inside again . . . not at my age . . ."

"Good thinking," Kenyon said. "Pity you didn't stick to it."

"I'd gone out for a paper," Bill said. "That happened to be the nearest boozer . . . I use it sometimes . . . not all that often . . . but I didn't go looking for him, Mr. Kenyon, and that's straight up."

"He just happened to be there," Kenyon said, neutrally, keeping an open mind.

"He came in," Bill said. "Sat there drinking pints, the rat-faced bastard . . . just sitting there, smirking . . . and I thought about young Katie . . . and him coming and going, free as air, and if ever a man deserved to be strung up . . ."

"So you decided to see to it yourself," Kenyon suggested.

"It wasn't like that," Bill Jarvis said. "Perhaps I should have pissed off as soon as he walked in . . . but anyway, I didn't . . . I had a few more doubles, and looked at him, so fucking pleased with himself . . . and I remembered how Katie used to be . . . and the more I looked at him, the more I could see it happening all over again." Bill sighed deeply. It turned into a coughing fit, and he got up and used the chamber pot again.

"Filthy habit, isn't it," he said. "But I can't help it." He lit another cigarette.

"It might help if you cut down on the fags," Kenyon said.

"There won't be any bloody women or booze inside," Bill said mournfully. "I must have something."

"Go on," Kenyon said.

"Well, eventually, he got up and went out the back,"

Bill said. "I'd had a few by then . . . more than a few . . . anyway, I followed him . . . I only meant to duff him up a bit, and that's the truth. But then he pulled his bleeding knife on me."

"You did a bit more than take it off him," Kenyon said.

"I know," Bill said. "But by then I'd got mad . . . I suppose it was the booze . . . I get like that when I've had a bit too much."

"I remember," Kenyon said. "Then what? Did you leave through the bar?"

Bill shook his head. "Through the guv'nor's living quarters, and out through the street door," he said. "He'd mentioned he was single-handed, so I knew there'd be no one around. Me hand was a bit of a mess."

"We'll have it seen to at the nick," Kenyon said. "Then we'll get all this down in writing."

He closed the lid of his briefcase, which had been open during Bill's recital, first switching off the small tape recorder which was concealed under some papers inside.

Kenyon had no great faith in verbal admissions obtained when there was no third party present. Villains had a habit of singing a very different tune once they had had the chance to think things over, and were confronted by a statement form.

The people in the bar might have been telling the truth. Conspicuous though the ape-like Bill Jarvis was, they *might* not have noticed him follow Archie Macintyre to the lavatory. The knife might not be conclusive, if there were no clear prints belonging to Macintyre, which was more than likely, after Bill had handled it. Even Forensic could prove to be a broken reed. Despite Kenyon's bluff, the blood on Bill's jacket might not be Macintyre's at all. Kenyon had been let down by Forensic before. He liked to make certain, if he could.

It was true that most courts would not accept a tape recording, obtained in these circumstances, as admissible evidence, but that was not the purpose. Once in the detention room at the nick, with the shadows of prison visibly closing round him, even the slow-witted Bill might come to the labored conclusion that he had everything to gain and nothing to lose by changing his story and denying everything. Kenyon did not think it likely, but he preferred to cover his bets. With the tape recording playing as a reminder, and himself and Malory leaning on Bill for an hour or two, or as long as it took, he thought that Bill would end up making the right kind of statement.

Kenyon was ready to go, but Bill Jarvis seemed disposed to linger for some reason.

"Come on," Kenyon said.

"I was wondering," Bill said. "If I could just have a word with Katie before we go . . . say goodbye, like."

"I don't think that's a very good idea," Kenyon said.

"The thing is," Bill Jarvis said, "she kind of takes me back . . . I had a kid like that, once, before her mother left, and took her away."

"You were never bloody married," Kenyon objected. Every known detail about Bill Jarvis had re-appeared in his mind like a computer printout, as soon as he saw the man's name on the list of tenants.

"I didn't say I was," Bill said. "Meant to . . . especially after the kid arrived . . . but then I got sent down . . . didn't get around to it somehow when I came out . . . eventually she got fed up and pissed off." He gave a deep sigh. "She was a respectable girl, really, and I was always in and out of trouble, even in them days. But I sent money for her upkeep . . . oh, for years."

"Where's your daughter now? Do you know?" Kenyon asked, marginally intrigued by the unlikely vision of Bill Jarvis as a parent of any kind.

"She must be forty years old," Bill said. "Or is it forty-one? I forgot. She lives at St. Albans, or she did. Husband in computers, or something. I never see her, of course. Never hear from her either, as a matter of fact, so she might not be in St. Albans, could be anywhere. But when she was little, before her mother went off . . . well, I see her in Katie, if you know what I mean."

"You could be a bloody grandad," Kenyon said.

"Yes, well, I'll never know about that, either," Bill said.

"OK," Kenyon said. "But tell Katie you're going on holiday, or something. Don't upset her."

"I won't," Bill promised.

"She'll forget all about you in a couple of months anyway," Kenyon said.

Bill looked at him with the injured gaze of a dog which

had been kicked for no reason. But it was true, Kenyon thought. The truth usually did hurt, for some reason.

"I nobbled one of them at home with his wife," Malory said. "She had a good go at him, didn't like her old man being involved with the police, and he admitted there was someone else in the bar he happened to have forgotten about. Didn't know his name, or so he claimed, but described him as a big ugly bloke about sixty years old."

"Bill Jarvis," Kenyon said, offhandedly. "He's stewing in the detention room now, waiting to cough."

"You've nailed him already?" Malory asked, put out. Kenyon nodded casually. "You smug bastard," Malory said.

They walked side by side from Kenyon's office, down the stairs to the detention room.

"Poor old Bill," Malory said. "Putting down scum like Archie Macintyre . . . hard to think of it as murder, somehow."

"Well, it is," Kenyon said, flatly.

There was no need for the tape recording. Bill Jarvis sang the same song. The Police Surgeon bandaged the cuts on his left hand, which were superficial, gave him something for his bronchitis, and advised him to give up smoking, unless he wanted to die before his time.

"Stupid bugger," Bill said bitterly, to Kenyon. "I ain't exactly got a lot to bloody live for now, have I?"

"I don't see that you ever did have much," Kenyon said.

"I took care of Archie Macintyre when you couldn't touch him," Bill pointed out. He might have a point there, Kenyon thought.

Time was getting on. Kenyon went back to his office, and wrote up his working diary for the day. It was a pleasure to be able to record exactly what had happened, for once, in accurate detail. The forthcoming evening would be another matter. Kenyon wanted some account of his movements in his diary, in case someone happened to notice him out and about, but it would bear more relation to fiction than fact. Oh, hell, he could cook that tomorrow, or the next day, when he had more time.

He turned his attention to Archie Macintyre's possessions, which had been cleared for handling. He flipped through the pocket diary. Archie Macintrye had been no Samuel Pepys. Where he had been, on any particular day, what he had done, and what his thoughts might have been, if the mental processes of a psychopathic creep like Archie could be so dignified, would forever remain a mystery. On the other hand, there were random, cryptic notes, dotted here and there, christian names, phone numbers, and odd words which might signify places, which could be worth looking into some time. Some other time, Kenyon thought, looking at his watch. He examined the contents of Archie's wallet, which he found much more interesting.

Archie's financial standing had dramatically improved since Nick had arrested him, Kenyon reflected, recalling the Detective Sergeant's reference to a few quid. The wallet contained four hundred and eighty pounds, mostly in twenties, with a few tens. What had Archie Macintyre been up to in order to acquire that kind of bread? But even more puzzling were the five one hundred dollar bills.

Kenyon had seen a fair number of forged notes in his time, and these appeared to be genuine. Archie was not exactly known to move in international circles. Knocked off then? Must be. But Archie operated in other ways. He had no form for robbery. Oh, well, Kenyon thought, a thousand times a year, in the course of his endless investigations, he came across inexplicable little things which did not fit, and nine hundred and ninety times they remained forever unexplained. Besides, Archie was dead. Still, it was funny . . .

Not enough to detain him today, though, and he shoved Archie's possessions away. If he did not get out of this place soon . . .

Malory walked in.

"I've gone," Kenyon said, putting his jacket on. "You just missed me."

"I was wondering if you were busy this evening," Malory said.

"Why?" Kenyon inquired. He had kept his plans for this evening, and other evenings, to himself. In the present climate of the Metropolitan force, where the CID were supposed to have been publicly laundered, whiter than white, the much vaunted "cleansing process," what he was about could look a bit dodgy.

It was not exactly that he did not trust Malory, but they were different animals. Both were dedicated career coppers, and both were ambitious, but the routes they chose to follow varied in accordance with their disparate characters. Kenyon was disposed to cut corners, play it by ear, ignore the book if necessary, and rely on it coming off, which so far it had done, touch wood. Given Kenyon's kind of success rate, even some of those at the Yard, whom he regarded as sanctimonious bastards, were unlikely to probe his methods too deeply.

Malory's route was to sail with the prevailing wind. He went by the book on the whole, took care not to stick his neck out, and played it safe. Even his working diary, Kenyon thought, unlike most of those in the CID, would stand up to the most rigorous investigation. Malory was also working on another aid to easing his path to the top, which, it transpired, looked like being successful.

"Well, you know I've been seeing quite a bit of Vera Drummond," Malory said.

"Yes," Kenyon said. He had met Vera Drummond at various functions. She was the apple of her doting father's eye. She was earnest, twenty-one years old, and a young Conservative. Kenyon would have been surprised if she were not also a virgin. He would have been even more surprised if she had found much difficulty in protecting her honor. He thought that, to any man who was not besotted with her, she was decidedly plain, the sort of girl you talked to politely at cocktail parties, while looking round to see if there was not some talent elsewhere in the room more worthy of your attentions. Kenyon was far from certain that Malory was all that besotted.

"We've decided to get engaged," Malory said.

"Congratulations," Kenyon said. Vera's father was Commander Christopher Drummond at Scotland Yard, well known to be highly regarded by the Commissioner. The word was that he was marked down to become the next Deputy Assistant Commissioner (Crime), a position Kenyon deeply coveted for himself in about fifteen or twenty years' time.

"Thanks," Malory said, with a somewhat sheepish grin. Being the future son-in-law of the next Deputy Assistant Commissioner (Crime) would do Len Malory's career no harm at all, Kenyon thought. He wondered how soon he would become Lionel Malory again.

"The thing is," Malory said, "she's just been on the phone. Her old man's having a bit of a get together tonight at his place. You know, announce it officially."

"With the top brass there, I suppose," Kenyon said.

"Well, the Commissioner, anyway," Malory said. "It's the only evening he's got free. That's why it's short notice."

"You must tell me how it goes," Kenyon said, searching for his car keys.

"I don't know if it's your scene, Sid," Malory said. "But I'd like you to come along, if you can. Give me a bit of moral support. Vera said to invite you. She thinks you're such a nice, polite man." He grinned. "I didn't put her right. Everybody needs a few illusions in this life."

"Well, thanks for the invite. I'd like to come along," Kenyon said, with hypocritical insincerity. "But I can't. Something I've been working on," he said vaguely, "and I've got a meet fixed for tonight."

"OK," Malory said. Normally, he was inquisitive about Kenyon's private ferretings, although he usually received a decidedly varnished version of the truth, but just now his curiosity, Kenyon guessed, was submerged under anxious anticipation of the big event. There was a faraway look in Malory's eyes, as though he were rehearsing what he would say to the Commissioner when the great man offered his congratulations. "We must fix something else," Malory said, abstractedly. "I'll have a word with Vera . . . perhaps we could all go out to dinner sometime, or something."

"Great," Kenyon said, heartily. "Give her my best, and I hope it all goes well."

Kenyon was heading for the car when the booming voice of his boss brought him to a halt.

"Just a minute, Sid," Detective Superintendent Pindar said. He came alongside Kenyon like an ocean liner berthing. "You've cracked another murder, then," he said, beaming. "Good work."

"Thank you, sir," Kenyon said. "But it was pure luck. I fell over Bill Jarvis by accident."

"Luck doesn't appear in the statistics," Pindar said. He liked Bayswater to show up well, which it usually did, against other and inferior Divisions, which did not have the good fortune to be commanded by Detective Superintendent Pindar.

They fell into step, and walked together into the car yard. "Besides," Pindar added, "a good copper makes his own luck."

Kenyon had no false modesty, and thoroughly agreed with the implied compliment, but he was beginning to get the feeling that his just and overdue reward seemed to be distinctly slow in arriving.

"There's something I'd like to have a word with you about sometime, sir," he said. "Sort of personal."

"I'm a bit pushed now," Pindar said. He unlocked his car. "We could have a chat tonight though, if you like."

"Tonight?" Kenyon was momentarily thrown.

"Len Malory's engagement party," Pindar said. "I don't suppose the Commissioner'll stay more than an hour, and after that . . ."

"I can't make it," Kenyon said. "Already had something arranged."

"Oh, well . . ." Pindar took a look at his watch. "I've got to get home and pick up the wife, and we'd better have something to eat before we go . . ."

Few of the CID in Bayswater Division lived in the manor. Flats were expensive, and houses were impossible. Detective Superintendent Pindar's home was in Slough.

"Oh, it'll keep," Kenyon said. "It's not important."

He took out his irritation on his gearbox, as he drove home, and nearly slaughtered a brooding Arab who casually decided to wander across Craven Road as though he were setting forth into the expanses of some desert.

Kenyon swore, avoiding mangling the burnoused visitor, and hence preventing him from spending his much needed foreign exchange, and turned into Gloucester Terrace.

Marvelous, he thought vindictively, how everyone could get to Malory's last minute party, as soon as they knew the Commissioner was going to be there. Perhaps he should have gone himself. He could easily have canceled his arrangements for tonight. No, sod it, he thought, let the Lionel Malorys of this world suck up to the Commissioner. That was not his, Kenyon's, way.

He collected his mail from the pigeonhole inside the street door, went downstairs to his basement flat, switched on all the lights, and opened the door leading on to his small patio to let in some fresh air.

He was being unfair, he knew that. Detective Superintendent Pindar was a decent, honest and able man, and Malory might be madly in love with Vera Drummond for all he knew. It was not his place to attribute unworthy motives to colleagues who had done him no harm. Yes, but where was the fairness in his own life?

He checked his mail while the steaming water ran into his bath. The letter from his father bothered him. It was bright and chatty, as usual, and the reference to hospital was a casual throwaway, ". . . just for a check up . . . nothing to worry about . . . wonder if that nurse that fancies me is still there . . ."

"Silly old fool," Kenyon muttered. He dialed his father's number, but there was no answer, which meant nothing, and might even be reassuring. The old boy always walked to the nearest pub for a couple of pints and a chat, at the same time every evening.

Kenyon climbed into his bath, and gave himself the luxury of soaking for five minutes.

He would phone again in the morning. When was he going into hospital? For how long? And why? The letter answered none of these questions. "Does he think I'm bloody psychic?" he thought, with frustrated irritability.

Kenyon's father had suffered a coronary, two years before, which he had been lucky to survive, but he still obstinately insisted on living alone. Was it about that? Or something else? Kenyon would have to try and take a weekend off, and drive up to Saffron Walden to see him. Make sure everything was all right. Oh, hell, something else to worry about.

Kenyon left his car parked where it was, and set out to walk to his destination. Too many people knew his car. He had no desire for the well-trained sharp eyes and retentive memories of the on or off duty coppers in Bayswater Division to automatically note the number, and wonder later why it was so often in a particular place.

Dusk was falling, the street lights glowed, and the trees in the squares and gardens wore their autumnal leaves of golden brown. This was London at its best, under a clear, darkening sky, the unjaundiced observer might have thought. Usually, Kenyon enjoyed the walk through Cleveland Gardens, Cleveland Square, across Leinster Gardens, into Queensway, and along Moscow Road, but tonight he was in a bad mood, and he chose to see it differently.

Coaches from all over Europe were infesting the gracious squares like overgrown lice, their great hulks parked in any available space, residents' parking strips, meters, yellow lines, anywhere the drivers could dump them overnight, ready for the morning's passengers. The small- and medium-sized hotels bulged to overflowing with the multilingual occupants of these coaches. Groups of them stood on pavements, impeding Kenyon's progress. Arabs squatted impassively on doorsteps, a natural habit in their own lands and their own climates, perhaps, but strangely incongruous in London.

A German coach disgorged its squad of late arrivals outside a hotel in Leinster Gardens as Kenyon was passing, swamping him in tired tourists. He picked his way round the luggage on the pavement bad-temperedly.

Queensway had always been a cosmopolitan kind of street, but now it seemed brash and garish, with its gift and souvenir shops displaying expensive rubbish, and the bright, neon-stripped restaurants, identical in their high prices and their indifferent food. Very little here was aimed at the Londoner anymore. The whole street was designed to suck in foreign cash.

No one in the passing crowds was speaking English, and Kenyon gained Moscow Road, relieved to leave the tourists behind him.

No one who read the newspapers could avoid knowing about the importance of the tourist trade to Britain's balance of payments. Politicians pontificated about it frequently. Kenyon wondered if the smug bastards ever noticed the effects on people who actually lived and tried to go about their business in their own city.

They were so bloody self-satisfied about it, Kenyon thought, remembering the way the politicians were prone to lecture their voters on the subject. What the hell did they have to be so satisfied about?

There they were, begging for votes, dying to run the

country, dead certain they knew what was best for other people, and what had they achieved?

They had done one thing, all right, Kenyon thought. Both political parties, between them. Since the days when, as a fresh-faced young constable, he had first walked the streets of London, they had turned the city into the bargain basement of Europe. A place where, if you were Japanese or Arab, Dutch or German, Belgian or French, everything was dead cheap, a city to flock into in your scores of thousands to pick up the goodies the natives could no longer afford. "They've made London the Woolworths of the world," Kenyon thought, sourly. "Some bloody achievement."

The villains prospered of course, providing whores, gambling, porn and clip joints for the jostling throngs with their hard currency, which went so much further in London than in Hamburg, or Beirut, or Amsterdam. Kenyon wondered if the villains' profits were counted among the "invisible exports" the Treasury assessed monthly. If so, presumably they were good guys, really, helping the old country's balance of payments.

He turned off Moscow Road into a network of side streets. The mews which he eventually reached was almost on the borders of Notting Hill.

He tried to shake off his depression, which was only partly caused by concern about his father. Also present was an uneasy foreboding, the roots of which he could not identify. Something, though. The vague feeling that things were amiss, that somewhere outside his ken something was happening which he was not being told about. What he needed was a few drinks, and a bit of pleasant company. Well, he would get those all right.

The mews was L-shaped, and looked much like any other, small cottages cramped together either side of the cobblestones. Built in Victorian times to house coachmen, grooms and their families, who were thus enabled to live on top of their jobs, their horses, manure, and swarms of flies, they still looked much the same, although the occupants were different, the stables had become garages, and the manure and flies had mercifully long since gone.

In Mayfair, or near Hyde Park, only the well-to-do could afford to live in such a mews these days. This one contained a mixture. A few cottages boasted yellow front doors and shutters on the windows which proclaimed the arrival of smart, professional people. Others, judging by their dilapidated condition, were still occupied by protected tenants, paying a controlled rent, to the distress of their landlords, who would have loved to have been able to get them out and sell the property, since the rents did little more than cover essential repairs, but could not.

The six cottages which formed the corner of the L were, in style, in between. There was a certain amount of wrought iron, and a parapet concealed the flat roof, but the decorations were discreet and in no way ostentatious. It was here that Kenyon pressed a doorbell. He glanced casually along the mews as he waited. One resident was reversing his car into his tiny garage, and making heavy weather of it. Others had obviously decided not to bother with this complicated maneuver. Three or four cars, and a van belonging to a television rental company were parked in the mews itself. Otherwise, there was no sign of life.

"Hi," Angela said. "Come in."

"Thanks," Kenyon said.

Angela closed the door behind him, and Kenyon moved into another world.

It was not, in fact, six cottages in the corner of the L at all. Inside, it had been gutted, and converted into one dwelling, if such a word was not ludicrously inappropriate.

"Where's Carmen?" Kenyon asked, slyly. He was beginning to cheer up a bit.

"Her English may be rudimentary," Angela said, "but there's nothing wrong with her memory. Gossip about you, I can do without."

He followed her into the living room. It usually was the Spanish maid's night off when he was due to call, but Angela's implied reason he did not buy. He might be hoping to use Angela, but he thought it was mutual, and that those who mattered in her life knew what was going on, at least in broad outline.

The living room was vast. A gallery ran round three sides. The pictures on the walls included two Picassos, a Monet, three Cezannes and a Utrillo. A fountain played in the middle of the room. Kenyon had always thought the fountain was a bit much.

"I'm surprised you don't get burgled," he had said, once. Angela had thought that was very funny indeed, which it was. It would be a bold burglar who would take anything from this place.

The house contained other amenities for day to day living, such as a sauna, a billiard room, a small but well equipped gymnasium, and a solarium on the roof. In this unlikely place, not all that far from the crowded supermarkets of Notting Hill Gate, a mini-palace had been created.

"In Xanadu did Kubla Khan . . ." Kenyon quoted.

"It's not much of a pleasure dome these days," Angela said. "Except when you come round."

He was ignorant of her prowess at billiards, but judging by her body, she put the other amenities to good use. It was as near the perfect female form as Kenyon had ever seen. Well, clothed anyway. He had never seen her without.

"God I needed that," Kenyon said, as he downed his first drink. The bottle stood at his elbow where she had left it. He helped himself to another.

Angela was curled up at one end of a huge couch fit for about twenty people. The glass she was holding would last her all evening. She drank very little at any time.

"One of those days?" she inquired.

"Someone elected to get himself murdered," Kenyon said. "As if I haven't got enough to do."

"Will it be in the papers?"

"I doubt it," Kenyon said. "I don't bloody care much, let alone the Great British Public."

Just the same, he would tell her about it, later on, when the bottle had gone down somewhat, and he could appear to become loose-tongued and indiscreet. He thought she could know something about both Archie Macintyre and Bill Jarvis. He would tell her, and watch her eyes. It was true that her eyes were so phenomenally lovely that it was hard, even for a copper going about his business in his own way, like Kenyon, to look into them and not get lost, and forget what he was about. But he would, just the same. It was that kind of game.

"How about you?" he asked. "Anything exciting?"

"Not really," Angela said. "A man from some stupid firm of estate agents came round. God knows how they heard about this place, but he said he had a client, an Arab, willing to offer two hundred and fifty thousand pounds." She smiled. "He was quite a sweet little chap, actually. He kept looking at my legs."

"Who wouldn't?" Kenyon said.

"His mind did seem to stray a bit from the commission he might earn," Angela admitted. Very justifiably, she had no false modesty about her appearance, or the effect she had on men. "I think he was quite disappointed when I told him to piss off."

She was prone to occasional vulgarities, which were strangely disarming, coming from such a poised, beautiful, ladylike creature.

"Quite right," Kenyon said. "Who needs a lousy quarter of a million quid anyway."

Angela had been christened Beryl Dobson. When she took up her chosen career, she became Angela Curzon. Angela was a good choice. With her long, natural honey blonde hair, her wide, deep blue eyes, her soft, shapely lips, and her perfect complexion, there was something angelic about her face. However, unlike some blondes, there was nothing vacuous or dim about her appearance. She was highly intelligent, with a lively, natural wit, and it showed.

Kenyon supposed, although he had never inquired, that she had picked on Curzon because her apartment, at that time, had been near Curzon Street in Mayfair. She was most certainly not related in any way to the noble family whose name she had borrowed.

She was now thirty-four years of age, a little older than Kenyon, but she still looked just as beautiful, just as youthful, and just as desirable as she had when Kenyon first met her, ten years before.

At that time, at the age of twenty-four, she had been the most exclusive, and the highest paid call girl in London.

"How's Tony?" Kenyon asked.

"Fine," Angela said. "Unless you hear anything different?"

"That's what I hear too," Kenyon said. "So everything's fine. No problems."

"Not so much as a parking ticket," Angela said.

"I didn't mean from the law," Kenyon said.

"No one else is going to give me a parking ticket," Angela said, smiling at him.

"I hear of a new firm," Kenyon said. "Supposed to be in the takeover business."

"What firm?"

"I thought I'd mention it," Kenyon said. He was far from sure if the vague rumor was true. He was always hearing things like that from dubious sources, who might have their own motives for feeding him moody information.

"They wouldn't be interested," Angela said.

"They might be," Kenyon said. "With no one minding the shop."

"There's no shop to mind," Angela said. "That's all over, Sid."

Kenyon suppressed a sigh. Who could fail to believe a woman who was capable of turning on such a candidly luminous gaze? She might even believe it. It might even be true. There was no doubt about it, he thought ruefully, it was hard work fencing with Angela. He had implicit faith in his skill at this kind of contest. Clever as Angela might be, she would give something away sometime. Assuming she had anything to give away. Perhaps all these visits were a waste of time after all.

He glanced at the level of whisky in the bottle, and decided he could safely start reminiscing about Archie Macintyre and Bill Jarvis. He held his drink somewhat better than he had led Angela to believe.

Angela had operated at the very top end of the market. Not for her, cards in shop windows, or advertisements in "friendship" magazines, or visits to hotel suites in response to phone calls from hall porters. In her case, it was by recommendation only, and even then she vetted prospective admirers first. It was infinitely more difficult to gain access to Angela's bed than it was to be invited to a garden party at Buckingham Palace.

In her own way, she had become a courtesan of her time. For a while, she was taken up by the jet set, but although they could meet her monetary requirements, she found them tediously superficial, as people, and dropped them. Angela liked men with brains and influence as well as wealth.

Her cabinet minister and her ambassador were her favorites. They always had some interesting gossip about what was really going on, as distinct from their public statements or the crap they gave to the press, and they had so much to lose, there was no risk of any scandal. Angela was averse to any publicity about herself—another drawback to the boring jet set crew.

Her high court judge was another one who was absolutely safe from that point of view, as were the more old-fashioned members of the aristocracy, with great estates and tweedy wives in their own wing of the house.

Businessmen she found dodgy, and after one unfortunate experience, she avoided them. The tycoon in question had been more than generous, but it transpired that he had been thriftily putting his expenditure through the company accounts. Some institutional shareholders asked awkward questions at an annual general meeting, and the tycoon was obliged to put matters right in a hurry. Tycoons, she discovered too late, often did not actually have money of their own. Angela lost a charming house at Sunningdale, set in two acres of land, with its own swimming pool, that way.

Occasionally, Angela would consent for curiosity as well as cash. A visiting American film star who was appearing in the West End was one example, although Angela found him disappointingly unlike his screen image. She was a straightforward girl when it came to sex, and what he had in mind offended her. She was also offended by his reaction to her refusal, which she thought coarsely rude, although she overlooked it, since he was drunk at the time.

A week later, at a quiet, expensively elegant restaurant, the American was hosting a celebration party. Angela was at a nearby table. The American called for the head waiter, and inquired loudly why a fucking tramp like that was allowed in.

Angela was with a group of friends, and friends of friends. One of the latter was Tony Vallenta, whom she knew only slightly. The head waiter knew him very much better, and was on the horns of an impossibly embarrassing dilemma. It was not a restaurant which cared for reports of ugly rows in the gossip columns, and yet on the other hand, he dare not upset Tony Vallenta, and from the look in Tony's brown eyes, he was more than a little upset.

Tony resolved the difficulty by quietly suggesting that Angela's party be moved to a private room upstairs. Face was saved all round, and the head waiter was suitably grateful.

The following day, Tony called on the American at his dressing room. What passed between them remained a matter for speculation, but soon after, Angela received a note of apology, the American developed nervous exhaustion, cut short his engagement, and flew back to New York.

Tony merely murmured, with his pleasantly open smile, that they had had a little chat, in the course of which they had discovered they had certain mutual acquaintances, and would say no more. But Angela thought that he had been very gallant and gentlemanly. They began to dine together alone, and shortly afterwards, Angela retired, at the age of twenty-six, when she was at the height of her career.

Kenyon focused on his watch, and decided it was time to go.

"Have one for the road," Angela suggested. "I know you're not driving."

"Carmen'll be back soon," Kenyon said. Like Cinderella, midnight was the witching hour for Carmen.

"She asked for the night off," Angela said. "She claims she's staying with relatives. I think she's found a boyfriend."

"If I have any more," Kenyon said, "I'm going to forget myself, and start making a pass."

It was a polite fiction, part of the game, that Kenyon only refrained from misbehaving himself with difficulty. Angela would have been insulted otherwise. Any man who did not desire her, she regarded as a pouff. It would also have been true, had Angela not been who she was. There could be some truth in it anyway.

"You're too arrogant to make passes," Angela said, with some accuracy. "A girl'd be bloody lucky if you condescended to meet her halfway."

"I'd better go," Kenyon said. He picked up his cigarettes and lighter, with the intention of putting them in his pocket.

"All right, Sid," Angela said. "You've been very kind to me, and I appreciate it. I want you to know that."

"That sounds like a goodbye speech," Kenyon said.

"There's something I haven't told you," Angela said. "At least, you may know . . . Tony's coming out on parole."

Kenyon changed his mind about putting his cigarettes away, and lit one instead. "I knew he'd applied," he said.

"It's been granted," Angela said.

Tony Vallenta was a businessman who liked to maximize profits. This had led him to place the law of supply and demand above that of the law of the land.

He was into many things, some of which were legitimate, some of which were not, and some of which merged from one into the other.

He ran property companies which, during the boom in the early seventies, had made money from breaking up blocks of flats, but their best returns always came from the Bayswater houses occupied by prostitutes who paid sky-high rents for their apartments.

His main front was a chauffeur-driven car hire service, whose Rolls Royces competed with Godfrey Davis. Behind that lay a web which no one had successfully untangled.

He was into the usual protection rackets, and he had gradually extended his territory from Bayswater and a modest slice of Mayfair, until it took in a lucrative section of Soho. He had also found the pornography business attractive.

Much of this the police knew but could not prove. Tony Vallenta had learned from the experience of those who had gone before him, and who in due course had gone down, and made strenuous efforts not to become too obvious. A so-called Mr. Big attracted intensive police attention. Special squads were liable to be formed, composed of patient detectives with one aim in view, willing to spend years if necessary to put their quarry away. Tony preferred a low profile.

47

Small teams ran each operation, and when the police broke one up, there was no apparent link with any other team, much less with Tony Vallenta.

"Christ," Kenyon had complained, after failing once to establish any connection with a team he had nailed and, for example, Tony Vallenta. "The day of the bloody conglomerate in crime has arrived."

Like any general, Tony Vallenta accepted casualties among the troops as part of the price of success, but stayed well clear himself from where the action was. The troops, for their part, accepted the risk of being put away. Like soldiers, each individual believed that it would never happen to him. If it did, well, their families would be looked after while they were inside and something akin to a bonus would be waiting for them when they came out. A kind of danger money. Tony Vallenta looked after those who comprised his empire a good deal better than any multi-national corporation.

Tony was finally done on two charges: unlawful possession of firearms, and conspiracy to murder. Tony claimed that the submachine gun found in the boot of his car had been planted by the police, but the jury thought otherwise, although it was certainly a remarkably careless thing for such a cautious man to have done. The conspiracy to murder charge was quashed on appeal, when perhaps the most brilliant Queen's Counsel in the land thoroughly earned his enormous fee, and Tony was left to serve six years for possessing firearms. Now, after serving less than three years, he was coming out on parole.

Kenyon's motives for slowly developing a relationship with Angela were mixed. First, although not foremost, he liked interesting feminine company, and Angela was about as interesting and feminine as you could get. Second, although personally he rather liked Tony Vallenta, finding him, as most people did, a thoroughly agreeable fellow, the Court of Appeal decision irritated him, although it was undoubtedly sound in law. Kenyon would agree, if one were to argue nice distinctions, that Tony was not guilty of conspiracy to murder, a charge which always had a faint air of desperation about it. Kenyon thought he was guilty of murder, period.

Finally, there was the question of money. Tony Vallenta

was thought to be a millionaire, several times over. Part of his wealth, the astonishing residence behind its modest facade, his legitimate companies, which were still operating, and his holdings in equities and gilt edged were out in the open, accounted for, and assessed for tax. The Inland Revenue could find no awkward questions to ask. Tony Vallenta was a great believer in always buying the best, and his accountants were no exception.

But while Kenyon had no firm facts to go on, he estimated that there must be some two to three million pounds unaccounted for somewhere. He wondered where it was, and what it was to be used for.

"You must come to dinner some time," Angela said. "I know Tony would like to see you." She uncurled herself, moved across to where he was sitting, lifted the whisky bottle, and looked at him inquiringly. "One more? Or not? Up to you."

"All right," Kenyon said. "Thanks."

Detective Inspector Sidney Kenyon was an ambitious copper, and saw himself as a hard, calculating man. But he had made a fair number of mistakes that day. And perhaps the most serious was the last drink which he allowed Tony Vallenta's wife to pour for him.

CHAPTER THREE

"Christ," Malory said. "You look worse than I feel."

"I didn't sleep very well," Kenyon said.

"I did," Malory said, yawning, "but not nearly long enough."

"How did it go? The Commissioner in good form?"

"He seems all right," Malory said. "No nonsense, but straight down the line. I was surprised how much he knew about me. Not only congratulated me on my last commendation, but remembered all the details as well."

The phone rang before Kenyon could frame a sour reply. Malory had thoroughly earned his last commendation which had involved tackling two armed bank raiders single-handed, but Kenyon very much doubted if the Commissioner's memory was that good. More likely, he had refreshed it, prior to attending the engagement party and, busy man that he was, he was only there because Malory's fiancee was the daughter of the next Deputy Assistant Commissioner (Crime). Full marks to the Commissioner for taking the trouble to glance at Malory's records first. Good on him for making the young Detective Sergeant feel that he mattered, and was not merely a cypher. Just the same, for whatever reason, he was not likely to forget Malory's name in future.

Kenyon wished that someone would refresh someone's memory about his own services rendered.

The phone call was the beginning of one of those not infrequent floods of cases during which Kenyon sometimes despairingly thought that the CID would be submerged.

It was like trying to swim against a fast-flowing current —desperately hard work just to stay where you were.

Besides trying to organize over-stretched resources,

there was all the paperwork as well, not to mention the necessary court appearances.

Bill Jarvis was remanded in custody at the Magistrate's Court. Bill's case was no trouble now, but the court appearance still took up the better part of a morning for Kenyon. Bill would continue to be remanded in custody in Brixton Prison, while he joined the long queue for trial in a higher court.

The Old Bailey was another day out of Kenyon's life, and put him further behind with his work load. He could not afford a weekend to reassure himself about his father, but grabbed a day, which did not leave him reassured but did mean that he was obliged to work eighteen hours out of the following twenty four, unavailingly trying to catch up.

Sleep became something he snatched at briefly, when and if he got the chance, and he had no opportunity to reflect on his evening with Angela. It was also much longer than he had intended before he got around to having a word with Detective Superintendent Pindar.

He tried to spare the time for a few minutes with Bill Jarvis now and then. Bill had sunk into a kind of dull lethargy, and Kenyon felt sorry for him. He made a point of keeping the big man supplied with cigarettes, and Bill was sadly grateful.

"Thanks, Mr. Kenyon," Bill said, one day.

Kenyon closed his briefcase, and shot a glance at his watch. He was due somewhere else half an hour ago.

"Nothing else I can do, Bill?"

"I don't think so," Bill said.

"What about your daughter?"

"What about her?"

"Do you want someone to find out where she is, and let her know what's happened?" Kenyon asked. "She might want to come and see you."

"No," Bill said. "She don't want to know about me."

"For Christ's sake," Kenyon said, harassed by the almost unbearable pressure he was working under into brutality. "You're going inside, and you're never going to bloody come out alive. She's all the family you've got. Still, if you don't care, that's your business."

"Hang on," Bill said, as Kenyon turned to go. "Look, I don't want her told, but if someone could find out where she is, find out if she's all right . . ."

"I'll see what I can do," Kenyon promised.

Kenyon did not feel obliged to keep all the promises he made to villains, not by a long way, but once they were safely locked up, he did his best. He told a young constable, who was dying to prove himself and get into the CID, what he wanted. The eager young man had little difficulty in tracing the whereabouts of Alice Brent, as she now was.

"She's moved from St. Albans," Kenyon told Bill, unloading cigarettes from his briefcase. "Ten years ago, as you'd have found out, if you'd ever taken the trouble to bloody inquire."

"I've been inside a lot of that time," Bill pointed out. "Where is she now then?"

"Cosham," Kenyon said. "Here's her address, in case you decide to write to her. Her husband's a big wheel in research and development now. And it seems you are a bloody grandfather."

"Well, I'm buggered," Bill said, astounded.

"I only hope their genes don't resemble yours, that's all," Kenyon said.

"What are you talking about? Jeans?" Bill said, baffled. "I wouldn't be seen dead in bloody jeans."

"Never mind," Kenyon said.

"Fancy her having a kid," Bill said in wonder. "How old's the little shaver then?"

"Bill," Kenyon said, with as much patience as he could muster, "there's more than one, and neither of them's little. The boy's sixteen, and the girl's fourteen."

"Well, sod me," Bill said.

"You can send them a Christmas card from Dartmoor," Kenyon said.

"They wouldn't put me in the bloody 'moor again, surely," Bill said. "Not with my chest."

Two of the other DIs came back off leave, and Kenyon was able to ease onto them some of his backlog of work. Meanwhile, Bill Jarvis, he was told, painfully composed a letter, beginning "Dear Alice, I trust you are in the pink.

Sorry I have never written before, but time flies, as they say . . ." and ending, "Yours faithfully . . ."

The letter asked for photographs of his grandchildren, ". . . so as I can look at them now and then like, as I am going to work in Australia and do not expect to be back . . ."

During one of his most hectic periods, Kenyon was surprised to be told that Mrs. Macintyre had arrived from Glasgow to claim Archie's belongings, and that she was accompanied by a solicitor, with all the necessary legal papers. The same solicitor, it seemed, who had successfully removed Archie from Nick Vardin's clutches. Somehow, it had never occurred to Kenyon that scum like Archie would have a mother, although obviously it was biologically necessary.

Kenyon found the presence of this same solicitor interesting. He also recalled his vague, and now half forgotten curiosity about Archie's possessions, and decided to act on a hunch, and deal with it himself.

Mrs. Macintyre and the solicitor were waiting in one of the Interview Rooms. Kenyon introduced himself. He had not met the solicitor before, but he knew the type. Clever, hard working, pillars of the legal profession, with large detached houses in Esher or the Thames Valley, they assiduously sought and often found any loophole in the law, any minute flaw in the way the police had behaved, which would protect their clients from the richly earned consequences of their criminal activities.

Such solicitors were few in number, but one was too many in Kenyon's book. He had a considerably higher regard for the villains themselves, than the tame lawyers who acted on their behalf.

Mrs. Macintyre was a gray, faded, subdued woman, who said little, and whose interest in what was going on seemed to be marginal. The solicitor was brisk and affable. Kenyon ignored him, and addressed himself to Mrs. Macintyre.

"These are the articles found in your son's possession, Mrs. Macintyre," he said. "If you'd be kind enough to make sure it's all there, and sign this receipt, please . . ."

"Where do you want me to sign?" Mrs. Macintyre said, dully.

"Just a moment," the solicitor said. "If you'd allow me, Mrs. Macintyre, before you sign anything . . ."

It took him about ten seconds. "There seems to be an error here, Inspector," he said. Most of his affability had gone.

"In what way, sir?" Kenyon inquired, ingenuously.

"According to your own record," the solicitor said, "Mr. Macintyre's possessions included a pocket diary, and five one hundred dollar bills. Those articles appear to be missing."

"Really, sir?" He diligently went through the motions of checking. "You appear to be right, sir," he said, surprised. "I don't understand this at all."

"I'd have thought you should do," the solicitor said, tartly, "since I believe you were the officer who handled the case."

"If you'll excuse me," Kenyon said, "I'll go and check with the clerk in charge of property."

Kenyon had not mentioned that he had handled the investigation into Archie Macintyre's death. He thought that the solicitor was extremely conscientious to have such information at his fingertips, when dealing with such a routine chore as assisting the man's next of kin to recover his possessions.

"Hurry up," Kenyon said.

"Talk to Rank Xerox, not me," Nick Vardin said. Nick was engaged in photocopying the contents of Archie Macintyre's diary. He had been the only occupant of the big room where the CID men had their desks, when Kenyon had decided to act on his hunch, and needed someone fast.

"These as well," Kenyon said, handing him the five one hundred dollar bills.

"Yes, I wondered what the evil little shit was doing with these," Nick said. "He never went in for mugging, as far as I know."

"I'm terribly sorry," Kenyon apologized. "I think you'll find it's all in order now."

"Perfectly," the solicitor said. "Though I don't really understand why it was not in order in the first place."

"We hold an enormous amount of property of one kind

and another in this police station," Kenyon said. "As I'm sure you know. Mistakes do unfortunately occur."

"And in this case, the mistake was . . . ?" the solicitor inquired.

"It was a large sum of money for a man to be carrying in his wallet," Kenyon said. "It was felt that certain inquiries were called for. The money was being held in a different safe."

"I presume your suspicions were unfounded," the solicitor said.

"We can't prove that the money was not lawfully acquired," Kenyon said, neutrally, for Mrs. Macintyre's sake.

"And the diary?" the solicitor asked, sarcastically. "Did you imagine that was stolen as well?"

"The diary was accidentally placed on the wrong shelf," Kenyon lied.

"I can't say that I'm much impressed by the efficiency with which you seem to handle matters here, Inspector," the solicitor said. "Perhaps you should review your system."

"It's all on the taxpayer here, so our resources are stretched. We're not in the happy position of being able to charge our clients forty pounds an hour," Kenyon said softly. "As you are, sir."

Mrs. Macintyre's eyes widened, and she became agitated. She turned on the solicitor. "You didn't tell me that," she said.

"Mrs. Macintyre," the solicitor began, "I assure you that . . ."

"If you'd said it was that much when you phoned, I'd have got someone else," Mrs. Macintyre said.

"The Inspector was being humorous or impertinent. I'm not sure which," the solicitor snapped. He squeezed Mrs. Macintyre's arm, reassuringly. His voice took on the warm, soothing tone which had mollified many a client. "As I told you, I had the pleasure of representing your poor son on several occasions. I felt it was no more than my duty to ensure that you receive what is rightfully yours as next of-kin. There is a considerable sum of money involved," he reminded her. "But I had no intention of making any charge whatsoever for my services."

Mrs. Macintyre sniffed a bit, but she was duly mollified. The solicitor looked at Kenyon vindictively.

"I'll see you out, sir," Kenyon offered, agreeably.

He watched them leave the premises, and noted that the solicitor courteously insisted on carrying the late Archie Macintyre's possessions.

That creep, he was reasonably confident, had never worked for anything in his life. If Mrs. Macintyre was not paying him, someone else was. Precisely what for remained a mystery.

A few days later, Malory told him, with many a chuckle, about the interview which had taken place between Bill Jarvis and his daughter.

It appeared that Mrs. Alice Brent was far from being as thick as her natural father, and found Brixton Prison, the address to which she was to forward the photographs, an unlikely jumping off point for a job in Australia. After an inner struggle, she had driven up to London.

"Apparently," Malory said, "they just sat there, old Bill, scratching himself and coughing, and his daughter tarted up like a dog's dinner. Bill kept clearing his throat, and she told him what the weather was like outside, and apart from that, they hardly said a word. When it was time to go, she said, "Well, goodbye . . . er . . . Dad. I hope your chest improves." And he said, "Thanks for the photos, Alice." And that was it. They took Bill back downstairs, and when they locked him in his cell, he was sitting on his bunk, crying like a baby." Malory grinned.

Kenyon thought that he had heard funnier stories, but he wondered if all that catharsis might have shaken Bill out of his torpor. He decided it was time to provide him with some more cigarettes, and drove to Brixton Prison.

Bill Jarvis was positively jaunty. He was also touchingly grateful.

"You don't know what you've done for me, Mr. Kenyon," he declared. "She's turned into a real smart woman, my little Alice, and the clothes she was wearing . . . did they tell you?"

Kenyon admitted that he had heard how smartly dressed she had been.

"And the photographs of her kids," Bill said. "Here,

57

have a look. No resemblance to me at all, is there?" he demanded proudly.

Kenyon agreed that indeed there was not. He let Bill carry on some more about how marvelous the two youngsters were. He felt that there would never be a better time than the present to try an idea he had been flirting with, and decided to give Bill an hour of his time. They were alone, the big man was in a good mood; no better occasion was likely to arise.

"I brought some fags, Bill," he said, unloading his briefcase.

"Well, that's very good of you, Mr. Kenyon," Bill said, uncomfortably. "But the truth is, I'm going to try and cut down. I mean, I've been working it out. If I keep my nose clean, I could still get out by the time I'm about seventy, if I don't pop off first. I wouldn't mind seeing those kids, just the once, you know, when they're grown up, like."

"I'll give them to someone else," Kenyon said.

"No, don't do that," Bill said hurriedly. "But I'll make them last."

"Mind if I pinch one?" Kenyon asked.

"Help yourself, Mr. Kenyon," Bill said. "Oh, shit, I may as well join you. Just the one."

Kenyon lit Bill's cigarette for him, put the lighter into his briefcase, and switched on the small tape recorder inside.

"Well, you've had quite a career, Bill," he said, reflectively.

"I have that," Bill said.

"The things you must know," Kenyon said.

"You're right there," Bill said. " 'Cor, what I could tell you about . . ." An idea occurred to him. "No reason why not, now, I suppose," he said.

"You don't have to talk to me, you know, Bill," Kenyon said. "You don't have to say anything you don't want to."

"Ah, what's it matter?" Bill said. "Not any more it don't. Besides, you've always been good to me. You know, dead straight, and I appreciate it."

There was a silence. Kenyon fancied he could hear the faint hum of the tape recorder, and he idly rustled some papers, in case Bill could hear it too.

"Mind you," Bill said, "the best time was just after the

war. You know, when everything was rationed. Christ, I was rolling in it then. It was dead easy. Every bugger was on the fiddle. I remember one time, we knocked off a lorry thinking it was a load of butter, and it turned out to be Scotch instead. 'Cor. . . ."

Kenyon let Bill get suitably warmed up with his reminiscences about the good old days of Black Markets and Spivs, although his interest in the years when he himself was little more than a toddler was zero.

"You know, Mr. Kenyon," Bill said, judiciously, "your firm was different in those days . . . you knew where you stood with Old Bill then . . . you know what I mean?"

"So they tell me," Kenyon said.

After that, he led Bill gently into what he hoped would be more fruitful pastures. He took care to say again, "You don't have to tell me if you don't want to, mind."

"It's nice, sitting here, having a bit of a chat," Bill said. "Did you ever hear about the night we duffed up Shorty Smith? He was called Shorty because he was seven feet tall. Well, anyway. . . ."

Kenyon rapidly lost interest in that story too, plus a few succeeding ones. It was ridiculous, he thought. Here was Bill Jarvis, happy to talk, a man with a criminal record stretching back for forty years. Never more than a tiny cog in a big machine, admittedly, but he knew them all, and had worked for most of them. Behind that lowering forehead must lurk some fragment of knowledge which Kenyon would ache to get his hands on, but all he was getting was anecdotes about punch-ups. If he were not fairly certain that Bill was too dim to deceive, he would have suspected the big ape of giving him the run-around.

Brooding over thoughts like these nearly made Kenyon miss the kind of thing he had been hopefully fishing for.

"Hang on," he said. "Who are you talking about?"

"The Colonel," Bill said. "You know . . ."

"Oh, yes," Kenyon said. "Nice chap."

"Funny, him going off like that," Bill said.

"People sometimes do," Kenyon said. "When accompanied by enough ready cash."

"Yes, I heard that yarn," Bill said. "But did anyone ever put it on the line, official like?"

"Could be they didn't want any trouble with the authorities," Kenyon said.

"Could be there wasn't any money missing at all," Bill said. "Could be that was spread around to account for *him* going missing."

"Someone's supposed to have seen him in Brazil," Kenyon said, keeping the ball in the air.

"From what I hear," Bill said, "he's a lot closer than Brazil."

"Like where?" Kenyon asked, idly.

Bill gave him a huge wink, grinned to himself, and said nothing. Kenyon waited patiently. The big man, once having started, was now like any gossip. He would not be able to bear to hug his secret to himself for long. He would have to reveal it. For what it was worth, which was not necessarily very much.

The Colonel was so called because he looked like one, with his silver gray hair and aquiline features, and he acted like one too, using a brisk, authoritative manner, and a clipped, Sandhurst accent, but he had not in fact been a regular officer at all. He had, however, briefly been an acting Major and acquired the Military Cross, during the Second World War, when it was possible for a young Territorial Army Officer to achieve such a relatively high rank in the Airborne Division, if he knew his stuff, and could contrive to stay alive. After the war, the Colonel had gone into business with, for a good many years, no more than modest success.

Kenyon lit another cigarette, and glanced at Bill inquiringly.

"I'd better not," Bill said, glumly.

"I'll send for some tea," Kenyon suggested.

"That only makes it worse," Bill said. "As long as I can remember, a cup of tea, light a fag . . . they kind of go together."

"Suck a mint," Kenyon said. He offered Bill the packet.

"Thanks," Bill said.

"Keep them," Kenyon said.

"Thanks," Bill said.

Opinion was casually divided at Bayswater nick about the Colonel. Some argued that he was as straight as he seemed, and pointed out that the Gaming Board's requirements were now so tough that no one got a license about whom there was the faintest breath of suspicion. This faction was somewhat surprised when it was rumored that he had departed with a suitcase full of the club's cash.

The others maintained cynically that anyone who appeared that straight had to be bent, and dismissed his impeccable references on the grounds that, since the criminals could no longer get their sticky fingers on gaming clubs themselves, they needed a perfect front man, behind whom they could operate. Like the Colonel.

Kenyon, without caring much one way or another, remained broadly neutral. By temperament far from being a trusting man, he tended to lean towards the cynical point of view, but there was one thing against it. For five years, until his fairly recent disappearance, the Colonel had run the Blue Otter, a lush, luxurious gaming club in a side street off Edgware Road, close to Marble Arch, just inside Kenyon's patch. And in all that time, there had never been the faintest breath of suspicion, not the merest whiff, that any villains were involved in that club, in any way.

"Well, don't you want to know?" Bill inquired. He seemed edgy and disappointed.

"Know about what?"

"The Colonel," Bill said.

"I thought you'd told me," Kenyon said.

"Well, if you're not interested," Bill said, miffed.

"Of course I am, Bill," Kenyon said, heartily. "I'm sorry. Let's see . . . you were saying he's not in Brazil . . ."

"An even hotter place," Bill said, mysteriously. "More like the temperature of molten iron, whatever that is."

"No idea," Kenyon said. "Are you sure you want to go on? You don't have to tell me, not if you were mixed up in anything."

"No, it's just what I hear," Bill said. "You know, around and about."

"What do you hear?"

Bill lowered his voice to a hoarse whisper. Kenyon moved his briefcase, hoping the microphone would pick it up.

"The word is," Bill breathed, "that he was knocked off in his own office. Then they put the body in the boot of an old car, and sent it to the breaker's yard. The car gets crushed for scrap, with the Colonel in the boot, and the whole lot goes into some furnace."

"Come on, Bill," Kenyon protested. "Do me a favor. That malarkey was used in bloody *Goldfinger*. You've been watching too many old films."

Bill grinned, unabashed. "Perhaps someone borrowed a good idea," he said. "Anyway, that's what one fellow told me. Another bloke reckoned it was done a different way."

"Try me on that one," Kenyon said.

"Well," Bill said, "he reckoned the Colonel's body was cut up first . . . four pieces, I think he said. They put the bits into plastic sacks, you know, the sort you shove rubbish in. Next morning, the sacks go into the dustcart, and the whole lot gets crushed to pulp on the spot."

Kenyon did not think much of that one either. It was true that dustcarts now mechanically ground refuse, with much clanking and groaning, into a mush . . . but human remains? And that bit about cutting up the body first . . .

"Do you know how much blood comes pouring out of a human being when you start cutting up the body?" he demanded. "All right," he said, "I take that back. You bloody should do. Anyway, you know what a mess it makes. People have tried carving up their nearest and dearest in the bath, before now, and traces of blood have always been found somewhere, no matter how careful they tried to be."

"They had a kitchen to work in," Bill pointed out. "Tiled walls, tiled floors, meat carvers, gulleys to carry water and junk away . . . and who's going to notice an extra spot of blood in a kitchen, for Christ's sake?"

The Blue Otter boasted an excellent restaurant. The kitchens were much as Bill described.

"Someone would have talked," Kenyon objected. "There must have been staff around."

"Not at four in the morning," Bill said.

"The dustcarts have to unload," Kenyon said. "Someone would have noticed all the blood and shit."

"With what they're used to collecting from restaurants," Bill said, "no one'd bleeding notice anything. Anyway, I'm only telling you what I heard. Perhaps he went to the breakers' yard, like I said first time. I don't know."

Or perhaps he was sunning himself in Brazil, with a suitcase full of money, Kenyon thought, unconvinced.

"Well, let's say he's dead, and never mind how," Kenyon said. "Why should anyone want to knock him off?"

"He's supposed to have been offered some sort of deal," Bill said. "But he turned it down. Only then he knew what the deal was, of course, so they had to shut him up."

"What kind of deal?" Kenyon asked.

"I don't know," Bill said.

"Well, who offered him this deal?" Kenyon tried.

"I don't know that either," Bill said. But for the first time, his glance shifted, and Kenyon knew he was lying, as distinct from repeating villains' gossip, or possibly fantasizing, if Bill Jarvis were capable of such a thing.

"Well, it's up to you," Kenyon said. "But there's no one else here, it's all off the record, I'm not going to tell anyone."

"I don't know," Bill said. "You'd have to promise to forget I ever said anything."

"Of course I will," Kenyon said. "You know me, Bill." He hoped that the tape had not run out.

"Well, I know I can always take your word, Mr. Kenyon," Bill said, then paused. "But I really can't tell you. Even if I knew, that is."

"Whisper it," Kenyon suggested.

"I'm sorry, Mr. Kenyon," Bill said, whispering all the same. "I'm an old man. I don't have that many friends now. Some nasty accidents can happen inside; I've seen them . . ."

Kenyon shrugged.

"Fair enough, Bill," he said. He picked up his case, reluctantly.

"Anything else, Mr. Kenyon. But not that, OK?"

Kenyon supposed that he could have squeezed Bill for the information, but felt he was bound to find out sooner or later for himself. He was not to know just how much that feeling was going to cost.

It was eleven o'clock when Kenyon, yawning, turned the lights on in his flat that night. Bill had cost him the better part of the afternoon, and he had slogged on into the evening until sheer exhaustion had threatened to switch him off whether he willed it or not.

At last, however, now that the other DIs were back in the swing, the horizon was in sight. Come the weekend, he could revert to his usual mere ten or twelve hours a day.

He played back the tape recording while he made coffee, and poured himself a whisky. Hearing it again did nothing to lessen his disappointment. It would always have been dodgy to try and use such a tape recording as evidence although, had there been anything really good, he might have argued that saying to Bill "you don't have to talk to me, you know, it's up to you" could have rated as a caution, even if some distance removed from that laid down in the Judge's Rules. Also, he would have hesitated anyway about putting Bill Jarvis into the box. The old villain was hardly likely to make an impressive witness. But he had hoped there might be something worth looking into, and what had he got? Bits from old films.

The phone rang halfway through. Kenyon turned the volume down, and answered it.

"I'm sorry to call you so late, Sid," Angela said. "But you're a hard man to get hold of."

"I haven't been in much," Kenyon said. "You should have left a message at the nick."

Angela laughed. Even down a telephone, even in his condition of advanced fatigue, that laugh of hers halfway turned him on. "I can't imagine why," she said, "but that didn't occur to me. Anyway, Tony's home now. He sends his regards, and hopes you'll be able to join us for a meal sometime soon."

Kenyon agreed, and they fixed a date. He switched off the tape recorder as he passed it on his way to bed. The old fool was rambling on about the Colonel and the Blue Otter. He could not be bothered with Bill Jarvis's meanderings tonight.

Somewhat fresher, in his office, first thing in the morning, he decided that, as a long shot, it might be worth finding out one or two things, provided he did not have to do it himself. Malory was nowhere in sight, but a message from him was. Special Branch was laying on some kind of protection for an Arab sheikh who was staying at the Royal Lancaster Hotel, and Malory had been hauled in to make up the numbers.

"Oh, hell," Kenyon muttered. His eye fell on Nick Vardin, who was sauntering towards his desk. Presumably it was football coupon day today.

"Nick," Kenyon called. "Come here a minute. Do me a favor, will you . . . ?"

He explained what he wanted. Nick did not ask why, as Malory would have done, but he did point out that his own guv'nor kept him quite busy enough, without any homework from Kenyon.

"Don't give me that eyewash," Kenyon said. He thought that Nick's DI was a lazy bastard with a genius for avoiding work, who let Nick do exactly as he liked. "We can make it official, if you like. If you're on anything important, tell me what it is, and I'll decide if you're entitled to refuse."

The older man, wise in the ways of avoiding trouble, grinned. "All right, Mr. Kenyon, sir," he said. "But is it OK if I fit it in as and when?"

"It's not urgent," Kenyon admitted.

His telephone rang. "Kenyon," Kenyon said.

"Hullo, Sid, it's Jim," a cheerful voice said. "Feel like a good piss up tonight? I've been made up to Chief Inspector. I've just heard."

"Congratulations," Kenyon said, flatly. Detective Inspector James Alleyn was an old friend, presently at West End Central, whose career, so far, had paralleled Kenyon's. "But I'm tied up tonight. Can't make it, mate. Sorry."

"I don't know why I bloody asked you anyway," Jim said, cheerfully. "You didn't invite me when you got your promotion."

"It hasn't come through yet," Kenyon said.

"You're kidding," Jim said.

"There's a call on the other line," Kenyon said. "Must go. Best of luck, Jim."

He hung up, and sat staring bitterly at his silent telephones. Jim Alleyn was a nice man, and a hard-working, if plodding detective, but he was not in Kenyon's street, and they both knew it. Kenyon put his jacket on, and walked along the corridor.

"Yes, Sid?" Detective Superintendent Pindar said. He was wearing his glasses, and was halfway through a file which was twelve inches thick.

"I'd like a word, off the record," Kenyon said.

"What about?"

"My promotion, sir," Kenyon said.

"Not now," Pindar said, gesturing at the file. "Are you free for a drink at lunch time?"

"Fine," Kenyon said. "The Back Door?"

The Back Door was a pub called the Horse and Jockey opposite the rear entrance to Bayswater Police Station, and was where the CID refreshed themselves. It was also where they held their meets with "official" informants.

"No," Pindar said. "I'll meet you in the Falcon. One o'clock."

That was odd. Pindar always used The Back Door. He did not believe that senior officers should be seen drinking in local pubs, except the semi-official one.

Kenyon sat at a table in the half empty bar, waiting. A DI was only the second step up the long ladder, and you had to reach it young if you were going to get anywhere.

Kenyon had done that. Subsequently, he had taken his promotion examinations, and appeared before a Selection Board. He was later informed that he had been selected for promotion to Chief Inspector, and would be made up as soon as a vacancy arose. Kenyon was one of thirty-eight men who had received a similar notification at the same time. It was a big force, the Met.

It had only gradually occurred to Kenyon that while he kept hearing about colleagues who had become Chief Inspectors, no vacancy was arising for him. Jim's happy phone call today had been the last straw.

Pindar lumbered in apologetically. Kenyon bought him a drink.

"Sorry," Pindar said. "The Assistant Commissioner chose to ring up . . . cheers."

Kenyon spoke his mind, ". . . nearly every bugger out of that thirty-eight's been made up except me," he said.

Pindar listened impassively.

". . . perhaps I'm getting paranoid about it," Kenyon

said. "And if so, you can put me down, but I don't think I am. Can you give me some sort of hint? Have I put up a black of some sort?"

"Not with me," Pindar said.

"There must be some reason," Kenyon said.

"Look, Sid," Pindar said. "On or off the record, I'm on your side. I always thought you'd go a long way. You know that. You're a damn good copper. One of the best. Any delay, it's not down to me."

"I didn't think it was, sir," Kenyon said. He had a considerable affection for this big, upright man. "But why the hold up? Do you have any idea?"

Pindar sipped his whisky, sighed, and finally spoke unhappily. "Don't be surprised if you have to go and see the CIB, Sid," he said.

Kenyon's stomach constricted. "Why? What are they looking into?"

"If I knew, I couldn't tell you," Pindar said. "But I don't. Something. That's all I know. And I shouldn't have said that much."

"I know," Kenyon said.

"Let's lay it on the line," Pindar said slowly. "They don't work on spec. They must have firm information of some sort. If it's good, you're the one who'll know what it is."

"I don't," Kenyon said helplessly. "I haven't got the first bloody idea."

"My turn," Pindar said. He got up and went to the bar. Kenyon racked his brains. Why would the CIB be after him? Why? But he came up with nothing. Just the same, over in Scotland Yard, on the seventeenth floor, there was now a file, with his name on it.

He lit a cigarette. He noticed that his hands were clammy. He wiped them on his handkerchief.

CHAPTER FOUR

Kenyon wanted to think. He did not feel like facing the four walls of his empty, silent flat. He badly needed a few drinks. He decided to spend the evening at The Pelican.

The Pelican was a small, luxurious night club on the fringes of Mayfair. It was not exactly exclusive, since enough money or the right credit card would purchase an entrée for anyone, and the glitter would only deceive the willingly gullible. But Kenyon had been accustomed to spending time if not money there in the old days, before detectives were discouraged from hanging around the clubs. Villains of many kinds enjoyed flashing their money about, and it was possible for a copper who kept his ears open to acquire interesting snippets of information which later came in useful, as well as a reasonably good meal.

It was also a practical way to ensure that clubs were not effectively controlled by the mobs. A club owner had only to give a CID man a free dinner and a bottle of wine, and he had cheap protection for the night. No team looking for easy pickings was going to cause trouble with a copper on the premises.

However, as soon as the CID were told to stop haunting the club, the protection racketeers moved in. Villains, like nature, abhor a vacuum.

No way were the club owners going to report anything to the police once they lost the reassurance of the CID as regular, if non-paying customers. They would rather cough up and have no trouble.

Kenyon regarded the restrictions placed on him and his kind as silly, if not downright stupid, and the results predictable.

The Yard achieved a public relations whitewash job,

and senior officers who enjoyed appearing on television were able to assure the public that the CID was being cleaned up.

So the CID were deprived of a valuable source of information, and the protection racket received a considerable boost.

Kenyon did not like it, but he contrived to conceal his contempt for those in authority who equated sanctimonious gestures with taking stern action, and placing the CID in unnecessary shackles with improving the police image, whatever that might mean. One day things might change, but in the meantime he had to make his way in the police force as it was, not as he would like it to be.

As soon as he walked in, he realized that The Pelican had changed since his day. It was relatively early, but it was crowded already. The lights were dimmer. The hostesses were more numerous. Arabs and Japanese, rarities when Kenyon had been a regular, were much in evidence.

Kenyon stood at the corner of the bar, waiting to be served. The only customer speaking English as his native language seemed to be an American, who wanted to change traveler's checks for a thousand dollars, partly, presumably, to ensure the amorous attentions of the redheaded hostess whose shapely young body was glued to his side. And who appeared to be single-mindedly devoted, either to him or, perhaps more likely, to the universally desirable product of American Express.

Kenyon gave up, and decided to have a drink at the table. The head waiter, instinctively suspecting, with some reason, that Kenyon was not likely to prove a free-spender, was some distance short of effusive.

"Tell Frank Granger I'd like to have a word with him," Kenyon said.

"Who?" the head waiter inquired, ungraciously.

"I want to see your boss," Kenyon said.

"He's busy," the head waiter said. He dropped the menu on the table.

"You need some lessons in good manners," Kenyon told him. "Fetch him, before I bloody give you some."

The head waiter thought about making an issue of it. Kenyon, none too good tempered anyway, looked at him

70

silently. The head waiter thought better of it and went off, muttering under his breath.

Kenyon lit a cigarette, and had half smoked it before a familiar face approached his table. But it was not that of Frank Granger. This one was black, matching his immaculate dinner jacket, smiling, and belonged to a young spade called Garry.

"Hullo, Mr. Kenyon," Garry said, shaking hands. "You should have phoned. I'd have made sure you had a better table."

"This one'll do fine," Kenyon said. "Where's Frank?"

"He sold out a couple of months ago," Garry said.

"I'm a bit out of touch," Kenyon said. "Is this your place now?"

"That's right," Garry said, beaming.

"Quite a little gold mine by the look of it," Kenyon said.

"The overheads are high," Garry said. "But I'm not complaining. Now you just tell me what you'd like, Mr. Kenyon. Myself, I'd recommend the whitebait to start with, followed by the fillet steak . . ."

The head waiter brought a large whisky which proved to be one of the best malts Kenyon had ever tasted. "I'm terribly sorry, sir," he apologized obsequiously. "I didn't realize you were a personal friend of . . ."

"Forget it," Kenyon said. "No hard feelings."

He munched his way through the whitebait and fillet steak, which both proved to be excellent. The recommended claret was even better. Garry inquired twice if everything was all right, and then left him alone.

Garry Bennett had come up fast in the world, Kenyon thought, idly. He had liked the young spade when he had first met him as a barman in an obscure drinking club off Spring Street. Later, Garry had taken on a new manifestation running a tourist guide service which might have proved to have made more money from pimping than guiding, had anyone cared to inquire deeply enough, which Kenyon did not. Garry was bright, pleasant and hard working, and Kenyon supposed he must have made a bob or two from the tourists, one way or another, but just the same . . .

Kenyon looked round the busy, smoothly organized night club. It would have taken a lot of cash to buy this place from Frank Granger. He wondered where Garry had got the money from, but not for more than a moment or two. He was more concerned with himself than with the achievements of ambitious young spades.

Kenyon drank and smoked reflectively, ignoring the discreet harmonies of the trio, the merrymaking Arabs, and the ubiquitous hostesses with their well-painted smiles.

How long had the Complaints Investigation Branch had any interest in him? Probably only since his Selection Board for promotion. If his card had been marked before that, it would have gone against him. Not so long, in that case.

All right. Were there any signs? Intercepted mail? Impossible to tell. His telephone? Was that being tapped? That was a question which, now he thought about it, was not difficult to answer.

For some time, Kenyon had been vaguely aware of growing crackling and interference on his line at home. Finally, it had become so bad that he had phoned the Post Office about it.

An engineer had called round, he remembered, thinking back, checked the wiring, and told him that the fault was in the road. Kenyon had groaned inwardly when he heard that. Faults in the road, he knew from bitter experience, had a nasty habit of not being fixed for a long time, and could turn into dead silence and a line totally out of order.

He had been pleasantly surprised when, only two days later, the engineers rang to say that the fault had been rectified. Considering that the Post Office ran the British telephone service with a truly Balkan degree of lackadaisical inefficiency, to find the fault at all was astonishing enough. To put it right in two days was moving like greased lightning, by their abysmally low standards.

Kenyon blew smoke at the pink candle on his table, watched it flicker, and thought grimly that he had been successfully conned.

Normally, had the clarity of his telephone line dramatically improved, he would have known at once that his phone was being tapped. It was one of the signs he was always, instinctively, on the lookout for. Like any experienced CID officer. Just in case. As a man risking being labeled a heretic centuries ago would have been on the watch for the first ominous sign of interest on the part of the Inquisition.

By degrading reception first, and then rectifying it, they had lulled him into overlooking that first, fatal indication. One up to them, the buggers.

He poured the last half glass of wine. OK. That gave him some idea of when. Had he spoken to anyone on the phone since then whom he should not have done? Said anything he ought not to have done?

Angela Vallenta, of course. But she had not identified herself. The conversation had been harmless. Anyone else? No. He was certain the answer was no.

Right. Since his line had been tapped, he had not said anything on the phone which even the CIB could regard as incriminating. But the bastards still had a file on him. There must be something in it. But what?

His visits to Angela Vallenta? But he had always taken great care. He was absolutely certain he had never been seen. And even if he had, which he had not . . . formally, his actions would attract disapproval, that was true . . . although there were many high-ranking detectives who would sympathize and exercise the Nelson touch . . . Even if the Yard *had* got to know somehow, would that be enough for the CIB to swing into action? No, never in a million years. Not just that on its own, not merely visiting Angela. The most that would have called for would be a sharp dressing down and a warning to lay off from Detective Superintendent Pindar, or perhaps the Assistant Commissioner if they really wanted to put the fear of God into him. But not the CIB . . . they fried bigger fish than that. All right then, what? What the hell did they have in that bloody file?

Kenyon stubbed out his cigarette. He would, he knew, find out soon enough, but he wanted to be able to field whatever they were going to throw at him. It was not a question of guilt or innocence. Kenyon did not feel guilty of anything, no matter what they had on him. But, these days, the CIB could fry a copper just for doing his job— at least, coppers who saw their job the way Kenyon did.

He became aware that something was intruding on his brooding introspection. He looked round, and realized what it was. Sitting at one of the tables behind him were three men. Their voices were raised in argument. Glasses shattered on the floor. One of them had an empty bottle in his hand.

Kenyon knew what was due to happen next. A phoney fight would break out. Crockery and glass would go flying everywhere and in the ensuing melée some of the guests would get hurt, while the remainder would decide to go somewhere quieter.

Later, Garry Bennett would receive a visit from a kind of businessman who would offer to prevent any repetition of such trouble—in return for a percentage of the take, of course.

Kenyon stood up and moved to the troublemakers' table. The one with the bottle in his fist was on his feet. Kenyon slammed him back into his chair.

"Sit down and shut up," Kenyon said.

"Who the fuck do you think you're talking to?" the aggressive one demanded, bouncing up again.

"Shut up, you fool," the one whom Kenyon knew said. "He's the law."

A general hush descended on the table. Kenyon sat down on the spare chair.

"Hullo, Alec," Kenyon said, nodding cordially.

"Evening, Mr. Kenyon," Alec Curtis said. Like the others, he was a big man in his twenties, expensively dressed.

"I expect you're just going," Kenyon said.

"That's right," Alec agreed.

"And pay for the breakages as well," Kenyon told him.

"We were going to do that anyway," Alec said.

"Of course you were," Kenyon said.

They paid the bill in silence, adding an extravagantly generous tip. The head waiter expressed humble gratitude, and went off, sliding one of the fivers discreetly into his back pocket. The three men got up to go.

"You can stay for a minute, Alec," Kenyon said. Alec sat down again. The other two goons hesitated, and then sloped off. Kenyon lit a cigarette.

"I came in here for a nice quiet evening," he said.

"We didn't know you still used this place, Mr. Kenyon," Alec said.

"Still working for Walter Flack, are you?"

"I see him around, now and then," Alec said.

Kenyon thought about the rumor, the bones of which he had retailed to Angela Vallenta.

"I hear that Walter's thinking of moving in on Tony Vallenta," he said.

"I wouldn't say that," Alec said.

"What would you say?"

"Walter don't like outsiders," Alec said.

"What sort of outsiders?"

"Any sort," Alec said, cryptically.

"Well, I don't much like Walter," Kenyon said. "Come to that, I've got mixed feelings about you, Alec. I expect that's mutual."

"Yes," Alec said. "Kind of."

"Good night, Alec," Kenyon said.

"Good night, Mr. Kenyon," Alec said.

Kenyon went back to his own table.

"I expect you'd like brandy and cigars, Mr. Kenyon," Garry said.

"That would round off a very pleasant meal," Kenyon agreed.

Garry offered a box of fine Havana cigars. Kenyon chose one. The brandy was Remy Martin VSOP. Garry poured it from a virgin bottle which he left on the table.

"This is Yvonne," Garry said. "If you should feel like a little agreeable company."

Yvonne smiled demurely. She was pretty, well shaped, and looked about nineteen years of age. For a fleeting instant, Kenyon was tempted, until he thought of the traffic a club like this would bear in the course of a week, let alone a month or even a year.

"Thanks all the same," he said. "But I'm not in a very sociable mood tonight." He smiled at Yvonne. "Sorry, love. Nothing personal. There'll be plenty of Arabs only too pleased, I know."

Yvonne's young lips compressed, making her look less young. "They're all bent," she said.

"Well, what do you expect?" Garry inquired. "That's what they're looking for." He sat down opposite Kenyon, and sighed. "A nice girl," he said, "but very choosy. Upsets the customers. I may have to let her go."

"Cheers," Kenyon said. "Join me. It's your brandy."

"I will," Garry said. He poured a measure into the balloon glass. "Thanks, Mr. Kenyon," he said. "That looked very nasty. I didn't recognize them when they came in. Who were they?"

"They're on Walter Flack's team," Kenyon said. "And by the way, your head waiter's a thief."

"I know," Garry said. "So are they all. If the staff weren't ripping me off, I could pretty well double my profits. Or halve my prices," he amended. "Still, that's the way it goes in this business. I suppose you wouldn't care to eat here regularly, Mr. Kenyon?"

"It would be a pleasure," Kenyon said. "But I daren't. Not any more. Times have changed."

Garry nodded acceptance of this statement. "Walter Flack'll try again in that case, I suppose," he said. "Eventually."

"You haven't got any . . . arrangement . . . of your own then?"

"I run a straight club," Garry said, which did not quite answer the question.

"Who's backing you, Garry?" Kenyon asked.

"No one," Garry said. "I'm on my own."

Kenyon did not believe him, but since Garry was clearly not going to volunteer anything, he did not press the point. In any case, he was not very interested. He was much more concerned with the looming problems in his own life, which the brandy was doing very little to dispel.

No word came from the CIB and Kenyon began to nurture the faint hope that Detective Superintendent Pindar had been misinformed. Except that there was no word about his overdue promotion either.

He considered canceling his dinner date with the Vallentas. It might be wise to do so. *If*, by some unknown means, they did know about his visits to Angela . . . But how could they know? No, it was impossible. They must have dreamed up something else. In which case, perhaps it would be even wiser to stay away . . .

Abruptly, Kenyon stopped worrying about it. He was

beginning to feel decidedly bloody minded about the whole thing. Sod the CIB. He would go. He did.

This time, it was dark when he arrived. Kenyon took an even more circuitous route, and he knew for certain that he had not been followed.

He stood at the entrance of the mews for several minutes before he approached Tony Vallenta's door. Once more, there were vehicles parked. Three cars. No one in them. Carefully, his eyes examined the windows of all the houses ovrelooking the L at the end. Finally, the parapets, silhouetted against the glow in the sky spilled over from London's lights. When he rang the doorbell, he was confident that no one was keeping observation on Tony Vallenta's house.

The meal, served by a silent manservant, would have been worthy of an inspired chef on a good day. Kenyon did not attribute it to Angela, whose talents did not lie in any kitchen, but he framed his complimentary remarks delicately, so that she could accept the credit if she wished.

Angela laughed, and said, "Nothing to do with me."

"A fellow I borrow on occasions," Tony said. "Thank him."

"Must make a nice change after the food inside," Kenyon said.

"Please. Don't remind me," Tony groaned. "It was awful. I had dyspepsia all the time." Kenyon made sympathetic noises.

Tony supposed they could manage some more wine, between them, and decanted the second bottle himself. He was careful about wine. They were drinking Mouton Rothschild. Kenyon caught sight of the year, and guessed that vintage retailed at about thirty pounds a bottle. Well worth it, too, provided someone else was paying.

Tony was wearing a handmade silk shirt, and cashmere trousers. Prison clothes had been another of the hardships he found hard to bear, it seemed.

"It must have been hell," Kenyon said, straight-faced.

"All right," Tony said. "Laugh at me. I'm a figure of fun." The last thing Kenyon regarded Tony Vallenta as was a figure of fun. Tony said, "But I have a grievance, remember. I was framed."

"Naturally," Kenyon said.

"Come on," Tony said. "Me carry a shooter in the boot of my car? A lunatic like Walter Flack, maybe. But me? Am I a lunatic?" he appealed to Angela.

"No, darling," Angela said.

"It was there," Kenyon said.

"Right," Tony said. "It was there. No denying that. So someone put it there. The law, maybe? That's how it seems to me. Who else?"

"I wouldn't know about that," Kenyon said.

"I thought you might," Tony said.

"I don't play that way," Kenyon said.

"You don't play all that straight either," Tony said.

Kenyon wondered if all this was the cheery badinage which it seemed to be, or if something else was going on beneath the surface.

"You did all right," Kenyon said. "You'd still be inside for a long time yet, if you hadn't eased your way out of that conspiracy to murder charge."

"I don't know what your lot have got against me," Tony said, plaintively. "I'm just a businessman, that's all. No one cooks up phony charges against the chairman of ICI. Why me?"

The comparison, and Tony's naive air of injured innocence tickled Kenyon, and he laughed. This was the Tony Vallenta whom he could not help but like. The other one, who trafficked, for profit, in extortion, human degradation and death, was absent, or at least well-concealed. "You're not exactly in the same line of business, Tony," he said.

"Business is business," Tony said. It probably was, to him, too. "And frankly, I feel I've been persecuted. People have taken advantage of my good nature." His bright, brown eyes stared at Kenyon. "I mean nothing personal, of course," he said.

"Tony has a great respect for you, Sid," Angela said.

"I have indeed," Tony said. "The highest possible regard."

"I'm flattered," Kenyon said.

"You should be," Tony said. "I don't rate all that many people, but I rate you in a very special kind of way."

Kenyon wondered if he was leading up to an offer of some sort.

"Suppose we go and have a game of billiards?" Tony inquired. "What do you say?"

Kenyon felt that the scenery, in the form of Angela, was superior here, but the man was his host for the evening, after all. He stood up, and followed Tony upstairs to the billiard room.

Tony chalked his cue in a businesslike fashion.

"A hundred up?" he inquired.

"Suits me," Kenyon said. "You're the expert. I'm only here to be beaten."

But early on, Tony missed an easy cannon and, aided by a couple of fluky in offs, Kenyon ran up a break of thirty. Tony groaned, and miscued. Kenyon notched up another twenty.

"I'm not back in practice yet," Tony said, bitterly. "Facilities for billiards in prison, they did not have."

Kenyon considered it tactful not to beat his host at his own game, and tried a fancy shot which he had not a hope of bringing off, and duly missed.

"You're getting too ambitious," Tony said, settling down into a series of kiss cannons.

Kenyon finally lost by three points, which restored Tony's good humor completely.

"You can tell a lot about a man's character by the way he plays billiards," Tony said, racking the cues. "You had me cold there, but you faded under pressure."

Kenyon thought that only a supreme egotist like Tony would have failed to see that he was being allowed to win, but chose not to say so. He lit a cigarette.

"Just the same," Tony said, "I'll make sure I'm back in form before I risk playing you again."

"In case you're not talking about billiards," Kenyon said, "I think you'll lose . . . in the end."

Tony shook his head. "I'm not chancing being set up again," he said. "A citizen above reproach from now on, that's me."

"Oh yes," Kenyon said.

"I've retired," Tony said.

"You're straining my credulity, Tony," Kenyon said.

"Look," Tony said, "why should I work my guts

out making more money? I'm not a rich man," he said, modestly, "but I've got enough to keep me and Angela in reasonable comfort. A man can't drive more than one car at once, or live in more than one house at the same time. Already, as well as this place, I've got a villa near Palermo, a beautiful spot, right by the sea. In fact, I've got all I'm ever going to need for the rest of my life. Why bother anymore? There's no reason."

"Habit," Kenyon suggested.

"Habit isn't worth prison," Tony said. "No, let other people do the work from here on."

"Like before," Kenyon said.

"Not like before," Tony said. "Like it's different from now on."

"I've got an open mind," Kenyon said. "We'll see."

Tony Vallenta was a small, slightly built man, no more than five feet six inches tall, although the lifts he wore added another couple of inches. His shining brown eyes had all the frank honesty of a Labrador's as he gazed up at Kenyon.

"You know," Tony said quietly, "I wasn't buttering you up downstairs. I've always had a lot of time for you. A lot of coppers, to be frank, are none too bright. You're bright. I've often wondered what a fellow like you gets out of the police force."

"I sometimes wonder myself," Kenyon said.

"I mean, the pay's disgraceful," Tony said.

"It's not the best way to get rich," Kenyon admitted.

"Take holidays, for instance," Tony said. "Going abroad these days costs you a grand before you can turn around."

"Not on a package tour," Kenyon said.

"I've sometimes thought," Tony said, "there's my villa doing nothing most of the time. Someone using it for a month, say, would be doing me a favor. Someone I could trust. It'd be worth my while to pay his expenses to keep the place aired, and so on."

"I suppose it would," Kenyon said.

"He'd have a marvelous holiday, in an idyllic spot, with everything found, including spending money," Tony said. "He could take a bird along, if he wanted, or if not, there's a pretty good selection on the spot."

"Sounds great," Kenyon said.

"It did cross my mind to suggest it to you, on a friendly basis," Tony said.

"Is that an offer?" Kenyon asked.

"No," Tony said. "I was tempted, but I thought you'd turn me down. You might have felt insulted, and I wouldn't like that. And I don't like being turned down."

"Why should I feel insulted?" Kenyon asked.

"You might have thought I'd want something in return," Tony said.

"Since you're not going to make an offer, we'll never know," Kenyon said.

Tony glanced at his gold Omega watch. "I ought to make the odd phone call," he said. "Suppose you go and keep Angela company. Can you find your own way downstairs?"

"I'll go via the kitchen," Kenyon said, "and give my compliments to the chef."

"I don't suppose he's there," Tony said, as he went off towards his study, which adjoined the billiard room. Angela had shown Kenyon all over the house, and he knew that Tony's study boasted a mahogany period desk, and the walls were lined with books, including a good many first editions, and two whole shelves of volumes about Napoleon Bonaparte, all of which, Angela told him, he had read many times. Tony admired Napoleon.

Kenyon paused as he passed the open door of the master bedroom, and glanced in at the opulent furnishings, and the king-sized round bed, with its silk sheets and satin bedspread. Tony must have missed all that in prison too. So had Angela, Kenyon thought.

He went down the stairs, and opened the kitchen door. The manservant was percolating coffee. The kitchen gleamed like a show place. There were no signs that a meal had been cooked there in living history.

"Can I help you, sir?" the manservant inquired.

"Is the chef around?"

"He's gone back to the restaurant, sir," the manservant said. "He likes to be there in time to supervise the entrées himself."

"All right," Kenyon said. "Never mind."

Angela had a large brandy ready for him. "Thanks," Kenyon said.

She sat down in her usual place on the huge couch and crossed her slim legs, which looked about six inches longer than any normal female's.

"You've been a long time," Angela said.

"It was a scrappy game, and then we got talking," Kenyon said. "Tony says he's retired."

"I've told you that," Angela said. "Repeatedly."

"I got the impression," Kenyon said, "that if I'd encouraged him a bit, he might have made me an offer."

He was watching her eyes casually, as he sipped his brandy, and he was almost certain that she was surprised.

"I can't imagine why," Angela said.

"Nor can I," Kenyon said. "Not if he's retired."

"Sid," Angela said, with a trace of impatience, "do you have to think like a policeman all the time? Can't you ever relax and take a night off?"

"Now and then," Kenyon said. "And very pleasant it is too. I enjoy it. But afterwards, I worry a bit."

"About what?"

"The reasons," Kenyon said.

"You're not married," Angela said. "You've no steady girl, as far as I know. You work like an obsessed beaver, but sublimation isn't terribly effective with men like you." She smiled with self-conscious self-deprecation. "At least, in my limited experience."

"I didn't mean *my* reasons," Kenyon said.

The manservant brought in the coffee.

"I'll see to it," Angela said. The manservant withdrew.

"Where's Carmen?" Kenyon asked.

"Gone back to Spain," Angela said. She poured two cups of coffee. "I missed Tony when he was inside," Angela said. "I missed him a lot."

"I expect you did," Kenyon said.

"One sometimes gets to the point," Angela said, delicately, "when what one needs most is a jolly good fuck."

A week later, at nine A.M., the telephone rang in Kenyon's office.

"Kenyon," Kenyon said, into the receiver.

"Good morning, Inspector," the voice said. "This is Detective Chief Superintendent Bernard Chandler, of the Complaints Investigation Branch."

"Good morning, sir," Kenyon said.

"I'd like to see you tomorrow morning at ten o'clock prompt," Detective Chief Superintendent Bernard Chandler said.

"Yes, sir," Kenyon said.

"And bring your diary," Chandler said. The line went dead. Kenyon hung up.

Half an hour later, Malory came in. He was shaken, and white faced.

"Sid, I need a bit of help," he said.

"If Vera's given you the brush-off," Kenyon said unsympathetically, "I've got more important things to worry about."

"It's not that," Mallory said, querulously, "though the odds are she bloody soon will. I've just had the CIB on. I've got to be there ten o'clock tomorrow morning."

"I wonder what we're supposed to have done," Kenyon said.

Malory stared. "You too?"

"Join the club," Kenyon said.

CHAPTER FIVE

They rode up in the lift to the seventeenth floor.

"If they lived much higher up, they'd need bloody oxygen," Malory said. His well-pressed suit was immaculate, he was showered, shaved and after-shaved, but a certain puffiness under his eyes hinted that he had not slept any too well.

They were shown into a waiting room by a Detective Sergeant who neutrally asked for their working diaries.

Kenyon eyed him as he checked the date on which Kenyon's diary commenced. He was interested to see if his previous diary would be required, but the Detective Sergeant took both diaries away without a word. So the CIB were only concerned with the last few months, or possibly weeks. They sat down and smoked in silence. The minutes dragged by, leaden footed. Malory grew restless.

"I wonder if there's any chance of getting some coffee," he said.

"Go and find out," Kenyon suggested.

Malory shook his head vaguely, and sat down again. No one appeared. Forty minutes went by. Malory got up, picked up the overflowing ashtray, and emptied it into a waste bin.

"Looks bad," he explained. Kenyon yawned. Tiredness, perversely, was overtaking him. He could cheerfully go to sleep.

"I told Vera last night," Malory said, unhappily. "In case her father had heard anything."

"Had he?"

"No," Mallory said. "But she was by no means overjoyed."

"I don't suppose she was," Kenyon said.

"I mean, it looks bad," Malory said. "Bloody bad."

"Like too many dog ends," Kenyon said.

"What? Oh." Malory gave his lip a chew. "Vera said, could there be anything I knew of . . . I said nothing . . . I've racked my brains, but . . ." He shot a quick, almost furtive glance at Kenyon. "Vera said, in that case, since they'd sent for you as well . . . it must be something you knew about."

"I don't," Kenyon said.

"Come on, Sid," Malory said, "if I'm going to have my balls chewed off, I've got a right to know what it's all about."

"If you're very lucky," Kenyon said, "they might tell you. But I wouldn't take any bets on it."

"Look," Malory said, urgently. "We've worked together for a long time now. We make a damn good team. All right, you're the best DI in the division, and I've learned a lot from you. But I think I've done my bit as well."

"You have," Kenyon said.

"Then give me a break, Sid," Malory said. "Fair's fair. At least give me some idea what I'm supposed to say."

"About what?" Kenyon inquired.

"I don't bloody know what," Malory said, agitatedly. "That's what I'm asking. It's nothing we've been in on together, I'm sure of that. The only thing I can come up with . . . you sometimes take off on your own . . . say you're doing one thing, but I know damn well that . . ."

"Why don't you shut up, Len," Kenyon said. "I can't get five minutes kip if you're going to rabbit on like an old woman." He closed his eyes.

It was widely believed that the waiting room was bugged, and that was why those summoned to the CIB were kept waiting interminably, until perhaps, under the nervous strain, one of them said something he should not.

Kenyon had no idea if this belief was well-founded or not. But he thought it best not to take any chances.

Malory fidgeted in silence after that. At the end of one hour precisely, as if on cue, the Detective Sergeant came in.

"Detective Chief Superintendent Chandler will see you now, sir," the Detective Sergeant said.

"Sit down, Inspector," Detective Chief Superintendent Bernard Chandler said. He was a stout, balding, placid-looking man with an affable, sympathetic face. His appearance was deceptive.

"Thank you, sir," Kenyon said. He sat down in the single, hard-backed chair facing the large desk, over which Bernard Chandler presided.

"Good morning, Inspector," the other one said.

Kenyon twisted his head round. "Good morning, sir," he said to Detective Chief Inspector Paul Stapleton, who was sitting behind Kenyon, ready to take notes. Paul Stapleton was younger than his chief. In his early forties, he had bushy reddish brown hair, and he showed a lot of white teeth when he smiled, which was frequently. The effect was by no means friendly, and reminded Kenyon of a fox contemplating a large, plump chicken.

Kenyon knew both men slightly. At one time, after becoming a Detective Superintendent at West End Central, and before returning to the CID on appointment to the Complaints Investigation Branch, Bernard Chandler had commanded a section of the Special Patrol Group, a body not renowned for its affability or sympathy. Paul Stapleton had been a rigidly efficient Detective Inspector at Camberwell, an immediate and enthusiastic convert to the 'clean up the CID' campaign, as soon as it was instituted, attracting favorable attention at the Yard in the process.

No one offered to shake hands. The formalities over, Detective Chief Superintendent Chandler got down to business.

"On the fourth of last month," he said, "you spent the hours between nineteen hundred and twenty-two hundred with an informant at a public house called The Grapes in the vicinity of Westbourne Grove."

So that was it. But what occasion was that? The fourth? "I'm sorry," Kenyon said, trying to remember for his own benefit, not theirs. "The fourth was . . . ?"

Chandler held up Kenyon's working diary. A stubby finger indicated the entry.

"Ah, yes," Kenyon said. He supposed some bastard

87

must have been in that pub who would have seen him had he been there, and for some reason they were checking. Well, he could skate round that all right.

"The informant's name was . . . ?" Chandler inquired.

"Vic Rowan," Kenyon said. "But we didn't stay. Vic spotted one of his cronies playing a fruit machine."

"Really. It says here . . ." Chandler began.

"It says we met at The Grapes," Kenyon said. "We talked for a while, and then caught a bus to North Acton, where he lives. I got the tube home."

"Arriving at twenty-three hundred," Chandler said.

"Yes, sir," Kenyon said.

"And the information you received . . . ?" Chandler inquired.

"A tip-off concerning a man involved in a raid on a jeweler's shop in Praed Street," Kenyon said. "Marty Doran. He was detained for questioning, I think, about ten days later."

Chandler methodically located the appropriate entry. "Yes, I see," he said.

Everything Kenyon had related was correct. It had all happened, although not on the fourth. Kenyon's diary was accurate enough in content. He simply shuffled dates now and then when he was engaged on something he preferred not to commit to paper.

"Bearing in mind," Chandler said, "the entry in your diary, and the further explanation you have provided in response to my questions, can you account for this?"

He held out a photograph. It showed Kenyon outside Tony Vallenta's house. Angela was standing in the doorway, smiling at him. The photograph carried a date and time. The date was the fourth.

Kenyon swore under his breath. He knew, without being told, where that photograph had come from. The Serious Crimes Squad, which operated out of Limehouse. They used photographs a lot these days, when keeping a target under observation. Villains could and did refrain from putting anything incriminating on paper, or saying anything on phones which might be tapped, but they had to go about their business, and they could not become invisible. Hence the widespread use of photographs.

He also knew, sickeningly and too late, how it had

been taken. From that bloody TV rental van, which he had looked at, and ignored. He must be going soft in the head. He should have known better.

He should also have known better than to underrate the CIB. They did not act on trivia or speculation, or without hard information or evidence. Well, they had that all right, he thought, glancing at that blasted photograph. By trying to be clever, he had dropped himself right in the shit. There was only one thing he could do now, which he should have done right from the beginning, and that was to tell the full and unvarnished truth.

"As a matter of fact," Kenyon said, "I can account for that photograph, yes."

"I'm glad to hear it," Chandler said.

"But I'd be obliged if we could start again, sir," Kenyon said.

"I want to be completely frank with you, Inspector," Chandler said. That would be the day, Kenyon thought sourly. Chandler riffled the pages of the diary. "I could take up a great deal of my time in questioning you about other entries where we have some reason to doubt their verisimilitude." He smiled faintly, pleased perhaps with his grandiloquence. "You may be able to set my mind at rest concerning these other entries, of course," he said.

"I believe I can set your mind at rest, sir," Kenyon said, "by explaining why some entries, while accurate and truthful in themselves, are written up for days and times other than that on which they actually took place."

"Please do," Chandler said.

"I was investigating a matter which it would have been premature to put on record," Kenyon said.

Chandler sat back expectantly. His kindly, crinkled eyes studied Kenyon benevolently. "Go on," he said.

Kenyon told them. Both men had been good experienced working coppers before they were appointed to the Complaints Investigation Branch. They knew what it was all about. They would understand. He explained that he had known Angela and Tony Vallenta for a long time. Why he had developed a relationship with Angela. His belief that Tony was responsible for at least one murder, despite the Court of Appeal decision, and possibly more. His suspicion that a large sum of money, perhaps as much as two or three million pounds, was unaccounted for. His private, and admittedly random speculations as to what kind of criminal use such an amount of money might be used for.

Long before he finished, he knew that he was not getting through. Both men were listening carefully, but in a remote, detached fashion. He was getting nothing back from either of them, not the slightest flicker of any indication that they identified with what he had done, in any way.

When he had finished, there was a long silence. Kenyon was dying for a cigarette, but he seemed to be in the presence of non-smokers. There were no ashtrays anywhere in the room. Chandler raised his eyebrows in the direction of his subordinate. A silent request for a comment, and permission to speak.

Detective Chief Inspector Paul Stapleton said from behind Kenyon, "The fact remains that his diary is no more than a tissue of lies, sir."

"I've explained that," Kenyon snapped, over his shoulder.

"Not to my satisfaction," Chandler said. He leaned sideways, shuffled through several photographs, and selected one.

"In the course of your inquiries," he said, "did you think it might be helpful to spend the night with the no doubt delectable Angela Vallenta?"

The photograph showed Kenyon leaving. In the doorway was a sleepy Angela, wearing a lace negligée. The date recorded was the fifth. The time, six fifty-one in the morning.

Kenyon said nothing. He felt ill. In his mind's eye, he walked again along the mews that morning. His heels clicked on the cobblestones. The air was crisp and fresh, cleansed by the night breezes, and as yet unpolluted by exhaust fumes. He felt good and bad at the same time, pleasantly drained and drowsy, but already beginning to feel that it might not be the most sensible thing he had ever done.

There was no TV rental van in the mews. That had gone. But, he now recalled, parked in a different place was a Dormobile. The bloody Serious Crimes Squad had stayed up all night and switched vehicles.

No wonder these skeptical pillars of the CIB had been none too impressed. A detective, known to have slept with the wife of one of London's most prominent villains was, prima facie, not going to be regarded as the most dedicated upholder of law and order.

Christ, what a mess. It was due to get steadily worse.

"Would you have any objection to your flat being searched, Inspector Kenyon?" Chandler asked.

"Why the hell should you want to do that?" Kenyon demanded, unpleasantly.

"I'm not satisfied with your answers, so far," Chandler said. "A careful examination of your flat might serve to set my mind at rest."

His mind seemed to be in permanent need of being set at rest, Kenyon thought. He wondered bitterly if it ever was. Up to now, it appeared to be in a continual state of unease.

"You are, of course, entitled to refuse," Chandler said, "and indeed, should you have something to hide, it might be wise for you to do so."

Kenyon took out his keys, and threw them on the desk. Detective Chief Inspector Stapleton stepped past him and picked them up.

"The search will take place with your permission, Inspector Kenyon?" Chandler inquired.

"With my permission," Kenyon said. He supposed the whole thing was being recorded, and they wanted his assent on tape. Detective Chief Superintendent Chandler looked at his watch, and then at Stapleton.

"I think we shall be quite a long time with Inspector Kenyon yet," he said. "You'd better tell Detective Sergeant Malory that he may take lunch in the canteen, but he is not to leave the building."

"Very well, sir," Stapleton said.

"Order something on a tray for us," Chandler said. "Cold meat and salad for me. I have to watch the calories these days."

"Cheese and biscuits as well, sir?" Stapleton asked.

"No, my wife keeps giving me cheese," Chandler said.

"She thinks I'm a bloody mouse. I'll have . . . let me see . . . apple pie . . . just a small portion," he qualified.

"Right, sir," Stapleton said.

"And perhaps a little cream," Chandler said. "I'm sure that can't do much harm. What would you like to eat, Inspector Kenyon?"

"I'm not bothered," Kenyon said curtly. "Just coffee and an ashtray."

Stapleton went out. "Do smoke, if you feel so inclined," Chandler said.

"Thank you," Kenyon said. He lit up, and inhaled gratefully. Chandler's nose wrinkled with distaste. Hard luck, Kenyon thought, as smoke drifted in Chandler's direction. The time had long passed since there was any point in worrying about such niceties, in the hope of making a good impression. The impression he was making was all bad. Irritating Chandler's nasal passages was not going to make much difference.

Stapleton came back in, gave Kenyon an ashtray, and sat down. A team of men armed with Kenyon's keys would be heading for his flat now. Bloody good luck to them, Kenyon thought. There was nothing in his flat which would worry a righteous archbishop, much less a worldly detective under investigation. He wondered how long it would take. Not long. He thought that could be the turning point, when they came back empty-handed.

"I suppose you support Queens Park Rangers," Chandler said to Kenyon.

"No," Kenyon said, taken aback. "Why?"

"About your nearest team, aren't they?" Chandler asked.

"I'm not much interested in football," Kenyon said.

"Really?" Chandler said. Kenyon thought that could be another black mark against him.

"You wait till we're in the First Division," Stapleton said.

Chandler chuckled benignly. "*You'll* have to do the waiting," he said.

"You'll see," Stapleton said.

"I still say Arsenal have got what it takes," Chandler said.

Kenyon wondered if the Star Chamber had taken time

out with their victims to discuss the merits of the various well known exponents of bear baiting, or cock fighting.

Lunch came in on trays, with a pot of coffee for Kenyon, and tea for the other two. The talk about soccer meandered on as they ate, covering the league, the FA Cup, and how soon America might be a force to be reckoned with in the World Cup.

Kenyon sipped coffee, and smoked one cigarette after another. He noticed that Stapleton kept glancing with yearning at Kenyon's cigarette. The man was probably a smoker who refrained, when on duty, out of deference to his boss. Kenyon offered him the packet out of devilment.

"Cigarette, sir?"

"I've given up," Stapleton said, displaying all the symptoms of the heavy smoker who needed one badly.

"You hypocritical, bloody liar," Kenyon thought, and left the packet, invitingly open, on the desk. Let the bastard suffer.

After thirty minutes precisely, the trays were removed, and Chandler resumed. Kenyon found the line he took unexpected.

"You own your flat, I believe," Chandler said.

"It's on a lease," Kenyon said.

"The unexpired portion being . . . ?"

"About a hundred and thirty years," Kenyon said.

"I'd call that ownership, for all practical purposes," Chandler said. "How much did you pay for it?"

"Five thousand, two hundred and fifty pounds," Kenyon said.

"You got it cheap."

"That was seven years ago," Kenyon pointed out.

"Of course," Chandler said. "What would you say was its present day value?"

"I don't know," Kenyon said. "Perhaps thirteen, fourteen thousand."

"I am advised," Chandler said, "that a reasonable asking price would be between sixteen or seventeen thousand pounds."

"You're better informed than I am," Kenyon said, shortly. He did not understand this line at all.

"You're sitting on a very nice capital gain," Chandler said.

"Only in paper money," Kenyon said. "We've had inflation of Christ knows how much since then."

"Just the same, you have trebled your money," Chandler murmured.

"Not in real terms," Kenyon argued.

"You've got a better asset than many of us," Chandler said. "I'd say it was a shrewd investment."

"Are we here to discuss my financial acumen, or otherwise?" Kenyon inquired, sarcastically.

"Yes, in a way," Chandler replied, blandly. "How did you happen to pick on that particular flat?"

"I don't understand the relevance of these questions," Kenyon said.

"Excellent," Chandler said. "Then you can have no objection to answering."

"I didn't pick on it," Kenyon said. Suppressed anger was boiling inside him. What bloody right had they to interrogate him about such a private matter as where he lived? The fact that he knew the answer did nothing to lessen his resentment. A policeman was not as other men. His duty was to enforce the law, which implied the preservation of the liberty of the subject to go about his lawful business without let or hindrance. But the policeman himself had his liberties curtailed. He was subject to discipline, not only on duty, but in his private life as well. It was a "crime" for a policeman to be in debt, or to have a second occupation, or to bring the police force into disrepute. Kenyon had been able to ignore these restrictions up to now because he had not been affected. Now he was finding out what it was like to have what normal men would regard as their personal privacy trampled on.

"Are you saying someone offered you the flat?" Chandler asked.

"No," Kenyon said. "I'd been living in the Section House, and I was fed up with that. I was looking round for a place of my own. I used to drive round on my day off . . . I liked Gloucester Terrace very much."

"A fine example of Georgian style architecture," Chandler agreed. "Those houses are the subject of preservation orders now, aren't they?"

"Yes," Kenyon said. "Anyway, one day I noticed workmen converting one of the houses. I went in on the off chance, and they let me look round. I liked the basement flat at once. I don't know why. The foreman told me who the agents were and I went along."

"Did you purchase the flat at once?" Chandler asked.

"Well, no . . ." Kenyon said.

"Why not?"

"The asking price was six thousand five hundred pounds," Kenyon said. "That was more than I'd bargained for. It may not sound much now, but in those days . . ."

"Quite so," Chandler murmured.

"I went to my building society, and they wouldn't even consider it," Kenyon said.

"Building Societies don't much like conversions, to the best of my knowledge," Chandler said.

"No," Kenyon said. "They advised me to find a purpose built flat, or a modern house. I said I'd be glad to if they'd tell me where to find one in W2 or anywhere near, at a price I could afford. We parted on somewhat bad terms."

"I wonder why Inspector Kenyon was so anxious to live in Central London, sir," Detective Chief Inspector Stapleton said from behind Kenyon, addressing his chief. "Most of us settle for what we can afford, and commute. I live in Uxbridge myself, for example."

"I don't like the suburban attitudes of people who live in places like Uxbridge," Kenyon said, with a glance over his shoulder.

Paul Stapleton acknowledged the remark with a smile which was not inspired by any great amusement.

"I'm finding your account a little confusing, Inspector Kenyon," Chandler said, professing to be baffled. "You seem to be implying that you couldn't afford this flat, or raise a mortgage, and yet you acquired it, and have lived there ever since."

"I left my name and address with the agents," Kenyon said. "Two or three weeks later, they rang me, and said that offers for the basement flat would be considered, if I was still interested."

"Oh, I see," Chandler said, as though light were dawning. "And you offered five thousand, two hundred and fifty pounds."

"Yes," Kenyon said.

"Asking price, six and a half," Chandler said. "You offer five and a quarter, which is accepted. That seems like one hell of a drop to me. Didn't that strike you at the time?"

"Apparently the other flats were selling all right," Kenyon said, "but no one except me wanted the basement flat."

"How strange," Chandler said. "Living room twenty-three feet long, private patio, good-sized bedroom with built-in wardrobes, bathroom with colored suite, fully equipped kitchen, with cooker hood, waste disposal unit, twin sinks, breakfast bar with pine fitted shelves forming a dividing unit . . ."

Kenyon's face was growing hot with anger. The bastard had the sale particulars. He was also flushing for another reason. It all sounded so unlikely, at that price, in the circumstances of today. But, God damn it, that was seven years ago, and before the property boom, when prices took off for the sky. He said so, again, putting it even more forcefully this time.

"No one's disputing that you made a highly advantageous purchase," Chandler said. "Quite the reverse."

"Money was tight in those days," Kenyon said. "Not only for people like me, but also for developers. The agents told me that the property company concerned wanted to recover their investment as fast as possible. That's why they were willing to accept my offer."

"Oh, that's why," Chandler said, cryptically.

"I've answered all your questions," Kenyon said, his anger finally boiling over. "And now I'd like to know by what bloody right you've been interrogating me about things, which are fuck all to do with you, Sir!"

Chandler hiccupped slightly, and said, "I should never have had that cream." He smiled at Kenyon kindly. "I expect we're about as impressed by injured innocence as you are, Inspector. When you're interviewing a suspect."

Kenyon was about to say that suspects knew what they were suspected of, but that would have been laughable to two men in the same trade, and he changed his mind. So this was what it was like to have apparently irrelevant and meaningless questions fired at you by men who knew which cards they held in their hands when you did not. He felt beads of perspiration trickling down his temples. How many times had he watched a man, and noted those first traces of sweat, while he himself remained cool and calm and unruffled. On how many occasions had he experienced that small thrill of pleasure as his questions induced those physical manifestations of fear and unease, and thought "He's going. It won't be long now. I've got him." So this was how it was to be on the other end. The wrong end.

"These developers," Chandler said. "This property company."

"They'd bought the house, and were converting it into modern flats," Kenyon said. "There were a lot of conversions going on at that time, all over, Fulham, Paddington, Chelsea. At first, I believe, it was very profitable, but by the time I bought mine . . ."

"Yes, I know all that," Chandler said. "I'm more concerned with who they are. Or were."

"Oh," Kenyon said, trying to remember. ". . . something Developments Ltd."

"The title of the company isn't important," Chandler said. "I'm referring to the identity of the principal shareholder."

"I don't know," Kenyon said.

"You don't know," Chandler said, flatly.

"There were dozens of companies in that game," Kenyon said. "Probably hundreds."

"Are you saying," Chandler inquired, "that you were not aware that the company from whom you purchased your flat was owned by Tony Vallenta?"

Kenyon stared at him. It was only by an effort that he stopped himself repeating vacantly "Tony Vallenta?", a response which he himself always found deeply suspicious, and regarded as a useless effort to gain time.

"I was not aware of that, sir," he said, as steadily as he could. A cold chill entered his guts. Now he understood their questions.

"If you were not aware of it," Chandler said, "it seems rather a surprising coincidence. You admitted yourself that you've known Tony Vallenta for a long time."

"I didn't admit it," Kenyon snapped. "I stated it. And I said I knew him, not that I lived in his pocket."

"Well enough to visit his wife frequently while he was in prison," Chandler smiled.

"I've explained that," Kenyon said.

"Having made a successful offer," Chandler said, "how much did you have in cash to put down?"

"Since you know so much else, sir," Kenyon said, "I'm sure you know that as well."

"I'd still like you to answer my question," Detective Chief Superintendent Chandler said, gently.

"One thousand, two hundred and fifty pounds," Kenyon said. "And if you care to go over my old bank statements, and Building Society passbook, you'll see how I'd managed to save that enormous sum out of my pay."

Chandler allowed all irony to pass him by. "Leaving you four thousand pounds to find," he said.

"I obtained a mortgage for that amount," Kenyon said.

"Was your building society more amenable after you'd secured this very substantial reduction in the price of your flat?" Chandler asked.

"No," Kenyon said. "They said their policy was not to lend against conversions. But the agents offered to make alternative arrangements."

"With whom?"

"A finance company willing to regard those conversions as adequate security," Kenyon said. "The interest rate was a bit higher, but . . ."

"And this finance company was . . . ?" Chandler inquired, sticking to his habit of not completing questions.

"Well, since then, they've been taken over by an insurance company," Kenyon said.

"Yes," Chandler said. "Tony Vallenta sold out before the fringe finance company bubble burst. A good businessman, Tony."

This time, Kenyon could not help himself, "Tony Vallenta?"

"Vallenta owned the finance company in question," Chandler said. "But I gather you are about to say that you were not aware of that either."

"I was not aware of it," Kenyon said. He had run out of cigarettes. His mouth was parched and dry, but he would have given anything for another pack, just now.

"You acquired a flat from Vallenta, on exceptionally

favorable terms," Chandler said, in a mild voice. "When you found difficulty in obtaining a mortgage, Vallenta arranged the necessary finance. Tony did you quite a favor. You could sell tomorrow, and make twelve grand profit. And yet you claim you had no knowledge that Vallenta was involved in any way."

"I don't claim it," Kenyon said. "I'm telling you."

Chandler nodded. "Has he ever suggested that you might be able to do him a service of any kind?" he asked.

Kenyon hesitated, thinking of that oblique conversation in Tony's billiard room. "No," he said.

"You took your time answering that one," Chandler observed.

"He has not," Kenyon said.

"Well, we all know what a generous man Tony Vallenta is," Chandler said. "Some former police officers now in prison for corruption could well be living testimony to his generosity, except that unfortunately we've never been able to prove that Vallenta was directly involved."

"Not up to now, sir," Stapleton observed.

"Can you think of any reason why Vallenta should surreptitiously help you in this way?" Chandler asked.

"Do you have any reason to suppose that the property and finance companies were not legitimate?" Kenyon asked in return.

"No," Chandler said. "Vallenta has always operated straight businesses, as well as his more questionable activities, as I'm sure you know. Which is one good reason why no one's been able to put him away for any length of time."

"He employs managers," Kenyon said. "Tony may not even have known it was me buying the flat."

"I suppose that's possible," Chandler said, although he did not seem to think much of the suggestion. "But on the hypothesis that he did know . . . and if we accept for one moment that he has never made any demands on you in return . . . why should he?"

Kenyon had been thinking about what he was forced to admit to himself was the more likely hypothesis ever since he had learned who his Fairy Godfather had been.

"Well," he said, "all I can imagine is . . ."

"Yes, Inspector Kenyon?" Chandler inquired. "What do you imagine?"

"It could have been a kind of investment on his part against a rainy day," Kenyon said. "After all, it wasn't costing him anything. He probably made a profit on the sale of the flat, or at least got his money back . . ."

"His own money," Chandler murmured, "since he lent it to you."

"On which he got damn good interest," Kenyon argued. "Besides, he might have known at the time that the insurance company would be taking over that firm. He wasn't really laying out anything."

"Sowing seeds which might blossom in due course," Chandler said. "As and when the need arose."

"Something like that." Kenyon said.

"Vallenta might sow, I suppose," Chandler said. "But he would most certainly reap, in due course."

"Perhaps that was in his mind," Kenyon said. "Put me in a position where I might appear to be in his debt, and then lean on me one day when he needed a bit of help."

"But according to you," Chandler said, "he has never attempted to foreclose on his investment, as it were."

"No," Kenyon said. "He hasn't."

"That's where it falls apart, sir," Stapleton said, putting in his four pennyworth. "If Tony did this without Inspector Kenyon's knowledge, he's had seven years to put the bite on. Inspector Kenyon claims he has not. I don't believe a man would do anyone a favor of that kind without a specific end in view in the very near future."

"You're thinking like a copper," Kenyon said, in Stapleton's direction. "Tony Vallenta thinks like a villain."

"Well," Stapleton said. "I'm prepared to bow to your superior knowledge in that respect."

"I think you've forgotten what it's like," Kenyon said. "You've sat up here on the seventeenth floor of Scotland Yard too long. Out on the streets, theory and procedure don't get you far. You have to get inside a villain's mind, you have to think the way he does."

Kenyon supposed that he was telling his grandmother how to suck eggs with a vengeance. The CIB might utilize a certain kind of man, but they were all senior officers with a good track record. Just the same, they *did* talk as though they had sat in comfortable offices, dealing with paper rather than people, for far too long.

Chandler leaned back in his chair, his hands folded on his protruding stomach, studying Kenyon.

There was a tap at the door. Chandler ignored it, and continued his benevolent examination of Kenyon's face. Stapleton got up, went to the door, opened it, held a whispered conversation with the man standing there, closed the door, and handed a large envelope to Chandler. Chandler examined the contents.

Kenyon supposed the large typewritten sheets contained an inventory of the contents of his flat. He waited. At least there would be nothing incriminating there, thank God, and he guessed that would tip the balance. The interview had gone far from well, but it had not amounted to a total disaster. Some serious question marks had been raised against him which he could well have done without, but he thought he could successfully work his passage from here on. He would have to watch his step in future, and there were one or two items which needed sorting out with Tony Vallenta, but . . .

"How much do you have in your bank account?" Detective Chief Superintendent Chandler inquired.

"Something over three hundred," Kenyon said. "I think you have my last statement there, sir." Chandler was fingering it.

"Yes," Chandler said. "Three hundred and thirty-seven pounds, forty-two pence."

Let the bastard try and make something out of that.

"Would you mind telephoning your bank for an up to date balance, please?" Chandler asked.

"It won't be much different," Kenyon said. "Since then, my pay's been credited, but I've drawn checks for . . ."

"Let's not speculate," Chandler interrupted. "Let's have an accurate figure."

Kenyon felt that he had taken all he was going to. Enough was enough. He seemed to have been sitting on this hard chair in front of his inquisitor for a week rather than half a day, and he was stiff, tired, and fed up to the back teeth with having doubt thrown on everything he said.

"A reasonably accurate figure would be about three hundred and fifty pounds, sir," he said. "I see no purpose in wasting the bank's time to find out if it's a few quid more or a few quid less."

"No one's interested in a few quid," Chandler agreed.

"Right," Kenyon said. "Is there anything else?"

"But are you sure that your bank balance might not approximate more closely to five thousand three hundred and fifty pounds?"

"Don't be bloody stupid," Kenyon said, tiredly.

"I always try not to be," Chandler said. He held up a small piece of paper.

Kenyon stared at it blankly. It was the counterfoil of a Giro pay in slip. The stamp was that of the Piccadilly branch of his bank. The amount paid in was £5,000 in £10 notes. It carried the initials "S.K."

"I know nothing about that," he said, shakily.

"It was found at the back of a drawer in the desk positioned beside the standard lamp in your flat," Chandler said. "It's true that the counterfoil does not carry any account number, and that the initials S.K. could stand for Stanley King, or Sally Kong. They could also refer to Sidney Kenyon. Are you prepared to settle any doubts on that score by telephoning your bank?" Chandler delicately moved one of the receivers across the desk to Kenyon's elbow.

Kenyon phoned his branch in Bayswater and spoke to the manager, who recognized his voice, but said he would call back, if Kenyon would give him the number, which was the usual procedure.

They sat in silence for two minutes. The phone rang. Kenyon picked it up.

"Including the recent large deposit," the bank manager said, "your balance as of today is five thousand, three hundred and fifty-eight pounds, ninety-two pence."

"Thank you," Kenyon said.

"Glad things are looking up for you," the manager said cheerfully.

"Yes," Kenyon said.

He hung up. So did Chandler. He had been listening in on an extension.

"Inspector Kenyon," Chandler said, "I want to be as fair as possible. Before this interview is concluded, I am willing to give you the opportunity to change any of the answers you have given in response to our questions. You can go back and start afresh if you wish to amend your statements in any way, or provide any additional information. Do you wish to avail yourself of that opportunity?"

"No, sir," Kenyon said.

"Very well," Chandler said. "Then can you account for this five thousand pounds?"

"Only in one way," Kenyon said. "I've been set up."

"For what reason?"

"I don't know," Kenyon said, tightly. "But if I had taken money from someone, I wouldn't be daft enough to leave evidence lying around my flat."

"It wasn't lying around," Chandler observed. "One might say it was concealed. And you weren't to know that your flat would be searched."

"I gave my bloody permission," Kenyon snarled.

"You had very little choice," Chandler said, accurately. "You could well have hoped it would be overlooked. The fact that you were so reluctant to telephone your bank might lend some credence to that possibility."

Kenyon did not think it worthwhile to try and explain his reluctance now. In the light of what had happened, his reasons would sound weak in the extreme.

"That pay in slip was planted in my flat," he said flatly.

"That implies someone knew we'd be searching it," Chandler said, skeptically.

"You may have done some digging before you saw me," Kenyon said. "But I think you've been fed information as well." He looked at Chandler. The stout man's eyes did not flicker. "I don't have to tell you," Kenyon went on, "how easy it is to plant moody information about a copper."

"We make a point," Chandler said, "of bearing all possibilities in mind."

They were not going to give anything away. Kenyon knew it. But he tried anyway.

"One possibility you might bear in mind, sir," Kenyon said, "is that I'm being framed."

"We weren't born yesterday, Inspector," Chandler said. For the first time, there was a tinge of asperity in his voice.

"It would help me to refute false allegations," Kenyon said, "if I knew what information about me had been fed to you."

Chandler said nothing. He clearly intended to say nothing. Kenyon supposed that, had he been in the stout man's place, he also would have said nothing. But that was poor consolation. He was not comfortably ensconced behind a big desk, playing his hand the way he chose. He was sitting in the hot seat, with no idea what the game was, let alone how many cards were being concealed.

"All right," Kenyon said. "Do you know who passed information about me?"

Again, Chandler said nothing, and of course it was almost certain that he did not know. It would have been done indirectly, or through a third party, who himself would be genuinely ignorant of the real source.

Chandler examined Kenyon's keys, and then passed them across the desk. Kenyon took them.

Chandler studied one of the typewritten sheets. "There were no signs of forced entry," he said. "Neither door nor windows. If the pay in slip was planted, a key was used to gain entry. Does anyone else have a set of keys to your flat? Caretaker, managing agents, friends?"

"No, sir," Kenyon said.

"How many sets of keys do you have?"

"Two," Kenyon said.

"One set now returned to you," Chandler said. He went back to the typewritten sheets, and studied another one. "And your spare set in the top right hand drawer of your dressing table."

"That's where I keep them," Kenyon said.

"Have you entertained anyone whom you might suspect of planting the pay in slip?" Chandler asked.

"No," Kenyon said.

"Then how do you suppose it was done?" Chandler inquired. "No forced entry, no one else has any keys, no one who might have done it been in your flat. Give me a suggestion."

"I can't," Kenyon said.

"Well, if you can't," Chandler said, "I don't know who can."

"But since I didn't pay that money in, and no one else

paid it in to my knowledge and handed me the slip, it must have been planted somehow," Kenyon said, doggedly.

"Well, I doubt if there's any chance of the individual who did pay it in being remembered," Chandler said judicially. "Piccadilly must be about the busiest branch in the land. But we'll make inquiries."

"Thank you very much," Kenyon said. There was not a hope, and Chandler knew it as well as he did. "But I'd suggest that's why they chose the Piccadilly branch."

"Who might 'they' be?" Chandler asked, with interest.

Kenyon saw no point in saying "I don't know" yet again. He contented himself with a brief, pleasant fantasy, in which he and certain members of the CIB were alone, on a piece of wasteland, with no one else within sight or earshot.

"For what purpose do you suppose you might have been set up?" Chandler asked, going through the motions of being fair, and giving his victim every chance.

"Well, I suppose it could be revenge," Kenyon said, uncertainly.

"Jesus Christ Almighty," Chandler said, moved for once to genuine emotion. "I can well believe, Inspector Kenyon, that a fair number of people in this world hate your guts. Personally, I find that entirely understandable . . . bearing in mind the number of good villains you've put away," he added. "But if it were revenge, why go through this rigmarole? I do vaguely remember the villains' mentality," he said pointedly, "from those distant days when I dealt with a few myself. A beating up, a kneecapping, or even your death would be much more satisfying to the average villain in my limited experience. Any of which events could be purchased a damn sight cheaper than five grand."

Chandler was right, and Kenyon knew it. "All right," he said. "If it's not that, it must be an attempt to discredit me."

"OK," Chandler said. "Why?"

"To get me off someone's back," Kenyon said.

"Who?" Chandler demanded. "And what are you on to that's so bloody important to anyone?"

"If I knew that," Kenyon said, "I'd have told you before now."

"Let me be perfectly frank," Chandler said. "I find it hard to believe you, and I'll tell you why. Dropping a man in the shit deliberately, that dodge has been tried before, and we're on the lookout for it. A villain might invest five hundred quid, or even a grand, to try and shop a copper who was getting in his way. But five thousand pounds? What the hell do you think you know that's worth five grand to anyone?"

Kenyon shook his head helplessly.

Detective Chief Superintendent Bernard Chandler said, "I have to tell you that the prima facie evidence against you is extremely strong, and I am not satisfied with the account you have given. Therefore, I shall recommend to the Commander that you be suspended from duty pending further investigation. Wait outside. The Commander will see you shortly, when he will explain your rights. That's all, Kenyon."

As Kenyon closed the door, he heard Chandler burp with profound relief.

CHAPTER SIX

Kenyon went back to his office. He was mentally numb with shock. Nothing made sense, and he could not even begin to think straight yet. The Commander had taken his warrant card from him, and explained his "rights," which amounted to none.

This day, guilty of nothing, he had been suspended. Suspension from duty was far worse than he had ever anticipated in his worst nightmares. Few men's careers ever recovered from a setback like that even if, in the end, they were reinstated.

Despite the prima facie evidence which Detective Chief Superintendent Chandler had found so impressive, Kenyon doubted if that "evidence" could ever be turned into the kind of proof which would enable them to make corruption charges against him. For that, witnesses were required. Circumstantial evidence was not enough. And since Kenyon had not in fact made any corrupt deal with anyone, he did not see where any witnesses were going to come from, prepared to stand up in open court, and be subjected to rigorous cross-examination.

The odds were that the CIB's investigation would drag on for months, or even a year or more, while Kenyon cooled his heels at home on full pay until, reluctantly, Detective Chief Superintendent Bernard Chandler noted "no further action." But, even if at that point he were reinstated, the file on him would not be closed.

The Metropolitan Police Force had other weapons at its disposal. Intense pressure would be brought upon him to resign. Well, he could resist that pressure. But that would not be the end of it either. He could be transferred to the uniformed branch in one of the Met's far flung, and more tedious, outposts. Promotion would be permanently blocked. He would be a marked man. They would be content to wait. He would either quit in the end, in despair and disgust, or soldier on, disillusioned and cynical, an ignored nobody, until he could get out with a pension. Either would suit their purposes, to some degree.

And whatever happened, if the wild, random speculation he had clutched at was right, if someone had set out to discredit him for some reason he could not imagine, that person could now sit back and forget about him. Kenyon was well and truly discredited, as of now.

The bush telegraph was obviously working at optimum efficiency. As Kenyon walked along the corridors and up the stairs of the busy Bayswater Police Station, everyone, miraculously, was deeply occupied with something else as he passed by. They all happened to be looking elsewhere, which saved them from noticing his presence, and the embarrassment of trying to think what to say.

When victims of the Black Death exhibited the first telltale signs of the disease, they might have felt something like Kenyon, as their neighbors and friends turned their backs.

Kenyon became aware that a large form had appeared in the doorway of his office. He continued emptying drawers.

"I'm clearing out my desk," he said.

Detective Superintendent Pindar nodded. "Make sure you don't have to come back for anything," he said. "You will remain available for further interviews, as required, but you'll have to stay away from here until this business is cleared up, one way or another."

"I know the form," Kenyon said.

"You didn't make a good impression on them," Pindar said.

"They didn't make much of an impression on me either," Kenyon said.

"Aggressive, disrespectful, unhelpful," Pindar said. "I choose some of the milder adjectives used to describe you. My phone practically bloody melted in my hand."

"Snide, hypocritical, suspicious shits," Kenyon said, "would be my understated response."

"They're only doing their job," Pindar said.

Kenyon closed his briefcase, and looked at the big man. "I've been set up," he said, steadily. "A good job, but a set-up."

"Everyone in your position says that," Pindar said.

Kenyon sighed. "I know," he admitted.

"Where's Malory?"

"I was first," Kenyon said. "With them now, I suppose."

"My guess is," Pindar said, "that they'll be using him to test your version."

"I wasn't able to give much of a version," Kenyon said. "I know bugger all."

"They may have given you a rough ride," Pindar said, "but they're not there for polite tea party conversation. Len Malory's steady, straightforward, and reliable. If he can back you up in any way, they're bound to take that into account."

"Perhaps someone's planted something on him too," Kenyon said. He was in no mood to detect silver linings.

"They'll look into your contention that you've been framed, you know," Pindar said. "They're not there to screw coppers as a hobby."

"You could have fooled me," Kenyon said, bitterly.

A couple of young Detective Constables strolled past Kenyon's office, and Pindar closed the door.

"Look, Sid," Pindar said, "some of the people who know you best, people like me, for instance, are going to want to believe you. But the CIB aren't idiots, and they've nothing against you personally, however you feel at the moment. If they say there's strong prima facie evidence, there is."

"Evidence fed to them," Kenyon said. "And planted."

"Quite a number of bent coppers have either resigned or gone inside," Pindar said, "because of investigations inspired in the first place by information received. Or, putting it another way, evidence fed to the CIB. As for the plant, they'll look into that possibility."

"I think I can convince you I was set up, sir," Kenyon said.

"If you can convince me," Pindar said, "you can convince the CIB. Did you tell them?"

"No," Kenyon said.

"Why not?"

"Five grand was paid into my bank account," Kenyon said, *"after* you'd given me the tip that the CIB had opened a file on me. I couldn't very well mention you'd done that."

"Some would have done," Pindar said.

"To accept a bribe after being told the CIB were on his tail," Kenyon said. "A man would have to be out of his mind to do that."

Pindar thought for a few seconds. Finally, he said slowly, "Or greedy."

"I'm not that greedy," Kenyon said.

"Tell them, if you think it would help you," Pindar said. "I'll confirm it, with pleasure."

Kenyon shook his head. "Thanks for the offer, sir," he said, "but I won't bother. If greed is the first likely explanation to cross your mind, it would sure as hell be in the forefront of theirs."

Pindar blinked unhappily, and reached for the door knob. "I don't suppose I shall be seeing you for a while, Sid," he said. "I'll wish you luck."

"Thank you, sir," Kenyon said.

He watched Pindar go, and scribbled a note to Malory, asking him to phone, during the evening, without fail. Then he went home.

Kenyon waited until the early evening news was over before he switched off his television set, and reached for the whisky bottle. Two large ones failed to have the desirable effect he was looking for. He poured a third, lay on the settee, smoked, and stared at the ceiling.

At seven thirty, he tipped the contents of a couple of tins at random into a saucepan, put it on the stove, and stared at it sightlessly until the strong smell of burning brought him back to the present.

"Oh, fuck the thing," Kenyon said uselessly.

He scraped out the revolting, blackened mess, threw it away, and spent twenty minutes scouring the saucepan. After that, he settled for topping up his glass, and a hunk of bread and cheese.

At eight forty-five, he started ringing around, but Malory seemed to have disappeared from the face of the earth. Kenyon resumed his horizontal position on the settee, and waited, but the telephone remained obstinately silent. At midnight he gave up, and went to bed. He slept very little.

Among Malory's sterling qualities was an almost fanatical regard for punctuality. At three minutes to nine every morning, his car could be virtually guaranteed to be seen turning into the car yard of Bayswater Police Station. Kenyon, waiting on the pavement, stepped in front of his bonnet. Malory jammed on his brakes. Kenyon wrenched open the passenger door, and got in.

"Let's go and have a cup of tea somewhere," he said.

"The thing is," Malory said, "there's rather a lot on my desk."

"Well, there's fuck all on mine, chum," Kenyon said, nastily.

Malory turned his car round, and drove in silence to Craven Terrace. He found a meter, reversed in, and they walked into a café well-populated with workmen taking a break, overcome by fatigue after an hour's work, from renovating a nearby hotel.

The tea was dark and strong, and presumably fortifying for those engaged in manual labor.

"I was expecting you to phone me last night," Kenyon said.

Malory stirred in sugar, which quite likely improved the brew no end. "Your phone's probably tapped," he said.

"So what?" Kenyon demanded. "Are you frightened of guilt by association if you turn up on their log?"

Malory stirred his tea miserably, long after the most obstinate lumps would have dissolved.

"All right, Len," Kenyon said. "I'm sorry. You're probably right. There's no reason why you should seem to be involved. Or do the CIB think you are?"

Malory shook his head.

"Good," Kenyon said. "I'm glad."

"So am I," Malory said.

"What happened?"

"They pushed me around a bit," Malory said. "Went through my diary with a fine-tooth comb, but in the end it was all right."

"I think you were sent for to shop me," Kenyon said, watching Malory's face. "Did you?"

"I wouldn't do that, Sid," Malory said. "I stood up for you . . . as best I could," he qualified.

"What does that mean?"

"I told them," Malory said, "what a good DI you were to work for. Hard on villains, yet always fair, never hogging the kudos, ready to give credit where it was due . . ."

"Never mind the crappy generalizations, Len," Kenyon said. "Specifically, what did they ask you about?"

"Tony Vallenta mostly," Malory said. He glanced at Kenyon. "And Angela," he added.

"That figures," Kenyon said. "What? Precisely?"

"Mostly," Malory said, "if you'd ever said anything to me about seeing Angela Vallenta as a cover for investigating her husband."

"I hope you told them I had," Kenyon said.

"How could I?" Malory said.

"You might have gone that far, Len," Kenyon said.

"If it was true," Malory said, "you . . ."

"It was true," Kenyon said.

"Well, if so, you kept it to yourself, Sid," Malory said, miserably. "How was I supposed to know?"

Kenyon stubbed out his cigarette. He could not help feeling that Malory had let him down, and yet, to be fair, Malory had to think of himself, and probably even more important these days, Vera, who was his key to the future.

"Fair enough," Kenyon said at last. "That'll teach me to bloody go off on my own without telling anyone."

"Another cup of tea?" Malory asked, more cheerfully. He had clearly been dreading this conversation, and despite what had happened would prefer to remain on friendly terms.

"No," Kenyon said. "But a bit of help wouldn't come amiss."

"Anything I can do, Sid," Malory said. "You know that."

"I've been doing a lot of thinking," Kenyon said. "I can't pretend I've come up with much so far, but some bastard's out to fix me, that's for certain. Well, I've no intention of being fixed, but if I'm going to get anywhere

I need the answers to a few questions. I can't get those answers, but you can."

Malory did not follow. "Why me?"

"Because I can't go back to the bloody nick," Kenyon said, "and get the information I want. Whereas, you're in and out every day, you can ask questions officially, get on to records, go through files . . ."

Malory followed now, and was indicating dissent. "You're asking too much, Sid," he said.

"I don't think so," Kenyon said. "I can tell you exactly what I want . . ."

"You're suspended from duty," Malory said. "And that means exactly what it says. Your warrant card's been withdrawn, you've no standing, you're off duty, period, until someone says otherwise, and you've no right of access to files, information, or anything else."

"I know the official position," Kenyon said, tartly. "This is unofficial, and comes under the old pals' act."

"The truth is, I suppose," Malory said, "that I'm not your kind of copper." He looked Kenyon straight in the eye. "You've always taken too many chances. I think you enjoy being on thin ice. Well, I don't. I never have. In the long run, it's not worth it. Now you've taken one chance too many. The ice has cracked, and the water's bloody cold. If what you told the CIB was true, you chose to keep me in the dark. You didn't ask for my help then. Now you want me to freeze to death with you. I don't think you've much right to expect that, do you?"

"No," Kenyon said. He stood up. "Give my regards to Vera."

"Thanks," Malory said.

Kenyon walked back towards his flat. He turned right at Chilworth Street, and stood outside the telephone box until the Pakistani inside had finished his interminable and mysterious monologue.

When the pips had finished bleeping, he said, "It's Sidney Kenyon."

"What on earth are you doing in a phone box?" Angela said.

"Oh, I'm out and about," Kenyon said. "Is Tony there?"

"He's playing golf," Angela said. "Can I give him a message?"

"No, it doesn't matter," Kenyon said. "But if he's gone to St. Andrews, I'll come and keep you company."

Angela laughed. "Sunningdale," she said. "And back for lunch. You can come and have coffee if you like."

"That's not what I had in mind," Kenyon said. "See you."

He walked to his car, got in, and drove to the golf course at Sunningdale. He parked next to Tony Vallenta's Rolls Royce. The chauffeur inside glanced with disdain at Kenyon's old Volvo, and went back to his newspaper.

Kenyon sat outside the club house until Tony appeared on the eighteenth green. The dignified man with him looked like a pillar of the Establishment, and probably was.

Tony saw Kenyon, waved, and sank a six foot putt with studied nonchalance. He handed his putter to the caddy, tipped him a fiver, and walked towards Kenyon, calling to his companion, "Your turn to set up the champagne, I believe, Jeremy."

"Who's Jeremy when he's at home?" Kenyon inquired, as Tony Vallenta arrived, and sat beside him.

"The father of Lady Rosemary, when she's at home," Tony Vallenta said. "Otherwise, a merchant banker, and a City Alderman. Nice fellow. We play golf together sometimes, that's all."

"I didn't suppose you needed any finance," Kenyon said.

"I didn't know you were a member here," Tony said.

"I'm not," Kenyon said.

"I'll put you up if you like," Tony offered. "Get Jeremy to second you."

"Too expensive for me," Kenyon said.

"We've got one policeman," Tony said. "Sits on the Green Committee. I think he's the Chief Constable."

"That settles it," Kenyon said. "He'd blackball me."

"Would he? Why?"

"I'm in a spot of bother," Kenyon said, "and it's partly down to you."

"Oh, my God," Tony groaned. "What have I done now?"

"It appears," Kenyon said, "that seven years ago, you sold me my flat, and also arranged the finance."

"Did I?" Tony frowned. "Which flat?"

"Gloucester Terrace," Kenyon said. "It was news to me, and the Yard have taken against it."

Tony's frown was clearing. "Yes, I do remember something about it," he said. "Basement flat was it?"

"You accepted an offer a grand and a quarter below asking price," Kenyon said. "And then arranged a loan. Why did you do that, Tony?"

"I don't know. That company was wound up years ago," Tony said. "I suppose the flat was sticking. You need to be a mole at heart to live below ground. You must have been the only mole in sight."

"If I'd known you were involved," Kenyon said, "I wouldn't have touched it with a barge pole."

"For Christ's sake," Tony said. "It was a normal commercial transaction. I didn't mind a copper buying it. I'm not proud," he joked.

"So you did know it was me," Kenyon said.

"I think my manager checked the offer with me," Tony said. "There aren't too many Sidney Kenyons around, occupation, police officer."

"The Yard think you did me quite a favor," Kenyon said. "And expected one in return."

"Well, you know that's not true," Tony said.

"*I* do, yes," Kenyon said.

"Suppose I make a sworn statement that they've got it wrong," Tony said. "I'll gladly do that for you."

"I doubt if anything you swear," Kenyon said, "would carry much weight at Scotland Yard. They'd be more likely to regard it as proof of complicity."

"I don't know how you put up with it," Tony said. "Surrounded by doubting Thomases. How about if I get my accountants to do it? Thoroughly respectable firm, the best in Europe for my money, let alone London . . ."

"Let's stop farting about," Kenyon said. "You weren't just selling a flat, you had a reason. I want to know what it was, just between you and me. There are no witnesses. You can level with me."

Tony Vallenta stared at Kenyon. His eyes ran down his suit, studying the line.

"No briefcase," Kenyon said. "No hidden tape recorder, no concealed microphone. Frisk me, if you like."

"I wouldn't dream of it," Tony said. "Not here. Some of the honorable members would have a fit. OK. You wanted a flat you couldn't afford. I was able to arrange that you could afford it. I had in mind that one day, you might be grateful."

"What form was this gratitude supposed to take?" Kenyon inquired.

"Nothing," Tony said. "Really, nothing, I assure you. Oiling the wheels here and there perhaps, smoothing out a few business problems, the occasional word of friendly advice . . ."

"I can imagine," Kenyon said. "But you've never tried to collect. Why not?"

"I got to know you a little better," Tony said. "I'm a good judge of character. I didn't think we'd be on the same wavelength after all. So I wrote it off to experience. What the hell, it didn't cost me much. No one but an idiot would have paid more than six grand for that flat, at the time, anyway."

"You've never found out what my wavelength is," Kenyon said. "I've had those bastards at the Yard in a big way. I could be quite receptive to new ideas just now."

"No, I don't think so," Tony Vallenta said, smiling. "I still think I've got you right. I believe you quite enjoy my company. You may even like me a little. But that's as far as it goes, and with you, that's not very far."

"You know how you hear about people in communist countries becoming non-persons," Kenyon said. "Well, I've become a non-copper."

"You mean you've been suspended?" If Tony Vallenta was not surprised, it was a first-rate imitation. Kenyon was not sure if that was suspicious or not. The word would get round among the villains, nearly as fast as it would in the police force, but it had, after all, only happened twenty-four hours before. Tony might well not have heard, unless he had had some special reason for finding out.

"A modern untouchable," Kenyon said.

"I'm sorry," Tony said, sincerely, "I truly am sorry. You've made me feel guilty about it, but I didn't imagine for one second they'd ever crack down on you just because you'd bought a flat from one of my companies. How did they find out?"

"I don't know," Kenyon said. He would be interested to know the answer to that himself. "Quite a few people knew, I suppose. The agents, your staff . . . somone could easily have sniffed it out. But should you ever happen to hear who it might have been . . ."

Tony said, "It it was anyone on my staff, I'll have his bloody balls for breakfast."

"It wasn't only the flat," Kenyon said. "They wouldn't have done me for that, although it didn't help. Something was planted on me."

"Like that gun in the boot of my car," Tony said. "I know how you feel."

"The bastard who did that really fixed me," Kenyon said.

"Who was it?" Tony asked.

"I haven't got the first idea," Kenyon said. This was not strictly true. He had developed an inkling as to how it might have been done, during his hours on the settee the night before, although he did not think much of the idea. Still, it was the only possibility he had, as yet. "But that one's not down to you. I know that."

"Well, I'm glad I'm in the clear over something, at least," Tony said. He looked at his watch. "I'm sorry, but . . ."

Kenyon stood up. "I know," he said. "The champagne's getting warm."

"I'll let you know if I find out who grassed on you," Tony promised.

"More to the point," Kenyon said, "bear in mind that my present occupation may be drawing to a close. It's not all locked away in files, you know. I carry a lot of useful stuff up here." He tapped his head.

"A few years ago," Tony said, "I'll admit, I'd have jumped at it. But I'm not in the market anymore. I've retired, for good. Still, if I hear of anyone else who might be interested . . ."

"Thanks," Kenyon said.

He drove back towards London along the A30, as far as Staines, and then cut across to join the M4. No one had followed him to Sunningdale, and no one was following him now. Neither the police, nor whoever had set out to break him, were showing the slightest interest in him.

Tony Vallenta had turned him down, and Kenyon thought that, at least, was genuine. There could be several reasons. It was conceivable that Vallenta was telling the truth, that he had retired. Villains did. Kenyon knew a number of them, now leading prosperous lives in leafy, well-heeled villages, donating generously to the Church Restoration Fund, popular fellows in the Lounge Bar of the local pub, most of them.

Then again, if Tony Vallenta was still in business, a suspended copper was precious little use to him. Like politicians out of office, a copper without access to up to the minute information soon became out of date. A tame copper on the payroll was only of use if he were above suspicion and had access to official plans, day in, day out. This line of thought did much to negate the vague possibility Kenyon had been flirting with, and which he did not much care for anyway.

There could be another explanation, but the more Kenyon looked at that, the more empty it seemed. For that, there not only had to be a reason, but a very big reason at that. Kenyon knew of no reason whatever, let alone a big one.

As the first day in what Kenyon, the previous evening, had mapped out as a determined effort to get himself off the hook, this was a washout. He had learned little from Tony Vallenta, and Malory did not intend to lift a finger, probably for very sound reasons, Kenyon admitted. It was asking a lot of any copper to stick his neck out like that. Probably too much. Kenyon would like to believe that he would have helped Malory, had their situations been reversed, but he could not be certain. The immediate, obvious, and sensible reaction was to think, "He's got himself into it. Let him get himself out. He's probably lying anyway. A copper doesn't get suspended for no reason. There's no smoke without fire."

Kenyon grimly suspected that all his friends would feel that way, in varying degrees. The police force was, and had to be, a cohesive, closed, and disciplined organization. It bred an attitude of mind. A copper was always dependent on his fellows, and if one of them dropped out, he was no longer part of that tight-knit group, and was inevitably regarded in a different way.

Yet Kenyon knew that he could no nothing on his own. Locked out, with no way of getting some of the answers he needed, he was finished before he started. Somehow, he had to get someone to help him. He desperately needed a way into the system from which he was now excluded.

Kenyon turned left at the Hogarth roundabout, drove through Chiswick and Shepherds Bush, and parked off Holland Road, on a yellow line. He went into a shop, bought some cigarettes, and asked for his change in 2p coins. Armed with these, he found an empty phone box, and monopolized it for over half an hour.

It was as he had anticipated. Those men whom he regarded as his friends were genuinely sympathetic, and commiserated warmly. They would be happy to meet him sometime, but, by some strange chance, none of them were free, for various reasons, in the near future. Next week perhaps . . . or the week after. Next week was no use to Kenyon, let alone the week after. He decided to try a very long shot indeed.

He did not expect to find his quarry easily, and so it proved. No one knew where he was, or if they did they were not prepared to reveal the information to a caller who merely muttered "It's personal" whenever he was asked for his name.

Kenyon tried all the likely pubs, cafés, dives, and drinking clubs without success. He was on the point of giving up, when someone guardedly, and suspiciously, said he might be reached at a certain number. Kenyon used his last coin. He was astounded when the owner of the phone number answered, and replied in the affirmative to Kenyon's inquiry.

"What the hell are you doing in a vicarage?" Kenyon demanded.

"Getting some good advice, Mr. Kenyon, sir," Detective Sergeant Nick Vardin said. "Also, some clown knocked off the altar cloth last night, plus a couple of valuable candlesticks."

"Someone getting ready for the next lot of power cuts," Kenyon suggested.

"I reckoned he was setting up in competition," Nick said, "but the Vicar didn't go a lot on that idea."

"Listen," Kenyon said. "Say no if you want to, but I was wondering if you'd have a drink with me sometime."

"Why should I say no?" Nick wondered. "I've never refused a drink in my life. This evening suit you?"

"Fine," Kenyon said. "Where?"

"What's wrong with your place?" Nick asked. "Then there won't be any nonsense about me buying a round."

"Perhaps you haven't heard that I'm persona non grata just now," Kenyon said.

"I've heard," Nick said. "It's all over the Met, let alone the nick."

"They might be keeping my place under observation," Kenyon said. "If they see you arriving, you could find yourself being interviewed as well."

"Sod that for a game of soldiers," Nick said. "They can . . . sorry, Vicar," he said, in an aside. "It's your invite," he said to Kenyon, "so it's your booze, or nothing."

"Suits me," Kenyon said.

"Eight o'clock. OK?"

"Right," Kenyon said.

He walked to an off-license, bought two bottles of scotch, and went back to his car. A traffic warden had given him a parking ticket, which he supposed he would have to pay, now that he could no longer write a note on official notepaper inventing some fictitious inquiry which had obliged him to park in that particular spot. Detectives were not accustomed to paying parking fines, on or off duty.

Kenyon shoved the ticket in his glove pocket, and started the engine. Six quid down the drain. But even that could not spoil his new found cheerfulness.

Fancy Nick Vardin, of all people, a desperate last resort, coming up trumps like that. But perhaps he should have thought of Nick first. Nick did not give a shit for anyone. It was ironic that the one man prepared to meet him without question should be a bent copper. But perhaps that was what he needed most, at this moment. A good, bent copper.

CHAPTER SEVEN

Kenyon's buzzer went at eight o'clock on the dot.

"Detective Sergeant Vardin, Mr. Kenyon, sir," Nick's voice said, on the entryphone.

"Come in, Nick," Kenyon said, and pressed the button to release the street door.

Nick came down the stairs, walked in, took off his raincoat, and threw it down. "There's a snotty-nosed young DC from the Yard sitting in his car outside," he said. "So I thought I'd better announce myself properly. May as well give the silly little bugger an easy life."

"So long as it doesn't make life difficult for you," Kenyon said.

Nick Vardin sat down, and poured himself a stiff drink from the waiting bottle. "I shall say," he announced, "that you invited me, which is true, and that I accepted your invitation, in case you wished to put any suggestions to me, which I might feel it my duty to pass on to the CIB." He swallowed half the contents of his glass. "Which would also be true," he added.

"I'll have to chance that," Kenyon said. It occurred to him a little late that Nick owed him nothing, and was not best known for his philanthropic nature. "Cheers."

"Down the hatch," Nick said. He gave himself a refill, lit a cigarette, and gazed at Kenyon with an ironic smile. "No one ever offered me five grand," he said. "That's a lot of loot."

"Planted," Kenyon said. "It's a frame."

"That's what I shall assert," Nick said, "if they catch up with me, God forbid."

"Yes, but I mean it," Kenyon said.

"I shall mean it too," Nick Vardin said. "I shall swear my innocence on my mother's grave, which may she

121

occupy soon, the drunken old faggot. I shall stick to my story, force the bastards to carry out a lengthy investigation, and meanwhile disperse the proceeds."

"I haven't got any proceeds," Kenyon said.

Nick raised his eyebrows. "Was the tale about five thousand quid exaggerated?" he asked.

Kenyon's euphoria at the prospect of having found a possible ally was rapidly seeping away. "I was going to ask you if you'd do something for me," he said. "But perhaps I'm wasting my time."

"I'm listening," Nick said.

"I don't like having this hung on me," Kenyon said. "I resent it, and I'm not going to bloody have it, if I can help it. I'm going to screw the bastard behind it, if it's the last thing I do."

"Could we tape record this?" Nick suggested. "That's exactly the right turn of phrase, the kind of outraged anger, that one day I may very well . . ."

"All right, Nick, I've made a mistake," Kenyon said. "Clear out now, before I knock your head off."

"Sorry, Mr. Kenyon, sir," Nick murmured. "I expect I've got a twisted sense of humor. You know the saying, the bigger they are the harder they fall. You're ten years younger than I am, probably the best DI in the force, headed straight for the top, everyone knew that, and suddenly . . ." He flicked ash from his cigarette. ". . . bingo . . . you're in the shit, up to your neck, and I look like collecting my pension after all. I suppose you wouldn't find the funny side uppermost . . ."

"Not noticeably," Kenyon said.

"It does have its comic aspect from my point of view," Nick said. "Still want me to go?"

"Finish your drink," Kenyon said. He knew the malicious pleasure which people experienced when someone, formerly riding high, came down with a crash. At least Nick Vardin was honest enough, in his own cynical way, to express it.

"OK," Nick said. He tilted the whisky bottle, and filled his glass to the brim. "But I'll have something worth finishing," he explained. He looked around the living room appraisingly. "Not a bad place you've got here," he said. "I wish I'd known Tony Vallenta was flogging flats like this cut price."

"Bloody marvelous how everyone knows everything in five minutes flat," Kenyon said, bitterly.

"The only gossip worth spreading," Nick said, "is the confidential and damaging kind. People can't resist passing it on. Len Malory for one. Only to his best friend of course. The number of people who've said to me today, 'Heard about Sidney Kenyon?' I said no, every time, in case there was some extra titbit I didn't know about. Yes," he went on, "a very nice flat indeed. I'd have struck a bargain with Tony Vallenta myself, if I'd had the chance."

"I suppose it's no use telling you," Kenyon said, "that I had no idea Tony owned the property company concerned."

"No, I'd believe that," Nick said. "Knowing the way Tony operates. He'd put the bite on later."

"He never did," Kenyon said.

"That's a little less easy to believe," Nick said.

"You belong to the same club as the bastards at the CIB," Kenyon said.

Nick said, "Now I think I'm offended."

"You've got a lot in common," Kenyon said. "Set a thief to catch a thief may be good practical politics, but if you're always looking for bent motives, you're going to find them, even when they're not there."

"I think I shall leave of my own accord," Nick said. He filled up his glass again.

"Someone fixed me," Kenyon said. "Because I was getting in their hair."

"By investing five grand?" Nick inquired, skeptically.

"It's the only conceivable explanation," Kenyon said.

"Not if you're sitting in this chair," Nick said.

"I'm not," Kenyon said.

"Five grand is too much," Nick objected. "Come on. What the hell do you know, what kind of muddy waters have you been fishing in, that's worth five grand to anyone?"

"If I knew that," Kenyon said, "I wouldn't be in trouble. But you've said much the same as the CIB."

"That's what anyone would say," Nick said.

"Whether you believe me or not doesn't matter twopence," Kenyon said. "All I want to know is if you'll do a bit of digging for me."

"I wouldn't rule it out," Nick said.

"Those phone numbers and things in Archie Macintyre's diary," Kenyon said. "Have you found out what they are yet?"

"Some," Nick said. He seemed surprised. "Not all."

"How soon can you get the rest?"

"What the hell has Archie Macintyre got to do with it?" Nick demanded.

"Nothing, for all I know," Kenyon said. "But all I've got to go on are dates, after which things started to happen. Archie's diary happens to be one of them, but there are others. Such as . . ."

"Hang on," Nick said. "Are you saying the CIB only put you in their sights for the first time as recently as that?"

"No," Kenyon said. "I wish it were that simple. But when nothing fits, you clutch at straws. They've had a file on me for quite a long time, enough to keep an eye on me, but not to do anything about it, except delay my promotion. But the money was planted recently. That must have been because of something I'd done, or stumbled across by accident. Some bit of information perhaps, and I don't even realize its significance, but important enough for someone to plant five grand on me."

"I see," Nick said, neutrally.

"Do you know anyone in the Serious Crimes Squad?"

"A mate from my army days," Nick said. "Why?"

"They've got photographs of me going into Tony Vallenta's house. I'd like to know when they first spotted me, and why they were watching Tony's house in the first place."

"Was this when Tony was inside?"

"Yes," Kenyon said.

"So the bit about Angela Vallenta was true as well," Nick said, grinning lasciviously. "What's she like?"

Kenyon ignored the question. "When you've got that . . ." he began.

"Just a minute," Nick said. "Hold hard. Whoa there, Mr. Kenyon, sir. Doing a bit of digging for you seems to be turning into a career. When am I supposed to find time to get the Vicar's altar cloth back?"

"It won't take all that long," Kenyon said, impatiently.

"I was looking at your car outside," Nick said.

"What?"

"I've always quite fancied a Volvo," Nick said. "What's she like?"

"Getting old," Kenyon said. "But in first class nick. Why?"

"Thinking of selling it?" Nick asked, casually.

"No," Kenyon said.

"I'll tell you what," Nick said. "I'll make you an offer. A thousand quid."

"That car," Kenyon said, "is worth at least fifteen hundred."

"Not to me," Nick said. "A thousand. Top whack."

Kenyon stared at Nick. Nick stared back, blandly. "I see," Kenyon said at last.

"Have we got a deal?" Nick asked.

"You greedy, grasping bastard," Kenyon said.

"That's me," Nick said. "No question."

"All right," Kenyon said, slowly. "Since there's not much of an alternative. If you get me the information I want, I'll . . ."

"We do a deal tonight," Nick said, "or I don't even begin."

"In that case," Kenyon said tightly, "I've got no guarantee you'll carry out your side of the bargain."

"That's true," Nick agreed. "But it seems to me you've got fuck all choice, Mr. Kenyon, sir."

Kenyon got out the registration documents. Nick Vardin wrote out a check for a thousand pounds. They completed the formalities. Kenyon handed over the car keys.

"She's gone to a good home," Nick said, "so you needn't fret. I'll take good care of her."

"Thanks very much," Kenyon said.

"Perhaps tomorrow," Nick said. "More likely the day after, I'll call you, just give you a time. That's when I'll be at the Serpentine." He grinned. "The Vicar'll have to wait."

Kenyon spent the following morning shopping for another car. He was tempted to go up market, and get something decent. He had, after all, five thousand pounds in his bank account, which everyone was convinced was his. But in the end, he settled for an aging Ford Capri.

The steering was lighter than Kenyon was accustomed to, but he did not like it. He had become attached to his Volvo, which was built like a tank, and handled like a tank. His dislike for the car grew as he drove home. The engine did not develop as much power as it should have done, and rattled unpleasantly. Still, he only needed something to get him from A to B. He was not going to be engaged in any races.

Observation on his flat seemed to be of the intermittent variety. There was no one there during the afternoon, but a Viva turned up halfway through the evening, and parked where the occupant could see Kenyon's building.

The man behind the steering wheel was young, had long hair, a Chinese moustache, and wore a leather jacket. In the old days, coppers were supposed to be conspicuous because of their size ten boots, short back and sides, large build, and broad shoulders. Today's young undercover trendies, convinced they were passing as students, or tearaways, stuck out even more, Kenyon thought disdainfully. What villain who was worth his salt would be taken in by that youngster's façade? Kenyon belonged to the suit and tie brigade. He supposed he was an old-fashioned copper all round, which was why he was in trouble.

For something to do, he played back Bill Jarvis's tape recorded ramblings. He noted the reference, scarcely audible, to the Colonel's death. But did it mean anything? Or was it, like so much else of the old villain's recollections, garbled, fourth hand, or plain invention?

The phone rang just before noon, next day.

"Is that double three, double oh?" the voice said.

"Wrong number," Kenyon said.

"Sorry," the voice said.

Kenyon left early, just in case, but the young trendy had not been replaced. He drove around for a while, entered Hyde Park, found a space in the car park, walked to the café beside the Serpentine, sat down, and ordered a pot of tea for two. At three o'clock exactly, Nick Vardin joined him. Both men knew that the other would have made certain that he was not being followed. Neither bothered to ask.

"I'll be mother, shall I?" Nick said. He poured two cups of tea.

"Anyone said anything?" Kenyon asked.

"About my visit?" Nick shook his head. "No. But I did. I told Mr. Pindar I'd bought your car."

"Stole it, you mean," Kenyon said. It still rankled.

"No, I didn't tell him that," Nick said, equably. "He just nodded, but he didn't warn me off. So provided we don't overdo it, I think I'm all right."

"Great," Kenyon said. "That really reassures me, to know *you're* all right."

"Don't be so ungrateful," Nick said. "I've been working like a black." He took a folder from his briefcase. Kenyon transferred it to his.

"Lots of snapshots," Nick said. "You turned up a month after they'd started. Apparently, everyone got very excited. An unknown face. Who can he be? Then one of the brass recognized you. Thought it could be a matter for the CIB."

"Why were the Serious Crimes Squad there in the first place?" Kenyon asked.

"I don't think they know themselves," Nick said. "Some sort of deal in the offing, my mate said."

"A deal?" Kenyon queried.

"Yes." Nick looked at him curiously. "Why?"

"What kind of deal?"

"It was one of those whispers that float around," Nick said. "No one can pin it down, nobody knows what it's about, but people keep hearing it." He studied Kenyon. "Have you heard it?"

"Indirectly," Kenyon said. He was in a hurry to get home.

Kenyon had seen the photographs of himself before, at Scotland Yard, and he discarded those. He sat down on his settee, and studied the rest. Few of them featured Angela Vallenta. Carmen had been on duty to let the others in.

One of the faces, Kenyon recognized at once. He stared at it. Walter Flack. Walter was an old-style protection racketeer with about as much finesse as a bulldozer. What the hell was Walter Flack doing, calling on Angela? Perhaps that rumor about a takeover bid had been right. Or a merger? But Walter had no time for Tony Vallenta, and Tony despised Walter Flack.

Kenyon subdued his instinctive professional interest, and put the photograph aside. Walter's visit had no relevance to him, that he could see.

Most of the others, Kenyon guessed, were there on legitimate business. One young man looked as though he might have been the estate agent Angela had mentioned. But there was another man who caught his eye, and Kenyon studied the photograph closely.

He was about forty, clean-cut, tall, well dressed, in a perfectly fitting suit. There was something familiar about him, which Kenyon could not place. He was about to add the photograph to the pile, defeated, when it came to him. The man looked, in the general sense, rather like Harry Coleman. Not that there was any facial resemblance, but the style of the man was similar. The way he held himself, the cut of his clothes, the impression that he had showered and put on a clean shirt just five minutes before.

Well, he meant nothing either, except perhaps in Angela's personal life. Kenyon would have been surprised if she had not taken more than one occasional lover while Tony was inside. A rich, good-looking American might well have appealed to her.

Kenyon turned to the typewritten sheets on which Nick had reproduced the jottings in Archie Macintyre's diary. Some had explanations, or possible explanations, alongside.

"E.S. last day,—could refer to Eddie Sirdar, a bookie at White City. Archie gambled on the dogs, and usually lost. Last day might mean settlement day."

Well, Nick should know about the dog scene all right, Kenyon thought, recalling his rumored venture into the ownership of greyhounds. Perhaps that was where Archie had acquired the substantial sum in cash found in his wallet. Except for those few one hundred dollar bills, though. Bookies at White City did not pay out in dollars.

A number of Archie's cryptic entries had temporarily defeated Nick, and carried a note, "don't know. Still checking." Others seemed to refer to various people of the kind Archie Macintyre might mix with, and implied the sort of activities one might expect. Nick's notes built up a skeleton, an admittedly speculative picture of a minor villain at work. " 'good jag to C.C.' . . . must be recent model Jaguar. C.C. = Clapham Common? Archie was skilled at knocking off expensive cars. That day, a Securicor Van was hijacked (two guards hurt) outside a bank in Clapham. (Unsolved). Team used a stolen Jaguar as switch car, later found abandoned in Croydon. . . ." And later, ". . . this bit sounds like Archie at work as a frightener for some money-lender. Putting the bite on some poor bastard with his knife . . ." Then later still, ". . . not sure about this. Did Archie go in for blackmail? Seems like it, but can't be certain. In any case, victim's (?) identity not clear . . ."

A couple of entries went against the trend. "S.S. for N.I. card" . . . Nick had appended, "S.S. = Social Security. Archie drew welfare regularly, like most petty villains. We support these bums while they rob us blind at the same time. I give up. This country has gone mad."

"Yes, Nick," Kenyon breathed impatiently. "I do know that. But the high moral tone lacks conviction, coming from you."

Further on was the second hint of Archie Macintyre as citizen of the U.K. "N.I. card to C.D." Nick had typed alongside, "Could Archie have taken a job? Hard to believe, but who else would want his National Insurance card? No idea what C.D. is, except that it is not Civil Defense. Not Archie."

Kenyon went back, and checked the relevant dates for these mystifying entries, but he could find no significance in them. He moved on.

Most of the phone numbers had turned out to be the kind one might have expected. Bookies, tawdry drinking clubs, sundry assorted low-grade villains, a fifty-year-old prostitute in Notting Hill. There was just one which made Kenyon decide that he had plans for the evening after all.

"This one is ex-directory," Nick had typed. "Seems above Archie's head to me. Tried it twice, but got no answer. Evenings only?"

Kenyon snatched up the A–D section of the London Telephone Directory. Two numbers were listed, Reception and Manager, for those wishing to telephone.

But, according to Nick, Archie had possessed a third,

ex-directory number, which also communicated with the Blue Otter.

Kenyon turfed out one of his desk drawers, and found a card which had once come in useful, and which gave him access to a number of legitimate, high-class clubs. He was relieved to find that it was still valid.

Behind a modest façade, the Blue Otter was as posh and plush as they came. Kenyon strolled across the lushly carpeted, discreetly lighted foyer. The sleek individual in the dinner jacket, who appeared to be the manager, but was in fact a security man, smiled, and said, "Good evening, sir." But his eyes were watchful, and Kenyon guessed that his presence was not welcome.

He wandered round for half an hour, reminding himself of the layout. After a while, the excitement he had felt began to ooze away. Nothing could have been more respectable than this place, which provided strictly controlled gambling, fenced in by innumerable rules and regulations under the Gambling Act.

The days when prominent Americans, suspected of being front men for various undesirable organizations, had been deported from Great Britain, were long since past.

Gambling Clubs were obvious targets for high-class villains, and there had been a time, years before, when several had come under criminal control. But since then, the whole thing had been radically tightened up. The requirements of the Gaming Board were now so rigid, and scrupulously enforced, that it was virtually impossible for the villains to move in.

Although nothing was utterly impossible, Kenyon thought, trying to cheer himself up again. But there was no sign of anyone moving in here who could not have provided impeccable personal and financial references.

Most of the action was centered around the roulette tables, where Americans and Arabs were playing for chillingly high stakes. Kenyon watched carefully, but he would swear an oath that the games were as straight as a die, and if that was the case, he might as well go home now. Only one thing attracted villains to gambling clubs, and that was the prospect of fixing the odds. What other reason was there?

Kenyon went to the bar, and ordered a large scotch.

"Will you be dining, sir?" the barman inquired, indicating a lavish menu, which stood on the bar.

"I don't think so," Kenyon said. He sipped his scotch, and then something about the menu struck him. It was a very, very long shot indeed, and the prices made him wince, but he was, he realized, hungry after all.

"I've changed my mind," he said.

"I'll inform the head waiter, sir," the barman said.

Kenyon went to the restaurant, and allowed himself to be cossetted. The prices they were charging allowed plenty of leeway for a lot of cossetting, but still, it was very pleasant.

When the first course he had ordered arrived he ate it delicately, carefully savoring every nuance of taste. He breathed a sigh of satisfaction. Quail's eggs were far from constituting a part of his normal diet, but unless he was very much mistaken, he had only eaten them, done in quite that way, once before in his life.

He attracted the attention of the head waiter, offered effusive congratulations, heavily implied that a very large tip was in the offing, and finally asked if it would be possible to see the kitchens, and offer his compliments to the chef.

"But of course, sir," the head waiter said.

The kitchen area was white tiled, spotlessly clean, and populated by busy, perspiring men presided over by a huge, fat, Gallic-looking character, who wore his chef's hat as though it were a royal crown.

The chef, who turned out to be as cockney as they come, responded instantly to flattery, and showed Kenyon round, proudly explaining how his marvels were produced.

"Those quail's eggs were marvelous," Kenyon said.

"My own secret," the chef said, proudly. "Always prepare them with my own hands."

"I've had them done that way before," Kenyon said.

"Not as good as mine, I'll bet," the chef said.

"They were," Kenyon said. "Just as good."

"Well, I'll have to take your word for that," the chef said, dubiously. "Where was this? Because if you're going to tell me the Connaught, five years ago . . ."

"More recently than that," Kenyon said. "At Mr. Vallenta's house."

The chef chuckled hugely. "In that case, I'll believe you," he said.

"You mean you did that meal?" Kenyon inquired, feigning astonishment.

"Followed by Sole Normandie, Boeuf Bourguignon, Crepes Suzette, and Lemon Sorbet," the chef said.

"Well, I'm damned," Kenyon said.

The door to a small office was open. Kenyon looked in. "Funny," he said. "You never think of chefs needing an office."

"It's not all inspiration," the chef said, modestly. "It's planning and administration as well."

Kenyon lingered in the office. There was a white telephone on a shelf, its dial turned away from him.

"I suppose you must work half the night," he said.

"No," the chef said. "The restaurant closes at midnight. Then it's all hands to the pumps, clearing up. I like to be out of here at one a.m. sharp."

In the course of his career, Kenyon had come to the conclusion that nearly all occupations harbored a certain proportion of those who were bent. But, somehow, he had never come across a bent chef before

"I'm dying for a cigarette," Kenyon said. "Would you mind?"

"I'm a smoker myself," the chef said. "Thanks," he added, accepting one from Kenyon's packet.

"Have you known Mr. Vallenta long?" Kenyon asked casually, as he lit the chef's cigarette.

"Mr. Vallenta was kind enough to be complimentary once when I was at the Connaught, years ago," the chef said. "He asked me if I'd do a private party for him. That was a great success, and he was pleased. Ever since then, I've attended his home on special occasions. Well, except for a period when Mr. Vallenta was away."

"Yes, quite," Kenyon said, joining the chef in avoiding the reason for Tony Vallenta's enforced deprivation from the delights of haute cuisine. "Though I suppose Mrs. Vallenta entertained now and then?"

"She had some Spanish girl living in," the chef said, with the faintest air of disapproval. "I believe she prepared the meals, although I must admit I'm a somewhat distant admirer of Spanish cooking, myself."

"Well, Mr. Vallenta always tells me he only employs the best," Kenyon said. "Although perhaps 'employs' isn't quite the right word in your case."

"We have an ad hoc arrangement," the chef said. "He always gives me a completely free hand, that's what makes it such a pleasure. Although Mr. Vallenta is always extremely generous," he admitted.

"Yes, that's true," Kenyon said. "I thought I might see him here tonight, but he doesn't seem to be around."

The chef seemed surprised. "As far as I know," he said, "Mr. Vallenta isn't even a member. I've certainly never seen him here."

Something going on outside the glass-walled office caught the chef's eagle eye. He put down his cigarette, said "Excuse me," and went out to rectify whatever mistakes his subordinates were making.

Kenyon leaned across to the ashtray, and stubbed out his own cigarette. He managed to catch an angled glimpse of the dial on the telephone. The number was the same as that which had appeared in Archie Macintyre's diary.

He crossed to the chef, thanked him warmly, and said goodbye.

"Just a minute," the chef said. "What did you order to follow your quail's eggs?"

"Only a boring steak," Kenyon said. "I'm an addict."

"Your steak tonight shall not be boring," the chef promised. "It will be the best steak you've ever had in your life. I shall see to it myself."

The chef was as good as his word, and Kenyon felt agreeably replete when he went back to the tables. He bought some chips, and began to play roulette for the sake of appearances, staking haphazardly, in sharp contrast to the dedicated, earnest care with which the Americans were playing.

An hour later, his twenty pounds had turned into two hundred. This, he thought, was undoubtedly his lucky night, all around. He decided to quit before his luck ran out. But when he passed a door marked PRIVATE. NO

ADMITTANCE he could not resist pushing his winning streak.

Beyond the door was a quiet corridor, lined with offices. At the far end, another door leading to the staff exit was closing, as a man carrying an attaché case went through it. Kenyon felt his heart leap with excitement, and he began to move, soft footed after him.

A middle-aged secretary emerged from one of the offices, carrying a sheaf of papers, and stared at him suspiciously.

"Can I help you, sir?" she asked, coolly.

"I'm looking for the cashier," Kenyon said, showing his chips.

"Back that way," the secretary said. "Off the foyer."

"Sorry," Kenyon apologized. "Wrong door." He did not know the secretary, and he hoped she did not know him. He retraced his footsteps.

But he was certain that the man whose back he had glimpsed was black, and that his name was Garry Bennett.

There were several Americans cashing in their chips, and Kenyon waited behind a tall Texan. His two hundred quid suddenly seemed like petty cash compared with the sums these men were dealing in, but of course, he did not know how much they had started with.

The cashier was a sleek young man, with butter-colored hair, lightning fingers, and a calculator for a brain. He also had a very soft voice, and it was not until the tall Texan in front of him was being dealt with that Kenyon heard the quiet inquiry.

"Would you prefer it in dollars, sir?" the cashier asked.

"Sure. Why not?" the Texan said. "Hell, I'm flying home tomorrow. I may as well have it in real money."

Kenyon watched for the fiddle, the manipulation of the exchange rate which would later put hard cash into the cashier's pocket when he balanced up for the night. But, surprisingly, the cashier paid out at the official rate, obtainable at any bank. This place, he thought, was so above board it wasn't true. Except for that ex-directory telephone in the chef's office, and a passing query as to what brought Garry Bennett to the PRIVATE. NO ADMITTANCE area.

The Texan moved away, and Kenyon took his place at the grille. On a hunch, he said briefly, "Dollars" in a low voice, and hoped his lack of the right accent would not show.

"Certainly, sir," the cashier said.

The cashier gave him three one hundred dollar bills, and the rest in smaller denominations. Kenyon nodded his thanks, and moved away.

He got five paces before the security man stepped in front of him.

"I'm very sorry, sir," the security man said, politely, "but only American nationals are allowed to take dollars. Exchange Control regulations," he explained. He took the notes from Kenyon's hand. "If you'll wait there, sir," he said, "I'll exchange this for sterling for you."

Outside, Kenyon spotted the tall Texan and his two companions. He strolled along behind them. They were debating the merits of a night club, as against going to bed. The Texan was against the idea of a night club. "You can count me out," he said, firmly. "I'm not getting mixed up with any of these London hookers. With these god-damned Arabs buying it like they've never seen a woman before? Think where they've been. Jesus!"

The Texan won the argument as they turned into Edgware Road, and they hailed a taxi.

"The Hilton Hotel," the Texan said.

As the tall man was about to close the door, Kenyon intervened.

"Excuse me," he said, "but are you going to the Hilton? I've been trying to get a taxi for ages. Would you mind terribly, if . . . ?"

"Climb in," the Texan said.

"Thanks very much," Kenyon said. He pushed down the folding seat, and sat on it. "I really am most obliged."

"Think nothing of it," the Texan said.

Kenyon thanked his stars for the inbuilt courtesy and natural kindness of the American. Most Englishmen would have glared at him, automatically suspected him of being drunk, and slammed the door in his face.

They chatted amiably on the way to the Hilton. Fortunately for Kenyon, there was a sizable traffic jam at

Marble Arch, which gave him the few extra minutes he wanted.

"What's your line of business, sir?" the Texan inquired.

"I work for IBM," Kenyon said.

"Is that so?" the Texan said. "Why, I use their computers myself."

The traffic jam began to clear, and Kenyon hurried on before the Texan started telling him what business he owned which called for the use of computers from IBM.

"Are you gentlemen over here on business?" he asked.

They all laughed at that. "We've come over for the gambling," the tall one explained. "A whole bunch of us, in a chartered 707 from Houston. We fly back tomorrow."

"It seems a long way to come to play roulette," Kenyon said. "What's wrong with Las Vegas?"

"London's the place for serious gambling," the tall one said. The others indicated assent. "Vegas is fine for entertainment, but if you want to play for real money, in real sophisticated surroundings, why it's London every time."

"So when you buy your ticket," Kenyon said, "is it all inclusive?"

"That's right," the tall Texan said. "Air fare, three nights at the Hilton, and membership of the Blue Otter. It's all in."

"I like the Blue Otter best of all," one of the others said.

"Well, the food's the best in town," the tall one said. "That's for sure."

The conversation digressed into the merits of the various London gambling clubs. They seemed to know them all.

"Well, I'd say the Blue Otter's on the up and up," the tall one said. "I met some fellows just flown in from Chicago, and there was another bunch from the West Coast . . ."

The taxi turned into the forecourt of the Hilton. Kenyon tried to pay the fare, but the tall Texan would not allow him. Kenyon followed them inside.

None of them were carrying cases, or briefcases, and the security men on duty just inside the door eyed them closely, but let them pass. The Hilton had been bombed more than once, and they were careful about security.

"What floor are you on, sir?" the tall Texan asked

Kenyon. "Because if you'd care to join us for a drink in my suite, why . . ."

"I'd love to," Kenyon said, "but I can't. I have to meet someone. But I don't know if you could do me a very great favor . . ."

"You want to ride up in the same elevator?" the tall one suggested, laughing.

"My colleague is an American," Kenyon said, "over here for a conference, and I owe him a hundred dollars. Like you, he's flying back tomorrow, and I'd like to pay him in US dollars." He hoped they would not suggest the excellent Hilton facilities for changing money. "So if you could possibly spare . . ."

"Hell, I thought you wanted a real favor," the tall one said. He carelessly peeled a hundred dollar bill from the large roll he had received at the Blue Otter. Kenyon gave him sterling in return.

"Hey, wait a minute, that's too much," the tall Texan said.

"It's worth it to me," Kenyon said, sincerely. "Call the difference my share of the cab fare." He bade them all a warm good night, waited until they had gone out of sight towards the lifts, walked outside, and took a taxi back to Connaught Square, where he had parked his car.

Early in the evening, Kenyon could usually find somewhere to park in Gloucester Terrace, outside his flat, but at this time of night, all the spaces had been filled. He turned into Cleveland Terrace, and left his Ford on a yellow line. He intended to be up early in the morning anyway, well before the traffic wardens started giving out tickets. He must remember to go to City Hall, among other things, and get the car number on his parking permit changed.

He walked back along Cleveland Terrace, turned into Gloucester Terrace, and crossed the road.

If anyone had been watching his flat during the evening, they had got fed up and gone home. Apart from the occasional car passing by, there was no one about.

Kenyon yawned as he ascended the steps outside the house. He suddenly realized how tired he was. He was selecting the key to the street door, when he caught a glimpse of them. They must have come up from the basement area outside the adjoining house.

There were three of them. Scarves covered the lower part of their faces. As they rushed him, he saw that they carried short iron bars.

CHAPTER EIGHT

It was all over in a few seconds. Not a word was said. Kenyon avoided the first blow, aimed at his head. It caught him on the shoulder, numbing his arm. Then he was bundled over by the oncoming bodies. His forehead hit the balustrade as he fell.

Someone kicked him in the guts. Expert hands rifled his pockets. Kenyon rolled over, and grabbed an ankle, bringing the owner down with a crash.

They came back at him. Kenyon closed inside those iron bars, and butted one of them in the face. Something gave under the scarf, and the man grunted with pain. Kenyon swung him bodily into the other two. They staggered, off balance, down the steps, and one of them sprawled on the pavement, but he picked himself up at once. Kenyon wondered if he had time to get inside his street door. They had him cut off at the top of the steps, and there was nowhere else he could go. If they took a little more care, now they knew their victim was going to fight back, and used those iron bars in earnest, they could beat him into a pulp.

Some such thoughts were probably passing through the minds of his assailants. There was a moment's hesitation on all sides. But then a car approached along Gloucester Terrace, headlights on. The three men decided to call it a day. They ran off, and turned into Chilworth Street.

Kenyon sat down on the top step, gasping for breath. Blood was running down his face. He eased his damaged shoulder, and wished it were still numb. Stabs of pain were biting deep into the muscles.

The approaching car had stopped outside Kenyon's house. It was a Volvo. Detective Sergeant Nick Vardin got out.

"Do you need a doctor, an ambulance, or a drink?" he inquired.

"I'll have those bastards first," Kenyon gasped. He stood up, lurched down the steps, and gestured with his good arm. "Chilworth Street. Come on."

Nick listened to the distant bark and roar of receding engines.

"I don't fancy my chances of following three motor bikes at the same time," he remarked.

"One'll do," Kenyon said, vindictively.

"Oh, come on," Nick said. "Fond as I've grown of your Volvo, it is not designed for chasing high-powered motor bikes."

The sound of engines had died away already. Kenyon thought they had headed for Bishops Bridge Road, but then where? Nick clearly had no enthusiasm for driving around on the off chance. All right, he would use the Ford, but when he started to walk, he became giddy, and had to support himself on the railings.

Nick read his thoughts. "Forget it," he said. "Not a hope."

"Well, at least try and summon up enough energy to use your radio," Kenyon said. "That's what it's for."

"Great. Waste everyone's time," Nick grumbled. "You used to know what a lost cause looked like, at one time, Mr. Kenyon, sir."

Nick called in, giving the sketchy descriptions which were all that Kenyon could provide. Afterwards, he followed Kenyon downstairs, sat him in a chair, poured a scotch, and thrust the glass in his hand.

"I reckon you need this more than medical attention," he said, cheerfully.

"Thanks for the expert diagnosis," Kenyon said, bitterly. But Nick was right. The rivulet of blood on his face had come from a scalp abrasion which was already beginning to congeal. His shoulder would be stiff and painful for some time, but there was nothing broken.

"I'm sorry," Nick said, grinning, "but I think it's hilarious. A copper mugged on his own doorstep. Where will these muggers stop, I ask myself?"

"What were you doing here, anyway?" Kenyon inquired ungraciously.

"You really are an ungrateful sod, Mr. Kenyon, sir," Nick Vardin said. "I called earlier with the results of some more labors on Archie's diary, found you were out, and deduced you were wining and dining somewhere. I was on my way home, and decided I'd try again on the off chance." He handed Kenyon a typewritten sheet.

"Thanks," Kenyon said. He scanned the sheet hopefully, but none of the additional information threw any light on anything. "Nothing there," he said, "but I'll tell you what I do want. The photostats of those dollar bills Archie was carrying."

"Why?" Nick asked, curiously.

"I don't know," Kenyon said, truthfully.

"Straw clutching time again, is it?" Nick supposed. "OK. Mine not to reason why."

They arranged where to meet on the following day, when Nick would hand over the photostats. Kenyon was not to know that he would not attend that meeting. Nick was to wait for an hour, tuck the envelope back in his briefcase, and go about his business. He did wonder later what had happened to Kenyon, but without very much interest.

Nick looked at his watch, and said, "OK if I use your phone?" Kenyon nodded. Nick dialed Bayswater Police Station, listened for a while, making noncommittal noises, and hung up.

"With those lousy descriptions, and no registration numbers," he said, "you will not be surprised to learn that no likely motorcyclists have been apprehended." He took out his notebook with a sigh. "I suppose you want me to take a statement from you."

"Never mind," Kenyon said. "What's the point?"

"Not a lot," Nick agreed. He put his notebook away with relief. "And it'll save me doing any paperwork, which I dislike at the best of times. What did they take? Your wallet?"

"Yes," Kenyon said.

"Money, checkbook, credit cards, that sort of thing?"

"That sort of thing," Kenyon said.

"Well, you'll be able to get most of it back, except the money," Nick said. "Perhaps somebody thought you might be carrying that five grand on you."

"Why don't you go home?" Kenyon demanded.

Nick grinned. "I'll let you know if the Paddington muggers strike again," he said.

Kenyon finished his drink, and crawled wearily into bed. He wondered why he had not told Nick Vardin about the hundred dollar bill. Yet, what was there to tell? All he had was a series of disconnected fragments with no link whatever. People were getting mugged in London with increasing frequency. Had they been waiting for *him?* Or were they just waiting for anyone who came along?

Apart from his state of near total ignorance, there was, he recognized, another reason for failing to confide fully in Nick. He did not trust the ruthlessly self-centered Detective Sergeant, and his resentment at being deprived of his beloved old Volvo only partly accounted for that.

Kenyon was sleepily pouring his first cup of tea at seven a.m. next morning, when the phone began to ring.

It was unexpected at this hour, and the shrilling bell made him start. He carried his cup of tea round the breakfast bar, lifted the receiver, and croaked "Hullo."

"Detective Inspector Sidney Kenyon?" The female voice was brisk, cool, and efficient.

"Speaking," Kenyon said. He swallowed a much-needed mouthful of tea.

"This is Sister Hurst, Inspector," the cool voice said. "We have met . . ."

Kenyon's stomach contracted abruptly with fear. His drowsiness vanished in an instant. Sister Hurst was in charge of the coronary ward at the hospital near Saffron Walden.

"What's happened?" Kenyon asked, as levelly as he could.

"I'm sorry to have to tell you," Sister Hurst said, "that your father suffered another coronary last night. He's in the Intensive Care Unit."

"Last night? When? What time?"

"Your father was on his way home from the annual dinner at the British Legion Club," Sister Hurst said. "He collapsed in the street. He was admitted at ten thirty."

"Ten thirty?" Kenyon demanded, his voice rising. "Why the bloody hell didn't you phone me at once?"

Sister Hurst's voice remained cool, unruffled and detached.

"The first priority," she said, "was to keep your father alive. By the time his condition stabilized, it was three a.m. It seemed better to wait a few hours, and inform you when you'd had a night's sleep."

"I'm sorry, sister," Kenyon apologized. "How is he?"

"It depends if he continues to respond," Sister Hurst said. "But I'm afraid his condition is certainly serious."

"I'll be there in two hours," Kenyon said.

"Very well," Sister Hurst said.

"No, hang on," Kenyon said, his mind for once confused, failing to cope. There were only two gallons of petrol left in the Ford's tank. He would need money, another checkbook. "I've just remembered . . . I can't leave at once . . . I'll try and get there by lunch time."

"It doesn't make much difference," Sister Hurst said. "You won't be able to see him, anyway."

Kenyon had his suitcase packed, and was ready to go by seven thirty. But the bank did not open until nine thirty. He chain smoked, and watched the minute hand of his watch crawl lethargically around the dial. At eight forty he could bear the inactivity no longer. He must *do* something. There was one quick call he could make. That would pass the time until the bank opened. Sitting here worrying himself sick would not help his father one iota.

He got into the Ford Capri, fought his way through the traffic to Grosvenor Square, and bullied his way into the last remaining parking meter, in front of a new Mercedes. The driver of the Mercedes mouthed angry criticism of the maneuver, but decided not to risk damage to his expensive bodywork by pressing the point, and drove off.

Kenyon ran up the steps of the American Embassy, and approached a soldier on duty.

"I want to see Ned Purcell, urgently," he said. "Detective Inspector Kenyon, CID."

"Wait here, sir, if you please," the soldier said, and went off to telephone.

Ned Purcell was the FBI man attached to the embassy whom Kenyon knew best.

The soldier came back. "I'm sorry, Inspector," he said.

"But Mr. Purcell isn't available. He sends his apologies, and suggests you leave a message."

"I don't want to leave a message," Kenyon said. "I want to talk to him. Did you say it was urgent?"

"I did," the soldier said, "but unfortunately he . . ."

"Let me speak to him on the phone," Kenyon said.

"I'm sorry," the soldier said. "He's in conference."

"I don't care if he's having a crap," Kenyon said viciously. "This is a police matter, and I want his co-operation, this minute."

The soldier went off again, and after a couple of minutes returned, and showed Kenyon to a telephone.

Kenyon lifted the receiver. "Since when do I get fed bullshit about conferences?" he demanded.

"Since when does a suspended detective have the right to demand my co-operation about anything?" Ned Purcell asked in return.

Kenyon had cherished some small hope that Purcell would not know. Christ, the word had been spread fast. "I only want ten minutes of your time," he said.

"I'm tied up," Purcell said.

"It's about your own lousy currency," Kenyon said. "Something I've come across during an investigation. It may be something, or it may be nothing, but at least you can look into it."

"Sidney," Purcell said patiently down the line, "you are not investigating anything. You are suspended, and that's it. Period. If," he went on, "you have any information, you can pass it to me through the proper channels, with whom I shall gladly co-operate. Fair enough? OK?"

Kenyon caught sight of his wristwatch. Perversely, the time had suddenly decided to race on. All this bloody hanging about. It was twenty past nine. He could not stay here and argue with Purcell.

"Look," he said, harassed, "my father's ill. I've got to go and see him. Can we meet for a drink and talk, off the record, when I get back?"

"Maybe," Purcell said, neutrally. "Sorry about your father."

Kenyon promised to phone Purcell again in a day or

two, and ran back to his car. But he never did make that phone call.

It seemed to take forever to complete the formalities at the bank. He shifted restlessly from one foot to another, and kept looking at his watch. Finally, they gave him a new checkbook. Replacing his credit card would take longer. He decided to draw out three hundred pounds, just in case. He kept fearing the worst. There might be expenses to meet in Saffron Walden.

He got back in his car and headed for the North Circular. God, he had forgotten to put any petrol in. He pulled into a filling station, and waited impatiently behind three other cars.

The North Circular Road was at its worst, slow moving queues of cars, line abreast. Kenyon bullied his way on as best he could, but the traffic was jammed for miles ahead. It was only when he gained the M11 that a clear road opened up in front of him.

The north-bound carriageway of the motorway was reasonably uncluttered, and he put his foot down. The Ford disliked this, and told him so. At anything over sixty miles an hour the engine developed an ominous clatter. Jesus, all he needed now was for this thing to blow up on him. He slowed down to a steady fifty-five and took a deep breath. Calm down. His father's life was in their hands. There was nothing he could do except pray to a God in whom he did not believe. The speed at which he drove would make no difference whatever.

Kenyon lit a cigarette, and settled down in the middle lane. Relax, he told himself, just relax. Drive carefully, the way you should. Watch the fellow in front, in case he pulls out without indicating. Keep an eye on your mirrors. Always know what's coming up behind you.

He concentrated purely and simply on driving, and it helped. His heart rate slowed, his breathing became easier. He returned to something like normal, pushing aside for the moment the helplessly frightened, worried young man, terrified lest death should snatch his father from him.

It was only then that something occurred to Kenyon. Since he had left his flat that morning, all the trained responses, which he had believed to be completely automatic and instinctive, had failed him. He had no idea if his flat was under observation, or if his car had been watched. He did not know if anyone had followed him or not. Or if anyone were following him now.

A Daimler and a new Rover went past him in the outside lane at well over the legal limit, and receded into the distance. He overtook a van in the inside lane, and watched it grow smaller in his rear-view mirror.

Way, way behind him was the only likely remaining candidate, a vehicle too far away to identify, also cruising in the middle lane. Kenyon kept an eye on that one, prepared to be suspicious should it remain at precisely the same distance.

Forgetting for a moment, he tried to accelerate, to see what the vehicle behind did. But the Ford's engine clanked horribly in protest. He slowed down again, cursing his bad buy, and sparing a few carefully chosen expletives for the avaricious Nick Vardin. His old Volvo had not been a notably nimble car, but at least it would cruise at eighty without any fuss. He put the speedo needle back on fifty-five, and the row subsided somewhat.

Slowly the vehicle behind grew larger in his mirror, and turned into an old Jaguar, with a tinted windscreen. Its approach was steady and unhurried, and Kenyon guessed that it was cruising perhaps two or three miles an hour faster than he was. He relaxed a little, waiting for it to overtake. But it came closer and closer, until it was sitting right on his tail in the way a lorry might try and intimidate a car into accelerating or moving aside.

Faster moving cars were now overtaking in the outside lane, but Kenyon considered there was plenty of room for the Jag to go past him normally. "Bloody cowboy," he muttered. Both the occupants were wearing sunglasses, he could now see. Had the Ford Capri had any guts left in it, he might have taken the Jag on, and accelerated away. He contented himself with a rude sign, directed behind him. The Jag sat impassively where it was, just over a car length behind.

An articulated lorry was lumbering along ahead in the inside lane. Once past that, Kenyon decided, he would move in ahead of it. He had better things to do than cope with idiots like the one behind him, whose submerged, suppressed aggressions blossomed into dangerous life once at the wheel of a car, and who were the cause of so many road accidents.

Safely clear of the articulated lorry, Kenyon signaled, and moved sedately into the inside lane. The Jaguar, continuing its progress, drew level with him, and then seemed to hesitate. Kenyon glanced sideways, and saw too late that the passenger window was wound down, and what the passenger was doing.

Kenyon's offside front tire burst at the moment the Jaguar cut in sharply in front of him, and accelerated away at full power. In the same second, he smelled petrol.

The Ford skidded across the motorway, metal on concrete howling as the rubber from the flat tire was torn off. The steering wheel was wrenched round as though by a giant hand. Kenyon fought to control the car and failed.

The Ford was spinning round, out of control. Kenyon caught a kaleidoscopic glimpse through the windscreen, of gyrating sky, trees, and an approaching motorway bridge.

There was nothing he could do. The uncontrollable Ford was due to hit the guard rails, other traffic, or blow up any moment. For Kenyon now realized that what he could smell was not just petrol, but burning petrol which was about to explode, and reduce him to an unidentifiable mess of charred, blackened remains.

Reason played no part in it. It was either instinctive self-preservation, or a desire to depart this life in a slightly less unpleasant way. He released the steering wheel, hit the seat belt release, forced the door open and somersaulted from the rotating car, trying to roll shoulder to hip across his spine.

The thump as he hit the concrete of the roadway knocked all the breath out of him. His chin was tucked down into his chest, but as he rolled over and over, he saw two images, frozen, like swiftly succeeding slides from an epidiascope.

The first was the Ford, exploding into a ball of fire as it hit the guard rails. The second was the huge bulk of the jackknifing articulated lorry as it bore down on his helpless body. Then blackness hit him.

The blackness turned into misty, wavering vision, combined with a thudding, splitting headache. He was lying on the verge, covered by a blanket. Warm air caressed his cheek. The stench of blazing petrol was in his nostrils. He turned his head. Fifty yards away, the Ford Capri was a roaring inferno.

"You'd better lie still, chum," a voice said. It belonged to a traffic cop who was standing over him. There were two police cars parked, their blue lights revolving silently. The jackknifed lorry was in front of him, blocking two lanes of the motorway. The driver was talking to another copper. Two more were settling out cones to guide oncoming traffic into the remaining open lane.

"The ambulance won't be long," the traffic policeman said.

Kenyon propped himself up into a sitting position, and shook his head, which reacted excruciatingly. "I don't want any bloody ambulance," he said. "You and your mate can take me to Saffron Walden." He threw the blanket off.

"You're going to stay where you are, chum," the traffic policeman said, putting it back again.

"Detective Inspector Kenyon to you, constable," Kenyon said. "Bayswater Division, Metropolitan Police." He held out one hand. The copper helped him uncertainly to his feet. Kenyon wobbled a bit, but he thought he could stay upright.

"I knew your name, Mr. Kenyon, from your checkbook," the copper said, wary, but not completely convinced. "But you had no wallet on you, no warrant card . . ."

Kenyon waved at the burning Ford, trusting the copper would deduce that his warrant card had been in the glove pocket. "Detective Superintendent Pindar's my boss at Bayswater. Check with him if you like," he said. He limped across to the lorry driver, and the copper with the notebook.

"I'm a DI in the Met," he told the copper, and turned

to the lorry driver. "Thanks for not mashing me into a pulp," he said sincerely.

"You were dead lucky," the lorry driver said. He was pale and shaken himself. "There was only inches in it."

"Did you see what happened?" Kenyon asked him.

"Your front tire burst when that Jag cut in in front of you," the lorry driver said. "Silly bugger. I took his number. I didn't see your lights go on, but I suppose you must have hit the brakes, and . . ."

"It wasn't that," Kenyon said. He waved at the Ford blazing merrily. "Did you notice if she was burning before she crashed?"

"Went up in flames when she hit," the lorry driver said. "You started spinning when your tire burst. I hit the brakes, tried to swerve, but then my bloody trailer started coming round . . ."

"Yes, all right," Kenyon said. "Thanks again."

He sat in the back of the police car, as it sped towards Saffron Walden. He had told them about his father, promised to have himself checked at the hospital, and the observer had radioed in to cancel the ambulance.

"You were lucky, sir," the driver said. "You should be dead."

"Yes," Kenyon said. "I should."

A fire engine passed in the opposite carriageway, heading south for the scene of the accident.

"I'd like you to ask Forensic to go over my car," Kenyon said.

The observer was puzzled. "Forensic, sir?"

"Yes," Kenyon said. "And that Jaguar. My guess is, it was stolen. Check it out. I want to know where it was knocked off."

"Right, sir," the observer said. He gave his colleague, who was driving expressionlessly, a sideways glance. The driver's eyes did not flicker, but an unspoken thought passed between them, as clear as a bell to Kenyon. "Poor devil. He's raving. Should have made him wait for the ambulance, Inspector or no Inspector."

His father, they told him at the hospital, was still in the Intensive Care Unit, and his condition was unchanged. Kenyon allowed himself to be examined by a doctor in Casualty who said "yes . . . m'm . . ." a good deal, and

149

wanted to keep him inside for twenty-four hours. Kenyon refused point blank.

"Well, there's no apparent concussion," the doctor said. "But just the same, it would be better if . . ."

"I'll get plenty of rest," Kenyon promised, "and come back if I feel any worse."

"It would be much better if you were kept under observation," the doctor said, annoyed. Patients were supposed to do as they were told.

A nurse dressed the abrasion on his face, and Kenyon went outside to find a taxi, but the patrol car was waiting for him. Kenyon gave them his father's address, and climbed in gratefully.

"Thanks very much," he said.

"Quite all right, sir," the observer said.

"Have you been on to Forensic?" Kenyon asked.

"Yes, sir," the observer said, politely.

They dropped him outside his father's house. Kenyon let himself in with the spare key his father had insisted on giving him. "I don't want to have to wait in for you whenever you might be coming," his father had said. "And it'd be daft for you to hang around outside, when I could be anywhere."

"Only the pub or the British Legion," Kenyon had said. "You're not the hardest man in the world to track down." But he had taken the keys anyway.

The small house was deathly quiet. There was too much old-fashioned furniture in all the tiny rooms, but his father had refused to discard any of it when he had retired, and left the larger house in Hounslow where Kenyon had been born and brought up. "Your mother chose it all, one time or another," his father had said. "Kind of a history of our marriage, all this stuff is."

Kenyon's grandparents had lived in a tied cottage outside Saffron Walden. His grandfather had been a taciturn farm laborer, who plodded through life from one season to the next.

"I always meant to come back, one day," his father had said. "Your mother knew that. She accepted it like . . . not that she cared for the country much . . . still, now she's gone, she won't have to put up with it. But there's been Kenyons buried in that churchyard for three hundred years, and, God willing, that's where I want to end up. Whether you care to join me, later on of course, that's up to you."

"Thanks very much," Kenyon had said.

That was when his father's eyesight had deteriorated to the point where he had been forced to finally give up his job as a London taxi driver.

The little house was one of a terrace, overlooking the Green, but it had no garden.

"I think it's ridiculous," Kenyon had said, "to come and live in a country town, and choose a house with no garden."

"I just want to see a bit of green," his father had said, obstinately. "But I don't want to have to do anything about it. What do I want with a bloody garden? Gardens need looking after. A garden would interfere with my social life."

For a time, Kenyon had hoped that his father might remarry, but the old chap showed no interest in any of the eligible widows who showed some interest in him. "Once is enough," he had explained to Kenyon. "Besides, suppose there is some sort of afterlife? You never know. There might be. What would your mother say if I were to arrive with some other woman in tow?"

"As I understand it," Kenyon had said, "that kind of thing doesn't arise on the other side, according to the Church of England."

"They could be wrong," his father had said.

"You should be a bloody Mohammedan," Kenyon had told him. His father had chuckled.

Kenyon lay on the bed in the silent house, dozed, and waited. They had promised to ring him as soon as there was any change, but the phone remained silent.

He phoned twice himself during the evening, and received phrases like "as well as can be expected." But he thought he detected a note of reserved anxiety at the other end.

He went to bed early, feeling that he should rest, even if he could not sleep. Contrary to his expectations, he dropped off at once, and slept deeply for twelve hours. He felt better when he awoke. More himself. Able to cope again. But there was nothing to cope with, except waiting.

He telephoned the hospital at intervals, but there was no news, or at least no good news. He filled in the time by going through his father's personal effects, which was easy enough. His father kept all his documents in an attaché case, a habit he had formed during the long blitz on London during the war. "As soon as the warning went," his father used to reminisce, "me and your mother, we'd go down the shelter, but I always had this case with me. I mean, there was petrol coupons for a start. More valuable than gold them petrol coupons were."

Inside the attaché case now, were a number of large envelopes, each neatly labeled, in block capitals. One said PHOTOGRAPHS. It contained his father's wedding photographs, a studio portrait of his mother as a young woman, and several snapshots, including a few of Kenyon himself as a child. There were also some of the taxis his father had driven. The early ones must have been drafty in the extreme.

Another envelope said CERTIFICATES. Creased, carefully preserved birth certificates, inluding Kenyon's, his mother's death certificate, his father's wedding certificate.

Kenyon wondered if his father thought he was supposed to take the attaché case with him, and present the relevant certificates for admission to the hereafter.

The deeds to the house, various insurance policies, and a will completed the documentation surrounding his father's life. "My son Sidney" was the sole heir. When his father died, Kenyon would be richer to the tune of one terrace house, and insurance policies totaling one thousand, four hundred pounds, originally taken out with the intention of preserving his mother from hardship, in the days when money had a very different value, and when the premiums must have been hard to find.

Kenyon sadly put the attaché case back where he had found it. It did not seem very much for one decent, hard-working, honest life. He wondered if there were still room in that churchyard where the Kenyons were buried. Even if there were not, his father would never know. But he hoped there was.

At six o'clock, the doorbell rang. Kenyon invited the uniformed Superintendent in. He took off his cap, and walked into the living room, but declined Kenyon's invitation to sit down, and refused the offer of a drink. Kenyon supposed they had done some checking, and picked someone to call who would outrank him. So it proved.

"The reasons don't matter to me," the Superintendent said. "But I believe you've been suspended from duty."

"Yes, that's so," Kenyon said.

"I want to be sure of my facts," the Superintendent said. "Certain actions were requested by one of the crew of a patrol car, and if he had been aware that you were suspended . . ."

"I don't think I made it plain," Kenyon said. "You must blame me. It certainly wasn't the Constable's fault."

"While you're suspended," the Superintendent said, "you have no authority to issue orders, or any right to information of the kind you asked for."

"I know, sir," Kenyon said. "But I'd just been involved in an accident in which I might have been killed. If it's caused any trouble, I can only apologize."

"Well, I suppose old habits die hard," the Superintendent said.

"I hope my suggestions will be followed, just the same," Kenyon said.

"There'll be the same investigation there would be into any serious road accident," the Superintendent said.

"Well, as you say, I've no right to insist," Kenyon said.

"No," the Superintendent said. He put his cap on, moved to the door, and hesitated. "I suppose there's no harm in saying, off the record," he said, "that you were right about the Jaguar. It was found abandoned in Bishop's Stortford. It had been stolen, the night before, from a long-term car park in White City."

"Any way of tracing who was driving it?" Kenyon asked. The Superintendent shook his head definitely. "And Forensic?" Kenyon went on.

"Your car's a burned-out, mangled heap of metal," the Superintendent said. "Forensic could spend weeks on it . . . and what are they supposed to be looking for?"

"I'm not sure," Kenyon admitted.

"Should we receive a request from the Yard," the Superintendent said, "or indeed from you, if you were returned to duty, then it might be another matter."

"If I'm returned to duty," Kenyon said, "it will only be of academic interest."

The following day, the voice on the telephone at the hospital stopped sounding as though she were trying to prepare him for the worst. Two days later, she was positively cheerful. His father was out of the Intensive Care Unit, and Kenyon could visit him.

Kenyon removed the dressing from his face, and cleaned it up as best he could. He bought some recent paperbacks. His father was a voracious reader.

Kenyon walked into the Coronary Ward, and crossed to his father's bed. The face that turned towards him was gray and exhausted. Deep lines hollowed his cheeks. The sparse gray hair was wispy and dull. But the blue eyes which focused on him still had a residual brightness, and the smile, if shaky, was as broad as ever.

"Hullo, son," his father said.

All the deep, profound feeling which Kenyon harbored for this man came flooding out of him.

"You silly old fool," he said.

The old man's smile broadened, and a trace of satisfaction entered it. "I'll go when I'm good and ready, and not before," he said. The grin faded, as he looked at Kenyon more carefully. "What's wrong with your face? What have you done to yourself?"

"I wasn't looking where I was going," Kenyon said. "I walked into a concrete lamp standard."

"Strikes me you're the silly fool, not me," his father said. "You're all right though? Are you sure someone hasn't been having a go at you?"

"I'm fine," Kenyon said. "Just concentrate on getting yourself out of this place. You don't have to worry about me."

He could not tell his father that someone, he knew not who, had set out to kill him, for reasons which he also did not know.

CHAPTER NINE

Two days later, Kenyon talked to the Consultant, who told him that his father would have to stay in hospital for at least a fortnight, and perhaps more. He was making satisfactory progress, but it was his second coronary, after all. It would help to significantly prolong Mr. Kenyon senior's life, the Consultant reflected ironically, if he were to avoid having a third.

His father was sitting up and enjoying a cup of tea when Kenyon went into the ward. He was looking much better already.

"They tell me you're not due to pop off just yet," Kenyon said, "so there's not much point in my hanging about waiting for the happy event. I've got a lot of work on my desk, and the pile's getting bigger by the minute." His suspension was something he had not mentioned to his father.

"Yes, you clear off," his father said. "You're only spoiling my chances with that nurse."

"I'll keep in touch," Kenyon promised, "and I'll come back to see you home and safely tucked in. I've arranged for a woman to come in and look after you, do your cooking and cleaning and so on. What's more, she used to do nursing, so she can keep an eye on you as well, and make sure you don't do anything stupid."

"I can look after myself," his father said. "I don't want no woman in my house."

"You'll do as you're told," Kenyon said.

He took a taxi to Audley End, and caught the train for London. He had considered buying another car, and decided against it. The feeling of safety engendered when climbing into one's own car was deceptive. A car was easier to keep tabs on than a pedestrian dodging in and out of cabs and tubes. He saw no good reason why, having tried and failed once, they would not try again, whoever "they" might be.

He collected his mail, and entered his flat cautiously. He had not had time to get the lock changed yet, and he believed that someone else still had a set of keys. But there was no one there, and no sign that anyone had been there during his absence.

He skimmed through the mail. Only one item was of any interest. That was an envelope, delivered by hand, containing photostats of hundred dollar bills, and a note from Nick Vardin, which read, "Waited for an hour. Gathered you had better things to do. Don't know if you still want these? Destroy if you don't. They are photostats of photostats. Hence the fuzziness." The quality of the copies was indeed poor. Kenyon rang around until he managed to track Nick Vardin down.

"When you bought my car," he said, for the benefit of the tape recorder locked into his tapped telephone, "you went off with my gloves. I'd like them back."

"OK," Nick said, indifferently. "Some time this evening, if you're in."

Kenyon hesitated before he made his next phone calls, but he could not be bothered to accumulate enough change, and go and find a vacant phone box. Besides, the odds were they would not make much sense anyway to an outsider.

The one to the American Embassy was abortive. Ned Purcell was in conference again. His movements thereafter appeared to be vague and mysterious, conceivably involving long journeys. "Well, when he gets back from Timbuctoo or Samarkand," Kenyon said, "tell him I called to say thanks for sticking his neck out for me." He hung up, and dialed a Paris number.

Mrs. Coleman, or Sarah Brooks, as Kenyon still somehow thought of her, answered the phone herself.

"I thought I was on your blacklist," she said, "when you didn't answer my letter."

"I was hoping to come and see you during the summer, but I couldn't get away," Kenyon lied. "Can I invite myself to dinner some time soon?"

"Well, yes," Sarah said. "When do you think you might be in Paris?"

"I've got a few days off," Kenyon said. "As soon as you like. I feel like a break. I'd like to meet your husband again. I assume he'll be there?"

"Of course," Sarah said. She sounded a little uncertain as to precisely what Kenyon was getting at. "At least . . . I'm just looking at his diary . . . after tomorrow, he's tied up with a visiting Senator, and then we have to come to London . . . perhaps we could . . ."

"Why don't we make it tomorrow?" Kenyon interjected. "Tell me what time, and I'll book a flight now."

Sarah seemed somewhat puzzled by the sudden urgency, after all this time, but she promised to check with her husband and ring back if, for some reason, the following evening was not convenient after all. Kenyon took a chance, rang British Airways, and booked a flight anyway.

Nick Vardin arrived soon after six p.m.

"A little bird tells me you've written your car off," he said. "Care to buy a Volvo in first class nick for two grand?"

"No," Kenyon said. "I want your opinion about something, as an ex-SAS man."

"Depends what it is," Nick said. "Some of the things we used to get up to still come under the Official Secrets Act."

"Since you're such a patriotic bugger," Kenyon said, "you'll have to use your discretion." He told Nick something, although not everything, about his accident. He paused and looked at Nick, who waited patiently, since no question had arisen yet.

"You may think this is a bit wild," Kenyon said at last, "but I know the SAS were equipped for all kinds of dirty tricks." Nick smiled deprecatingly. Kenyon said, "Suppose you wanted a car to crash and blow up? With very little risk of there being any trace of how you'd done it? I've got my own ideas, but how would you go about it?"

"From another car?" Nick mused. "Well, could be a special type of incendiary bullet, made of very soft metal, with a low melting point. Fire one into the petrol tank, and after a few seconds, up she goes. The casing melts along with half the car. It'd be a clever boffin who could track down one tiny piece of shapeless metal and say what it was, in a burned-out wreck."

"That's what I thought," Kenyon said. "But suppose you used the same type of bullet to puncture a tire? That casing's not going to get melted down."

"It'd go straight through the tire," Nick said. "Ricochet off the road, and end up Christ knows where in some field. Even if you could find it, all you've got is a small piece of mis-shapen metal. What would that prove?"

"Yes," Kenyon said. "Tire ripped to bits when it went flat, and burned up anyway. No one's going to find any holes in it."

"Is that what you reckon some well-wisher did to you?" Nick inquired.

Kenyon said, "I think it's possible."

"Anything's possible," Nick said. "But we're talking about pretty sophisticated gear. I don't know any villains who have access to that sort of thing. Shooters, yes, but special incendiaries . . . ?" He shook his head. "I'll tell you what I think," he said. "Your front tire burst, because it blew out. Tires do. You crashed, and the car caught fire. That happens too."

"Not as often as the movies would have us believe," Kenyon said.

"No," Nick said. "But more often than London coppers get uncommon bullets pumped into their cars. Jesus, the ones we used were manufactured in the USA. Even I wouldn't have the first idea how to get hold of any now, let alone some domestic villain who's decided he doesn't much like Sidney Kenyon."

Nick clearly believed that Kenyon was raving. Kenyon did not blame him. Perhaps he was. And yet he was certain that the Ford Capri had started to burn a second or two before it crashed. Well, almost certain.

He caught a late afternoon flight to Paris the following day, freshened up in a wash-room at Charles de Gaulle Airport, climbed into a taxi, and gave Sarah's address.

The first floor apartment was elegant, spacious, and overlooked the Avenue du Bois de Boulogne. Only a rich man could afford to live in such a place, but Harry Coleman *was* rich. He probably did not even draw his salary from the American Government, for whatever task he was now performing which called for him to be attached to the Paris embassy. Kenyon was far from clear what Coleman's present function was. He just knew he was a very influential man indeed, who owed Kenyon a favor.

Kenyon shook Sarah's hand politely, and smiled his way through the usual courtesies. He was appalled. Not by Sarah. She looked exactly the same. But by himself.

Anyone, he knew, could live without anyone else. No one ever died of a so-called broken heart. Broken heads, bullets, accident, disease, yes. Broken hearts, no. Devoted widows might weep, but they managed. Dead children were mourned, but the parents went on living. Lovers who had sworn eternal fidelity, parted, were miserable, and later swore eternal fidelity, to someone else. That was how human beings behaved during their brief span, that was how the world was. People got over it. They always did.

The affair with Sarah had only lasted a few months, a fair proportion of that, if passionate, less than contented, until she flew off to America to marry Harry Coleman. It was a long time ago now. It was all over and done with.

He was appalled to find, as he watched her, that it was not all over and done with at all. She moved serenely around this, her home, unself-consciously adjusting, chameleon-like, to her new environment, cool, impeccably groomed, beautiful, the smiling hostess, another man's wife.

But Kenyon kept seeing her in her small, top floor flat in Paddington. The way she came to meet him as he closed her front door, and put the keys in his pocket. The look in her eyes. The way her lips parted as she kissed him "hullo." And he remembered, uncomfortably, that sometimes the kiss had grown, and they had got out of bed an hour later, and eaten supper picnic style on the settee, in front of the electric fire, glancing now and then at each other, not saying much. He remembered the small, secret smile she gave him when she caught him looking at her.

All that was another time, and another place, with another woman—Sarah Brooks, not Mrs. Harry Coleman—and as dead as the cold ashes of an extinct fire. Or so Kenyon had believed. Or perhaps wanted to believe.

Harry Coleman was natural, welcoming, courteous and friendly. He shook Kenyon's hand with honest warmth and chatted in his articulate, fluent, American way. He was grateful to Kenyon for saving his life once, and Sarah's, on the island of Gotland, which was probably true although Kenyon had also been deeply concerned with preserving his own, at the time.

Coleman had also, it seemed, come to the conclusion that he owed his self-evident happiness with Sarah to Kenyon. This was also quite likely true, although not perhaps for reasons which Coleman knew about, and the thought gave Kenyon no pleasure whatever.

Harry Coleman was such a thoroughly likable man, his friendliness so patently sincere, his warmth so natural and unassumed, that it was hard not be drawn to him. It was also very hard not to envy him, and envy was not an emotion, Kenyon thought, that helped you to like someone very much.

But he played his part through all the civilities, the reminiscences, the casually wide-ranging conversation. Coleman fixed dry martinis himself, American style, and the potent brew did something to anesthetize Kenyon's unexpected sense of pain. Afterwards, they moved through into a paneled dining room, and dinner was served by the resident French staff.

He had taken to moving in affluent circles of late, Kenyon reflected, thinking of his dinner with Angela and Tony Vallenta, who were probably just as rich as the Colemans. What a deep-rooted difference there was though. All the carefully selected items in Tony's mini-palace added up collectively to unwitting, gutter bad taste. Here, everything was the opposite. Harry Coleman had always had money, and it meant nothing to him. His possessions were intrinsically beautiful, but might not be individually valuable. Everything Tony owned had a price, and he knew exactly what it had cost, and how much it would fetch.

Kenyon inquired what Harry Coleman was doing now. "Are you still with the State Department?"

"In a way," Coleman said. "Kind of."

It was "kind of" before, Kenyon recollected. Coleman had been an adviser on some of the early SALT negotiations.

"But then I had contacts with the other side, face to face," Coleman said. "That wouldn't be tactful anymore."

Kenyon had once, briefly and by chance, crossed the periphery of Coleman's world, which was what had taken him to Gotland. A world where power meant the life and death of nations, where both sides struggled for advantage under the guise of diplomacy, where a losing bluff might be paid for by nuclear war. Harry Coleman believed in peace, but a secure peace, founded on a strong Europe, not Fortress America. The other side had misjudged him, in their attempt to use him, and he had almost ended up a prisoner behind the Iron Curtain, or dead.

"I guess you might say," Coleman went on, "that I'm concerned with informational aspects which precede various policy decisions."

"You mean Intelligence," Kenyon hazarded.

Coleman smiled. "Sabotage and interference in domestic affairs, according to some," he said. "Human Rights is our name for it, and I think we're right." He went into a general explanation of his role in co-ordinating the follow-up to Helsinki and Belgrade, and the importance he attached to supporting various dissident movements.

Kenyon only half listened. He was watching the two of them, noting the tiny, almost invisible glances and minute changes of expression which passed between them, as between any two people who lived in the same house, and were concerned with each other's lives.

Harry Coleman adored Sarah, that was obvious. He smiled at her often, mutely appealing, even though not talking to her directly, for some silent signal of her approval, which made this vigorous, middle-aged man appear curiously vulnerable, and dependent.

Sarah was intrinsically the stronger of the two, Kenyon thought. She was proud of him, there was no doubt about that, and with reason. Harry Coleman was that rarity in Kenyon's experience, a man who was mostly good, although presumably his ex-wife might have reservations in that direction. Was there much more than pride and admiration in her attitude towards him? Gratitude, of a kind, he thought, yes, there was that.

Over the first glass of cognac, Kenyon asked "Do you ever see your children?"

"It's kind of difficult," Coleman said. "They're at school in the States, of course, and I've been too busy to take a real vacation . . ." For the first time, the adoration in his eyes, for Sarah, was qualified by something else. Something akin to regret and remorse.

"We're hoping they might be able to come and stay with us, perhaps next summer," Sarah said. "I'm sure they'd love it here, in Paris, and it would be fun, showing them round."

"It'll be great," Coleman said, heartily. "I'm really looking forward to it."

But neither of them believed that this visit would ever take place, Kenyon realized, and Coleman was relieved when Sarah changed the subject.

Coleman and his first wife were both practicing Catholics. It must have been hard for Coleman to insist on the divorce which all his upbringing told him was wrong. It said a lot about his feelings for Sarah, and had required considerable courage, but there was a price to be paid, for him, and he would always have to pay it.

"Where are you staying?" Coleman asked Kenyon.

"I'm not," Kenyon said. "When you throw me out, I'm catching the next plane back."

"That's crazy," Coleman said. "I don't think there's another flight now until seven thirty in the morning. You can stay with us. There's a guest room always ready for unexpected visitors, and in the morning . . ."

Sarah did not reinforce her husband's urgings. She was gazing at Kenyon speculatively. She knew him rather better than Harry Coleman did.

"I think Sid must have had a special reason for coming to see us," she said quietly. "I expect this is when we hear what it is."

"The lady is this week's Mastermind, and will undoubtedly appear in the finals," Kenyon said. He lifted his glass and toasted Sarah ironically. "Yes, you're quite right. There's a spot of bother, and I think Harry may be able to help me."

He told them nearly everything that had happened, including his suspension from duty. They listened in silence, but both seemed to accept what he said. Neither exhibited the skepticism to which Kenyon had become accustomed.

"Well, I'm sorry you're in that kind of trouble," Coleman said, when Kenyon had finished, "and if I could help in any way, I certainly would. I owe you a hell of a lot, I know that." His eyes sought Sarah's, and he smiled at her briefly. "But I don't honestly see what I can do."

Kenyon took the photostats from his pocket, and handed them over.

"See what you can find out about these," he said.

Coleman studied the blurred reproductions. "You think these hundred dollar bills might be forgeries?" he asked.

"I'm pretty sure they're not," Kenyon said.

"Then what do you expect me to come up with?"

"I don't know," Kenyon said. "Perhaps nothing. Perhaps I'm on the wrong track entirely. But I think they're part of it. How, I don't know, and I could be mistaken. But you're in a position to lean on people I can't even get near anymore. You can get answers. Is there something about those notes? God knows what. Anything. That's what I want to know."

"OK," Harry Coleman said. "I'll get our Federal people on to it. It may take a day or two though."

"Keep it confidential," Kenyon said. "If there is an answer, I don't want it to get around."

He gave Coleman the photograph of the clean-cut man outside Tony Vallenta's house. "It's a long shot," he said, "but perhaps you'd see if they can identify this merchant as well. I'm only guessing, but I think he could be American."

"That would be my guess as well," Coleman said. He smiled. "Funny how some of us kind of conform to a pattern."

Kenyon resisted Coleman's renewed invitation to stay the night. Now that he had done what he came for, he wanted to get out of this apartment, and away from Sarah.

He strolled at random through the night streets, for half an hour, and then hailed a cab. At Charles de Gaulle Airport, he settled himself comfortably into a seat to await the first plane, closed his eyes, and tried to sleep, but his mind insisted on coming back to the same thing over and over, and would not let him rest. In the end, he sat up, and lit a cigarette.

It was nothing to do with his suspension, or even who was trying to kill him, or why. It was Sarah's face which would not go away. There had been a time, when, he

163

believed later, Sarah would have married him. But he had said nothing, and she had flown off to New York, to Harry Coleman.

For months after she left him, Kenyon had wondered if he should have said something. Eventually, he had evicted such thoughts from his mind. Or so he had imagined. He stubbed out his cigarette and lit another one. Jesus, he told himself, there was nothing unique about Sarah Coleman, née Brooks. She possessed exactly the same equipment as any other woman. Any differences were marginal. There were thousands of females around just as good-looking as Sarah, and many of them more so. So forget it. Forget it.

He was weary when he let himself into his flat. There was no mail. He phoned the hospital. His father was making, they said, "Good progress." He considered going to bed, but decided against it. He had the distinct feeling, after being nearly burned to death on the motorway, that time was not on his side. He shaved and took a cold shower, which had served him in place of a night's sleep many times before.

There was a bitterly chill North wind, and he lengthened his stride as he walked briskly away from his flat. A man behind him seemed intent on going in the same direction. Kenyon made his way to Paddington Station, mingled with the arriving commuters, heading for the Underground, and slipped into the rear entrance of the Great Western Hotel instead.

His would-be shadow hurried past, and into the Underground. "Good luck, mate," Kenyon thought. He went through the hotel, across the foyer, and out into Praed Street. By the time he was satisfied that his tail had lost him for good, it did not seem worth hailing a taxi.

He circled the Blue Otter, and walked along the service road at the rear, slowing his pace. The back door of the building opened into a small, walled enclosure, where the dustbins stood. Kenyon took the lid off one of them. Inside was a green plastic sack, sealed at the top. He put the lid back, and sighed. He still thought Bill Jarvis was probably potty, or very gullible, but he could not wait around for Harry Coleman to get in touch with him. Coleman might come up with nothing.

Kenyon walked on through the service road, crossed Edgware Road, and hailed a taxi. He gave an address in Charing Cross Road.

"Detective Inspector Kenyon, Bayswater Division," he told the receptionist. It was odd. Normally, he carried his warrant card around for weeks, without ever showing it to anyone. Only occasional members of the awkward squad ever demanded to see it. Now that he had no warrant card to show, he was suddenly apprehensive. But of course no one questioned that he was a copper making inquiries. They never did.

He was shown into an office, where a Mr. Murchison introduced himself. Murchison was about thirty, a bright, able man who wore horn-rimmed glasses.

"I'm looking into a man's disappearance," Kenyon said. "The establishment where he was last seen is in the area you cover. The Blue Otter."

"Yes," Murchison said. He took his glasses off, gave them a polish, and put them back on again.

"According to information received," Kenyon said, "his body may have been cut up, placed in plastic sacks, and left for the Cleansing Department to remove when the rubbish was collected in the normal way."

"I see," Murchison said. He seemed none too impressed.

"I'd like to establish if such a method would be practical, or even possible," Kenyon said.

"I suppose it's not completely impossible," Murchison said, dubiously.

"Your refuse lorries grind up all the garbage as they go," Kenyon said, echoing Bill Jarvis.

"It's more a question of compression than grinding," Murchison said.

"But you end up with a kind of mash," Kenyon said.

"The mechanism allows quite large items to slip through," Murchison said. "And a human body . . . even cut up first . . . you must remember our collectors are always on the lookout for anything of value. That's the form their perks take."

"All right, there might be some blood and shit," Kenyon argued, against his better judgment. "But there's a busy restaurant at the Blue Otter. Fellows used to collecting garbage from restaurants wouldn't necessarily take much notice of blood and bones."

"There's no special restaurant collection," Murchison pointed out. "A crew covers a certain area, houses, flats, restaurants, business premises—they take it as it comes."

"Are you saying that human remains would necessarily be detected?" Kenyon asked.

"No, of course not," Murchison said. "Our job is the collection and disposal of refuse. We're not detectives, so it's not our job to detect things." His horn-rimmed spectacles glimmered. "I'm saying there's a chance something might be spotted."

"Suppose it weren't," Kenyon said. "What happens to the refuse?"

"I can only answer for the City of Westminster," Murchison said.

"Refuse from the Blue Otter," Kenyon said.

"That's in W2," Murchison said. "Right. It would be taken direct to our depot at Gatliffe Road, SW1, where it would be transferred by hopper into barges. There again, the barge trimmers would be on the lookout for any items of value."

"Something resembling bits of a carcass might not immediately appear to be of much value," Kenyon said.

"That's true," Murchison said.

"Where do the barges go?"

"Out to Pitsea, on the Thames Estuary," Murchison said. "There, the refuse is discharged by grab crane into vehicles or trucks."

"Then what?"

"Dumped for land reclamation," Murchison said.

"So if this method of disposing of the body was used," Kenyon said, "that's where it'll be."

"Yes," Murchison said. "Somewhere. Bulldozed in with hard core."

Somewhere is right, Kenyon thought gloomily. He looked at the area of reclaimed land at Pitsea which Murchison was pointing out on a map. He remembered Nick's sardonic words, "straw clutching time." Straws were not built to carry much weight. This one had duly collapsed, as he might have expected. In any case, there was not one shred of evidence to support the old villain's yarn.

"Is there anything else I can do for you, Inspector?" Murchison asked politely, breaking the silence.

Kenyon gave him the date of the Colonel's disappearance. "I'd like to know if there was in fact a collection from the Blue Otter the following morning," he said, "and if so, which was the crew concerned?"

Murchison did not have this information to hand, but he telephoned a colleague. Kenyon refused the offer of a cup of tea while they waited. They chatted idly for a few minutes, until a secretary brought in a couple of folders. Murchison scanned the records they contained.

"Yes, there was a collection," he said. "Early in the round, so it would be perhaps, oh, I don't know, about seven o'clock. As for the crew . . ." He consulted another set of documents. "That was . . . do you want their names?"

"If you've got them," Kenyon said.

Murchison passed the sheet over. One name leaped out at Kenyon as though it were in neon lights. This, he thought, must be how an old time prospector in California must have felt when he caught sight of the first glimmer of gold in his pan.

"Was this fellow with you long?" he asked, pointing at the neon-lighted name.

Murchison said, "Just a minute." He shuffled through other sheets of paper. "No, he joined the week before, and left the week after. We have quite a large staff turnover, I'm afraid. Why? Do you know him?"

"I did," Kenyon said. He asked for a copy of the crew list, in case there were any others who collected refuse from the Blue Otter that morning who might figure in Criminal Records, and who might still be alive.

He cursed himself for his slowness. The information had been presented to him before in that diary entry, "N.I. to C.D.," and he had ignored it. C.D. meant Cleansing Department.

According to Bill Jarvis, the Colonel's body had been cut-up, and disposed of with the refuse. The driver of the vehicle which had collected refuse from the Blue Otter that morning was Archibald Macintyre. Kenyon thought that was altogether too much of a coincidence.

The last remaining vestiges of tiredness had disappeared.

The adrenaline induced by this, his first real break, had seen to that. He found a pay phone, called Nick Vardin, and told him what he wanted. Nick grumbled, but finally agreed to do what he could.

Kenyon decided to treat himself to a good lunch, and walked to Wheeler's in Old Compton Street. He ordered Dover Sole, and toyed with a glass of Puligny Montrechat. He wondered if the Complaints Investigation Branch would be impressed by his morning's work, and decided they would not. He now believed Bill Jarvis's story. The Colonel's remains were buried somewhere at Pitsea, bull-dozed into reclaimed land, but there was not one chance in a million of ever finding them. Archie Macintyre's brief period of employment added up to Kenyon, but then he wanted it to add up. Detective Chief Superintendent Bernard Chandler would inquire what earthly connection there was between these unsupported snippets and the evidence of corruption against Kenyon. Kenyon would not be able to tell him that. He could see no connection himself. He was, he realized, not very much further forward.

He spun out his meal, sitting, drinking coffee, until all the other customers had gone. He knew in his guts that he was inching his way into the right ball game. But he needed proof, and a gut reaction cut no ice. Besides which, he was still guessing at random. He did not even know what he was supposed to be trying to prove.

He strolled through Soho to the Regent Palace Hotel, bought a newspaper, sat in the foyer, and read it from beginning to end, to pass the time until he could phone Nick again. At five o'clock Nick was "out." He tried twice more, without success, and finally reached him just after six.

"You're costing me a fortune in phone calls," Kenyon told him.

"I'm being underpaid for the amount of work I'm doing," Nick said. "If you take my meaning. You owe me several stiff drinks."

"See you at the Pelican," Kenyon said. "I'll buy you dinner as well."

"Buy nothing," Nick said. "It's not one of my haunts, but I'll bet you're on Freeman's there."

"I doubt it," Kenyon said.

He was right. The young dinner-jacketed spade, Garry Bennett, chose not to notice Kenyon, and the head waiter was back to his normal, surly self.

"I see Walter Flack's moved in," Nick said.

"Yes," Kenyon said. He had noticed Walter Flack lording it at the best table, with a couple of his minions. And when Walter snapped his fingers, it was Garry Bennett himself who hurried over obsequiously to see what he wanted.

There was one advantage to being shoved into a far corner, behind some potted palms and away from the dance floor. The service might be lousy, but it was safe to talk.

"Any of those names turn up in Records?" Kenyon asked.

"Why you should be interested in dustmen beats me," Nick said. "Only one. Oliver Clark, known inevitably as Nobby."

Kenyon had not mentioned Archie Macintyre, more from his ingrained habit of keeping his cards close to his chest than anything. He no longer actively distrusted Nick Vardin, but he did not regard him as all that reliable either.

The villains' world was freely populated with Nobby Clarks, and Kenyon could not recall one called Oliver. "Who's he?" he asked.

"Aged twenty-nine," Nick said. "No fixed address. Used to shack up with a whore in Chalk Farm. A graduate of Borstal. Done time for grievous bodily harm, robbery and attempted rape. One of those thick, petty villains, good for anything, just gets hired for a job as and when."

"Is he still with the same Tom?" Kenyon asked. "I want to talk to him."

"Well, as it happens," Nick said, "he seems to have disappeared."

"When?"

"No one's seen him around for two or three weeks," Nick said.

"Marvelous," Kenyon said, bitterly. "Bloody marvelous."

Nick's first course belatedly arrived. Kenyon had decided to skip the hors d'oeuvre, and he smoked while Nick ate his way through a plate of whitebait.

"What about our respected friend Mr. Samuel Ashby?" Kenyon inquired impatiently.

"I don't like trying to talk while I'm eating," Nick said. "One thing at a time."

Samuel Ashby was the man who had taken over the Blue Otter after the Colonel's departure, either for the sunny clime of South America with a suitcase full of money or, hacked into small pieces, for a less salubrious destination in reclaimed land at Pitsea. Kenyon finished his large scotch, and glared at the head waiter.

"I ordered a bottle of wine half an hour ago," he snarled. "Unless it appears in thirty seconds flat, no bugger gets a tip, and especially not you, sunshine."

The head waiter muttered something inaudibly, but the wine arrived not more than five minutes later.

"The way they look after you here," Nick remarked, "you must be an old and valued customer." He pushed his plate aside, drank a glass of wine as though it were beer, and poured another. "Right," he said. "Samuel Ashby. Respectable, spotless, whiter than white, or he wouldn't have got the license anyway. Fifty-five years old, married to the same woman for thirty years, one grown-up son, who works for the EEC in Brussels. Formerly financial adviser to a firm in the City. Retired three years ago with a handsome golden handshake. Treasurer to a couple of charities. Chairman of a Boys Club. Lives in a converted oast house in Kent, but he stays three or four nights a week in his London flat in Camden Town. Financially sound, handled money all his life, with never a hint that so much as a penny ever stuck to his fingers. General opinion, he could be trusted alone all night with the Crown Jewels, and they'd still be there in the morning."

Kenyon was shifting in his seat restlessly. "I know most of that already," he complained. "That's not what I asked for."

"What you asked for," Nick said softly, "might be regarded as criminal libel, if anyone was fool enough to write it down."

Kenyon stared at him. "Then there is something?"

"There's always something about anybody," Nick said. "I hear gossip about the Royal Family. Whether it's true or not is another matter."

"I'm not interested in proving anything about Samuel Ashby, one way or another," Kenyon said. "I just want to know if there's any way someone might have put the bite on him. Despite his impeccable references."

"You think Ashby's fronting for someone at the Blue Otter," Nick said.

"I think he may have been obliged to agree to something against his will," Kenyon said.

"A front man's no use unless he's got something to front for," Nick objected. "So what's bent about the Blue Otter?"

"If I knew that," Kenyon said, frustrated, "I wouldn't need a copper who has the doubtful distinction of being friendly with the worst scum in London."

Nick grinned, unperturbed. "It pays dividends," he said. "One way or another."

"The dirt on Samuel Ashby," Kenyon reminded him.

"There's a problem," Nick said. "The info didn't come for nothing. Before I could get my snout to open his mouth, it cost me."

"You've ripped me off for my car already," Kenyon said.

"Because I purchase a car," Nick said piously, "that does not cover my out of pocket expenses."

"All right," Kenyon said, wearily, "but if I ever get back on duty, I shall be the poorest copper in London."

"I'm working on it," Nick said. "Twenty quid, please."

"This had better be good," Kenyon said, putting the money on the table.

"It's probably a pack of lies," Nick said, cheerfully. He tucked the notes in his pocket. "There's a drinking club I use off Praed Street." Kenyon knew the place. It was a dark, scruffy hole, inhabited mostly by villains, including Detective Sergeant Nick Vardin. "One of the customers is called Barry," Nick went on. "He's a male prostitute. A dreadful old queen. I'll do the evil sod for something or another one of these days, but meanwhile, Barry thinks I'm rather sweet." He smiled grimly. "Very proud of his teeth, Barry is. Had them all capped. He'll cry like a baby when he resists arrest, and I accidentally break them all for him."

"Get to the point," Kenyon said.

"According to Barry," Nick said, "Samuel Ashby is the other way, at heart, despite his loving wife and his grown-up son."

Kenyon shrugged. "What about it?" There were plenty of respectably married men who were pouffters on the side. "That's not illegal anymore."

"It is with twelve-year-old boys," Nick remarked. "Which Barry claims are Samuel Ashby's special taste."

Kenyon nibbled his lip. "Queers on the game are always on the lookout for a spot of blackmail," he objected. "If this is true, why hasn't your charming friend put the bite on Ashby himself?"

"Could be he's never been able to get hold of the right kind of proof," Nick said, indifferently. "Or could be he invented it to get hold of your twenty quid."

Kenyon chewed his way through half his steak, left the remainder and reverted to cigarettes. He supposed the story was not beyond the bounds of possibility. If someone had needed Ashby badly, they could have set him up with some kid, and then threatened to expose him if he did not play ball. But it was thin. Like everything else he had been groping for, it was a vague half possibility impossible to prove, and which did not fit in anywhere even if it were true.

Nick was looking at a stunningly beautiful West Indian girl in a tight red dress. She smiled at him.

"I wouldn't mind some company a bit more interesting than yours," Nick said. "Black girls like that turn me on. Do you fancy the blonde she's with?"

"No," Kenyon said. He stood up. "There's someone I want to talk to. If you don't want to wait for me, you can pay the bill before you go."

"You're kidding," Nick said.

Kenyon moved away from the table, and the West Indian girl took his place. He heard Nick call for the obligatory bottle of champagne. Kenyon estimated the evening was liable to cost him about a hundred quid. He was not, he thought, getting value for money.

He moved alongside Garry Bennett, took hold of the young spade's arm, and propelled him forcibly towards the private office at the far end of the bar.

"We're going to have a little talk, Garry," Kenyon said.

"I'm busy," Garry said, dragging his feet.

"You'll be busy trying to explain a few things," Kenyon

said, "if you make any bloody trouble." He dug his fingers viciously into the spade's biceps.

He pushed Garry into the office, and closed the door. The sound of music outside was cut off at once. The office was soundproofed.

Kenyon released Bennett. The spade rubbed his arm. "You've no right to lay a finger on me, Mr. Kenyon," he said. "I know you've been suspended. Everyone knows. All I've got to do is make one phone call."

"I thought we were friends," Kenyon said.

"I don't want to make things worse for you," Garry Bennett said, "but you've no call to push me around either."

"I'll decide that," Kenyon said, "after we've had a quiet, friendly chat, off the record."

He heard the music again. The vocalist was warbling. Walter Flack came in with his two heavies, and closed the door. The vocalist was cut off in mid-warble.

"This place is infested," Kenyon told Garry Bennett. "You need the pest control people."

Walter Flack smiled politely. He was an ugly man of forty, with thinning hair, brushed carefully across the top of his head. The two heavies were younger, and looked like heavyweight refugees from a boxing booth.

"It seems to me," Walter Flack said to Bennett, "that this person forced his way in here without an invitation."

"Watch it, Walter," Kenyon said. "Don't get above yourself."

"You've stepped out of line," Walter Flack said, "not me. Unless Mr. Bennett wishes to talk to you. And you don't, do you," he informed Bennett.

"No," Garry Bennett said.

"Even a nigger's got a right to privacy," Walter Flack said. "Except of course if you were a policeman on duty. Are you on duty?" He stared at Kenyon with gray, empty eyes. "If so, just show us your warrant card, and we'll go at once."

"I'm clocking all this up, Walter," Kenyon said. "You're marking your own card for the future, if you go on like this." Walter Flack was unimpressed. Tony Vallenta regarded him as a "lunatic," Kenyon remembered. The heavies were not even listening. They were flexing large fists in anticipation.

"Failing any warrant card," Walter Flack said, "you'll be escorted off the premises as an unwelcome intruder."

"No rough stuff," Garry Bennett said, anxiously.

Walter Flack laughed. "Certainly not," he said. "Just a little discussion about a few old scores, that's all."

Garry Bennett opened his mouth to protest.

But the heavies had already begun.

CHAPTER TEN

"What game are we playing?" Detective Sergeant Nick Vardin asked. "Hunt the thimble? Can anyone join in?"

Kenyon heard the vocalist ending her love song as sincerely as though any of the customers had such a commodity in mind. The closing door imposed silence on the applause, or perhaps there was none. He picked himself up from the floor. His jaw ached, and his mouth was bleeding.

"Did you fall down, Mr. Kenyon, sir?" Nick asked.

"Yes," Kenyon said. He dabbed at his lips with his handkerchief. The heavy responsible looked innocent, and took out a cigarette.

"I suppose it's his turn to fall down now," Nick suggested.

"Some other time," Kenyon said. "When we have a replay."

"I'll be referee," Nick said. He wagged his finger at the heavy. "You see," he told him, "policemen do not fall down. It's against the rules."

"Walter likes to see warrant cards all of a sudden," Kenyon said.

"Evening, Walter," Nick said.

"Evening, Mr. Vardin," Walter Flack said.

"My warrant card," Nick said, showing it.

"No question, Mr. Vardin," Walter said.

"I don't think you've met Mr. Garry Bennett," Kenyon said. "Detective Sergeant Vardin."

"How do you do, Mr. Bennett," Nick said.

"Sergeant," Bennett said nervously.

"I've heard about you, of course, Mr. Bennett," Nick said. "Are you another one who's anxious to see warrant cards?"

Bennett shook his head.

"Well, I left a lovely lady all on her own for the pleasure of a word with you, Walter," Nick said. "Suppose we go back to our tables, and you can send a bottle of champagne over for me."

"My pleasure," Walter Flack said.

"I knew it would be," Nick said.

He ushered them out. Kenyon explored the inside of his mouth with his tongue. The bleeding seemed to have lessened.

"I'm sorry," Garry Bennett said. "I didn't want you roughed over."

"I didn't notice you doing anything to stop it," Kenyon said.

"What could I have done?" Bennett pleaded, helplessly. "Do you think I want my club to catch fire one night?"

"Sit down," Kenyon said. Bennett sat in his leather, revolving chair. Kenyon perched on the edge of the desk. "I've got nothing against you personally, Garry," Kenyon said. "But I'm in a corner, and if I have to tear you to bits, that's just too bad. You've got problems, because I can get this place closed down faster than Walter Flack can burn it, and don't think I can't just because I'm suspended. I've still got friends, like Detective Sergeant Vardin. One word from me, and you'll find the law going through this place like a dose of salts."

He hoped that Garry Bennett was nervous enough to believe this outrageous eyewash. Nick's assistance was strictly in return for cash, apart from his recent intervention, for which Kenyon was grateful. Otherwise, Kenyon's present influence on the forces of law and order was zero.

"I don't know what you want, Mr. Kenyon," Garry Bennett said.

"I'll make you a promise," Kenyon said. "Anything you say to me, I'll keep you out of it. Provided you level with me, you'll end up smelling of roses. I can't be fairer than that."

It was a large promise to make, but Kenyon was so desperate that he would have guaranteed salvation and eternal bliss to Himmler, Jack the Ripper and Al Capone separately or jointly if he had believed that any of them could be used to help him.

Garry Bennett said, "Keep me out of what? I just run a straight club, that's all."

"You're mixed up with Tony Vallenta," Kenyon said, gambling on an outsider because there was no favorite in the running.

"I haven't even seen Tony since before he went inside," Garry Bennett said.

"I haven't seen much of you lately," Kenyon said. "But one minute you're nothing very much, and the next you've got the Pelican. How much would it cost to walk into a place like this? A hundred thousand pounds? You haven't got that kind of money, and I don't believe in Santa Claus. Someone put it up."

"OK, I've been financed," Garry Bennett said. "But it's all legitimate. I've got the documents here." He opened one of the desk drawers.

"Don't waste my time," Kenyon said. "Your backer can screw you legally. Great. He still coughed up one hundred grand or more. That's sweet money for a spade whose idea of big business used to be pimping."

Garry Bennett flared up. "Because I've got a black skin doesn't make me a moron," he said. "I've got brains, and I can use them given the chance. Some people can see that, even if you can't."

"Like Tony Vallenta," Kenyon said. "Come on. If it's all on the up and up, why make a big secret of it?"

"Listen," Garry Bennett said, tightly. He was still angry. "I deal with businessmen and accountants. If I ask who's finding the money, I get told it's a consortium. Maybe it's Tony Vallenta, and maybe it's the man in the moon, and I don't give a damn. I've got the kind of club I've always wanted, and that's all I care about."

"OK," Kenyon said. "We've made progress. It just might be Tony Vallenta. And yet Walter Flack's moved in on you."

"I couldn't stop him," Garry Bennett said.

"If Tony's got an interest," Kenyon said, "I'd have thought he might have looked after that problem for you."

Garry Bennett hesitated. "Well," he said at last, "I did speak to the lawyer who fixed things up. He said he'd take advice."

"And what advice did he get?"

"He said it was up to me to handle that kind of thing," Garry Bennett said.

"Funny," Kenyon said. "Unless Walter's been put in to keep an eye on you."

"Tony and Walter Flack can't stand each other," Garry Bennett said.

"History is full of unlikely alliances," Kenyon said. He lit a cigarette. It was just plain unlikely, he thought. "All right. What does your backer get for staking you to this club?"

"A share of the profits," Garry Bennett said.

"Apart from that?" Kenyon said.

"Nothing," Garry Bennett said.

"And that's what takes you to the Blue Otter," Kenyon said. "Nothing." For the first time, Garry Bennett registered genuine discomfort. "You were seen," Kenyon told him. "Come on, Garry, you know me. I don't ask questions unless I've got a damn good idea what the answers are."

Garry Bennett made the mistake of swallowing this empty bluff. "It's not illegal," he said, plaintively.

"Convince me," Kenyon said.

"It's a service for the customers," Garry Bennett said. "I get lots of Americans in here, and the Arabs like dollars as well . . ."

"And the dollars come from the Blue Otter," Kenyon said. Garry Bennett did not register disagreement. "In one hundred dollar bills."

Garry Bennett said, "They take them in from gamblers at the usual rate, but I have to buy them dear. Pay over the odds." He shrugged. "Still, that was the deal. It was worth it to me."

Kenyon said, "Let's get this straight. You have to go to the Blue Otter and pick up dollars . . . how often?"

"I've only been a few times," Garry Bennett said. "Before that, someone used to bring them, but that arrangement went sour."

"How?" Kenyon asked. Garry Bennett seemed loth to answer. "Listen," Kenyon said. "I made a promise, and I'll keep it. Provided you're straight with me."

"Apparently he couldn't resist knocking off a few hundred dollar bills for himself," Garry Bennett said unwillingly. "At least, that's what I heard."

"Archie Macintyre," Kenyon said, joyfully.

"How did you know that?" Garry Bennett asked, blankly.

"I know a lot of things," Kenyon said, hypocritically.

"Look," Garry Bennett said, "I know he got himself knocked off, but I swear to God, I . . ."

"Never mind that," Kenyon said. "Show me some of this money."

"I can't," Garry Bennett said. "I haven't got any. The arrangement's been stopped."

"Since when?"

"A few days ago," Garry Bennett said.

Kenyon said, "A word of advice. I wouldn't tell any of these lawyers or accountants about any of the things you've mentioned to me, if I were you."

Garry Bennett looked worried. "What's going on, Mr. Kenyon?" he asked.

"I can't tell you that, Garry," Kenyon said, for the best of all possible reasons, which was that he did not know. "But play it cool with these people. Keep your distance. I don't suppose you want to be mixed up in a murder inquiry."

Genetically, Garry Bennett was incapable of turning pale, but he ran his finger round his collar nervously.

"I don't think Archie Macintyre was knocked off because of that," he said.

"I know he wasn't," Kenyon said. "I'm talking about the Colonel. His remains may be moldering in reclaimed land at Pitsea, but bones don't decompose. I know exactly the area to search," he lied. "And identity can be established from a skull by means of dental records."

"By all that's holy," Garry Bennett said, fear in his eyes, "I've never been involved in anything like that."

"If anyone should inquire what I wanted to talk to you about," Kenyon said, "tell them that. Say I don't like being fixed, and I'm after the bastard who did it. Tell them I know he had the Colonel knocked off, and once I've located the old boy's remains, I can prove it. That'll keep you in the clear as far as they're concerned."

It might also stir up something or another, he thought.

"If you keep a shooter in this office, Garry," he said, "I'd like to borrow it."

Garry Bennett shook his head. "I've never touched a gun in my life, Mr. Kenyon," he said.

Kenyon believed him.

The beautiful West Indian girl was doing her stuff, and knocking back the club's grotesquely over-priced champagne. There was also a bottle of brandy on the table. Nick Vardin was drinking that.

"I need a bit more cash," Nick Vardin said, to Kenyon. "Lend me thirty quid, will you?"

The beautiful West Indian girl lit a cigarette.

"They cash checks here," Kenyon said. "Write one out. You don't need to borrow money from me to subsidize your amorous plans."

"Those jokers would have beaten your head in," Nick reminded him.

Kenyon sighed, and counted out the money. "I should have known that nothing's for free where you're concerned," he said.

"Too bloody true," Nick said.

"But you earn it," Kenyon said. "Shift your chair sideways, so that Walter Flack can see you round these potted bloody palms, and then keep staring at him as if you don't like him."

"That won't be too difficult," Nick said.

Kenyon edged his way round the dance floor, pulled up a chair, and sat beside Walter Flack. The heavies watched him.

"Tell your morons to go somewhere else," Kenyon said.

The heavies did not wait to be told. They got up and went.

"You've really blotted your copybook tonight, Walter," Kenyon said. He glanced towards Nick.

Walter Flack's eyes flickered. Beyond the potted palms, Nick was regarding him with all the amiability of a hungry wolf.

"Me, I live and let live," Kenyon said. "But once that one takes against a man, he's for it. Funny how people always seem to resist arrest, when Nick's on the job. Or fall down a flight of stairs. Still, you must know his reputation. Pity you got on the wrong side of him. And there's plenty like him," Kenyon embroidered. "You see, Walter, you got it wrong. Just because a copper's been suspended doesn't mean it's open season, and you can lay hands on him. You can't."

Walter Flack puffed at his cigar, and waited for the "or else." He was an old hand. He knew there would be one.

"Do you want to put things right, Walter?" Kenyon asked. "Up to you. I'm easy. I'll get up and go now, if you like."

"I'm listening," Walter Flack said, grudgingly.

"I think you planted that shooter in the boot of Tony Vallenta's car," Kenyon said.

Walter Flack found a shred of tobacco on his tongue. He picked at it, gave up, and spat it out, on to the table-cloth.

"Tony thinks it was the law," he said, at last.

"We're all entitled to our own opinions," Kenyon said.

"It's a free country," Walter Flack agreed.

"I might mention it to him, though," Kenyon said.

"I reckon it was the law too," Walter Flack said. "Besides, I wouldn't do a thing like that. No reason."

"Get Tony put out of the way, and then move in," Kenyon said. "That sounds like a reason to me."

"I'm not greedy," Walter Flack said.

"Jesus," Kenyon said, with feeling.

Walter Flack caught sight of Nick's basilisk glare again, and shifted his chair uneasily, angling it sideways.

"I heard there was a team on the takeover trail," Kenyon said, "while Tony was inside."

"I mind my own business," Walter Flack said.

"I heard it was you," Kenyon said.

"There's been no trouble," Walter Flack said.

"Perhaps you made peace," Kenyon said. "Decided to work in harness."

"I don't work with bloody women," Walter Flack said.

"Or perhaps Angela proved to be a tougher nut than you'd imagined," Kenyon said. "She seems to have kept things going pretty well in Tony's absence. But then, she had help, didn't she," he said, fishing.

He eyed Walter Flack. Flack's cigar had gone out. He struck a match, and re-lit it.

"I'm told you don't like outsiders," Kenyon said.

"Me and Tony get on all right," Walter Flack said, "so

long as we never see each other. It's that whore he married who's got the big ideas."

"You don't blame Tony then," Kenyon said, groping through the fog of words in the hope of finding out what the hell Walter Flack was talking about.

"I blame him for not keeping her in her place," Walter Flack said.

"You could be right," Kenyon said, none the wiser.

Walter Flack gave up chewing the remains, mashed his cigar into an ashtray, and concentrated on lighting another one.

"Do one thing for me, Walter," Kenyon said, "and I'll forget about tonight. Tell Nick and the others you've squared things."

"I'm open to suggestions," Walter Flack said.

"Get me a shooter, Walter," Kenyon said softly. "No names, no pack drill."

Walter Flack glanced at Kenyon, puffed out clouds of blue smoke, and blew out his match.

"You must think I'm simple," he said. "You expect me to set up a meet, hand over a shooter, and then find the cuffs on, and me done for possessing firearms? No, thanks."

"I'm in the phone book," Kenyon said. "A plain package delivered to that address. No one knows where it's come from, least of all me. And if I did, I couldn't prove it."

He stood up. "Think it over, Walter," he said. "If it's delivered within twenty-four hours, we're quits. Otherwise, I tell Nick and a few other hard men like him that they can start leaning on you. You, personally, Walter," he said. Walter Flack studied the end of his cigar. Kenyon walked away.

Nick Vardin gave him a wink. The beautiful West Indian girl was now wearing a white fur wrap.

"I asked for your bill," Nick said. "I'm feeling a bit tired."

Kenyon looked at the total. "God Almighty," he said.

Late the following afternoon, Kenyon's doorbell rang.

"Hullo," he said into the entryphone. "Who is it?" There was no reply.

Cautiously, he went upstairs into the hall. A flat package

was lying on the floor, underneath the letter box. There was no one outside. The package was addressed in block capitals, with a felt tipped pen. Kenyon picked it up, and took it downstairs.

He cut the string, and peeled off the brown paper. Inside was a cardboard box. He opened it.

He squinted down the barrel, and grunted with disgust. Villains had no respect for firearms. It was filthy. He stripped the automatic down, cleaned it carefully, and reassembled it. He was loading it again, when something struck him. He ejected one bullet, and examined it minutely. He had been right. There were tiny, almost invisible scratches at the top of the casing.

He searched for a suitable implement, found an old penknife, gently levered open the casing, extracted the bullet, and shook the contents of the casing into the palm of his hand.

He kicked open the wastebin, and threw the cartridge and the bullet away. Walter Flack had a warped sense of humor.

The phone rang. Kenyon left the gun on the breakfast bar, and answered it.

"We shall be in London tomorrow," Sarah said. "Harry has a lunch date, but if you're free around eleven thirty . . ."

"That'll be fine," Kenyon said.

It was a filthy day, cold and misty, drizzling persistently. Kenyon did not want to rely on taxis today. He walked to the nearest self-drive firm, and hired a car. As he drove away, a green Allegro followed him, but he made no attempt to shake it off. No one would try anything at Claridges. It would be sacrilegious.

There was a grand piano in Harry Coleman's suite. Perhaps they assumed the guests were all music lovers, or concert pianists.

Sarah refused a drink. Kenyon accepted a whisky.

"I had hoped we could spend another evening together," Harry Coleman said. "But I'm on a pretty tight schedule. We're dining with the Ambassador this evening, and early tomorrow morning, I have to fly to Geneva."

"What then?" Kenyon asked politely. "A little skiing?"

"No," Coleman said. "After that, I go on to the Middle East. Sarah's staying in London for a few days to do some shopping."

"I see," Kenyon said.

"Anyway," Coleman said. He opened his briefcase. "The information you asked for."

"You've moved fast," Kenyon said.

"I've done very little," Coleman said. "Except use some pressure. Other people have done the work." He smiled his warm, attractive smile. "And the telex service has been kept pretty busy." He put on a pair of gold-rimmed glasses, and glanced at his papers. "First, the hundred dollar bills. The FBI can't be one hundred per cent certain, but they could be of interest."

"In what way?" Kenyon asked.

"Related bills have turned up in the USA. They've been impossible to trace back to source. Various outlets," Coleman explained, "such as supermarkets, stores, gas stations, and so on. Mostly in Texas and Ohio. More recently the West Coast."

"You mean they *are* forgeries?" Kenyon asked. He was surprised.

"No, they're perfectly good notes," Coleman said. "It's where they might have originated from that's the point. I say 'might have' because it appears that, not for the first time, science has not entirely lived up to its claims."

Sarah was sitting, smoking a cigarette, apparently deep in her own thoughts. She noticed Kenyon looking at her, and asked "Another drink?"

"No, thanks," Kenyon said.

"You'll be aware that kidnaping is by way of being a major industry in Italy." Harry Coleman said. Kenyon nodded. "There was a notorious case nearly a year ago," Coleman went on. "A child, a nine-year-old girl, the daughter of a banker in Turin. Her name was Giuletta. He knew the risk, of course, and the child was always heavily guarded. Two men died when the car in which she was traveling was ambushed."

"I vaguely remember it," Kenyon said.

"The ransom demanded was three million dollars," Coleman said. "It was to be paid in used one hundred dollar US bills. Giuletta was the only child. Her father worshiped her. He saw no choice. You know the complicated kind of way ransom money is handed over . . ."

"Yes," Kenyon said.

"Right," Coleman said. "There's no way the kidnapers can be traced or identified."

"Except possibly by the child," Kenyon said. "They killed her, didn't they?"

"Her body was found in a sewer," Coleman said. "Her throat had been cut."

Sarah got up, and stood looking out of the window.

"When the ransom money was assembled," Coleman said, "the banknotes were computer-monitored, in the hope that they would be relatively easy to trace. I'm told that for technical reasons it doesn't always work that way. Maybe through human error, I don't know." He handed the photostats to Kenyon. "It's thought these *could* have been part of the ransom money, but the FBI can't be any more positive than that."

"These were found on a dead man in London," Kenyon said. "I'd have thought the best place to dispose of large sums of American money would be in the USA."

"Well," Coleman said, "the FBI mentioned something else. Again, this is at best well-founded suspicion. They can't prove it for certain."

"I'm familiar with that situation," Kenyon said, drily.

"There's a weekly flight from Palermo to Chicago," Coleman said. "A 707. Known colloquially as the Palermo Express. The FBI had become very interested in that flight, and some of the people and cargo it might be carrying. Eight months ago, they were ready to move in. They were waiting for it at Chicago. The plane was late. It had landed at Marseilles to offload a passenger who'd been taken ill in flight. They went over it at Chicago anyway, but it was clean."

"I suppose the French police didn't go over it at Marseilles," Kenyon said.

"They had no reason to," Coleman said. "Now maybe that passenger really was sick. Or maybe there was a leak. Either way, there was nothing they could pin on the Palermo Express, then or later." He took the photograph Kenyon had given him from an envelope.

"Did the FBI know him, by any chance?" Kenyon asked.

Coleman said, "His name is Clifford Warren. He's forty four years old, a clever, wealthy New York lawyer."

"A corporation lawyer, or what?"

Coleman said, carefully, "He spends most of his time advising various business interests."

"You wouldn't mean the Mafia, by any chance," Kenyon supposed.

Coleman smiled faintly. "We'd say the organization," he said. "But while the FBI were able to identify him, he is, of course, a reputable lawyer who merely represents his clients to the best of his ability."

"Of course," Kenyon said. "Perhaps he's taken to advising English villains as well."

"He is known to have visited the United Kingdom several times in the last few months," Coleman said. "In fact, he's believed to be in London now. I expect you could find out where he was staying, if you wanted to."

"The police could," Kenyon said. "But even if I'm still drawing my pay, I'm on the sidelines. In any case, I'm sure he takes care to be as reputable here as he does in New York."

"Well, that's all I've got," Coleman said. "Is it any help to you?"

"I don't know," Kenyon said. "But I can tell you what's happened to that ransom money. It's being laundered, here in London through a gambling club, and at least one night club."

"Can you prove that?" Coleman asked.

"Only by proving that I was fixed," Kenyon said, "which is frankly my main concern. And while you've been a great help, and I'm grateful, what you've told me doesn't get me off the hook." There was one more thing he had to do. "Do you mind if I make some phone calls?"

Coleman showed him into the bedroom, and closed the door. Kenyon sat on the edge of the bed. Sarah's hairbrush and her pots of cream were on the dressing table. It reminded him of those months, when he saw her things, and her, nearly every morning, when he woke up. He pushed the thought to the back of his mind, and lifted the telephone.

Garry Bennett sounded edgy. Kenyon hoped he was right about the young spade, but he had no alternative.

Normally, he would never dream of trusting a man, just because he liked him. Now, there was nothing else he could do. Garry Bennett confirmed that inquiries had been made about Kenyon's visit. And yes, as Kenyon had expected, it had been suggested that Bennett should do a little fishing. Kenyon told him what to say, and hung up.

Then he made another phone call.

Afterwards, he sat sipping whisky, until it was time for Coleman to leave for his lunch date.

"Why don't you stay here and have lunch with Sarah?" Coleman suggested.

Sarah was fiddling with a vase of flowers which looked fine as they were, to the untutored eye. She glanced quickly at Kenyon, and he wondered if she sometimes remembered waking up with him during those few months.

"I can't," Kenyon said. "Perhaps some other time."

He had the impression that Sarah was relieved.

Kenyon retrieved his hired car from the nearby car park. As he passed Claridges, the usual bevy of chauffeur-driven limousines were picking up and setting down their passengers outside. He headed east.

The weather had decided not to improve. The wet, unending drizzle smeared his windows, limiting his vision. The windscreen wipers clacked to and fro monotonously. The rear window was not fitted with a demister. He opened the driver's window, and turned up the heat, but the rear window still refused to clear, and he had to rely on his wing mirrors.

He drove through the East End of London, Stepney and West Ham. The road ran more or less parallel to the River Thames.

It was not until he was past Dagenham that he was fairly certain, from the occasional glimpses in his wing mirrors, that the same car had remained stationed about a hundred yards behind him. It was a chauffeur-driven Rolls. Kenyon was almost certain that the driver was the only occupant.

He turned northeast, away from Tilbury, and the Rolls followed suit. Kenyon watched out for the next turning, signaled his intention, turned left, and parked. He craned round, peering through his open window. The Rolls sailed straight on. Kenyon waited. After a few seconds, his old Volvo went by, Detective Sergeant Nick Vardin at the wheel. Kenyon did a three-point turn, and re-joined the main road.

He accelerated until he could see the Volvo up ahead, and settled down to identify the car which he was pretty certain would have been backing up the Rolls, on the alert for his maneuver, and which should now be somewhere behind him. A Datsun appeared to be a possible candidate, but it turned off into a housing estate, and did not re-appear. Kenyon kept on glancing at his wing mirrors anxiously, but all he could see behind him was half a mile of empty road. After a few minutes, he was certain there was no backup car after all, which was strange. Perhaps his double-guessing had all been wrong. Perhaps no one was in the least interested in his journey. And yes, there was still the Rolls, which he could see up front, ahead of Nick.

At the next roundabout, the Rolls turned left, heading due north, along a road which would eventually take him to Brentwood. Nick circled the roundabout, gestured his intentions to Kenyon, and followed the Rolls north. Kenyon carried straight on, heading for Pitsea.

By the time Kenyon neared the reclaimed land, he knew that he was alone. No one was following him. The Rolls might double back of course, but Nick was taking care of him. In any case, what could one man achieve? Kenyon had at first assumed that the Rolls belonged to Vallenta's chauffeur-driven limousine company. But if so, why had it gone ahead of him, with no backup car, and finally been happy to lose him? No, he had assumed too much, altogether.

Kenyon turned into the vast, flat area which constituted the reclaimed land, dotted with puddles of water. He felt deflated. If no one cared, he had been wrong from beginning to end. And if there was nothing to care about, he was finished.

He stopped the car, and consulted the map of the area which Murchison had given him. The section where rubbish was being dumped at the time of the Colonel's disappearance was marked in red.

"I can't be any more precise than that," Murchison had

warned him. "Over that period, dumping was going on over at least a square mile, and perhaps more."

Kenyon thought it was more. It was strangely silent in this desolate, deserted place. He started his engine, and drove on. There were few identifiable features. He passed some empty huts, which were marked on the map, and turned off on to a muddy track. He thought he was moving in the right direction. He also thought that it did not matter much. He was tempted to turn round and go home. So far, he had not seen a living soul. But having come this far, he supposed he might as well go through with it.

The track petered out. Kenyon reversed on to some hard core and walked.

Faintly, through the silence which embraced him, he could hear mechanical groaning and clanking. Grab cranes and trucks. He could not see the source of the far-off noise. He was well away from the inlet in the Thames where the barges were unloaded, and the lowering clouds were blackening with the approach of nightfall. The drizzle was heavier here, and banks of mist were rolling gently in from the river. His car, behind him, was lost in the gray, enveloping swirls of moisture. He plodded on, skirting the puddles, but it did not make much difference. The ground was soft and muddy, and soon he felt the dampness seeping through into his shoes.

He stopped and consulted the map again. There were no visible points of reference left now. He had been counting his strides since he left the car. He guessed that another two hundred yards would take him to a point somewhere near the center of the area. He paced on across the soggy ground. In the combination of drifting mist and failing light, he could not see more than twenty or thirty yards in front of him, and he was startled when he first caught sight of the gaunt, strange silhouette. He stopped for a moment, and then moved on. It was a bulldozer, silent and inactive.

He circled the machine, and looked around him. The mechanical clanking was even fainter now. He could scarcely hear it. Drizzle soaked his hair, and ran down his face. Here he was, Sidney Kenyon, detective, wet, and shivering with cold. This was where the trail ended. He decided to smoke a cigarette, and then go. No one else was coming. It was a waste of time.

Kenyon heard the squelch of approaching footsteps as he put the cigarette in his mouth. The approaching figure materialized through the mist. It was a man, wearing a plastic helmet, overalls, and rubber boots. He stared at Kenyon.

"Hullo, squire," he said. "Lost are you?"

"No," Kenyon said. "Who are you?"

"Jack Holmes, bulldozer driver," the man said. "Who might you be, come to that?"

"Detective Inspector Kenyon, CID," Kenyon said.

"Yes?" Holmes said. "Something going on is there?"

"I want this area turned over," Kenyon said. "Something we're looking for."

"What, now?" Holmes asked.

"Now," Kenyon said. He wanted to know if Jack Holmes, bulldozer driver, could actually drive a bulldozer.

"OK," Holmes said, indifferently. He paused as he was about to climb into the cab. "Have you cleared this with the foreman?"

"He knows all about it," Kenyon lied.

"How deep do you want to go? Six or eight feet?"

"Something like that," Kenyon said. "Straight ahead."

"What do you think you're going to find?"

"If any human remains turn up," Kenyon said, "I'd be interested."

"Jesus," Holmes said. "Well, if it's bones and things you're after, I'll take it easy."

He started the engine, and the bulldozer roared into life. Holmes moved levers, and the great blade cut into the ground.

Kenyon stood back, pretending to scan the upturned earth, in fact watching Holmes. But the man was what he claimed to be. He handled the cumbersome great rumbling, clanking machine with the dexterity of an artist. To and fro, to the accompaniment of the deafening noise, the bulldozer moved, the blade slicing delicately away, layer after layer.

Holmes leaned out of his cab, mouthing something, apparently shouting. Kenyon shook his head. Holmes switched the machine off. After the terrifying racket, the silence was a relief.

"I said how much more do you want?" Holmes said.

"That'll do," Kenyon said. He looked at his watch.

"Yes, it will," Holmes said. "It'll do nicely."

Kenyon froze. Blue steel glinted dully in Holmes's hand. The barrel was aimed at Kenyon's stomach.

Too late, he cursed himself for being all kinds of a fool. Of course. There had to be someone else. A man, above suspicion, employed on the site. A man who would make sure that the Colonel's remains were dug in safe, and snug and deep.

He could hear the squelch of footsteps again. More than one man. He turned and peered into the gloom. The noise of the bulldozer would have masked the sound of any car arriving.

Three shapes came towards him, emerging through the mist. Kenyon knew one of them. The small, neat figure, delicately picking his way round the puddles.

It was Tony Vallenta.

CHAPTER ELEVEN

Tony Vallenta regarded the hole in the ground, a swathe twenty feet long, the width of the bulldozer blade, eight feet deep. Black, muddy water was seeping into the bottom of it.

"Well done, Jack," Tony Vallenta said.

"Thank you, Mr. Vallenta," Holmes said, respectfully. That ugly hole in the ground, Kenyon realized, constituted his own grave. Holmes would be on a nice fat bonus for his good work.

"It's your own fault, Sid," Tony Vallenta said. "You can't leave well alone, can you." His hands were thrust deep into the pockets of his elegant raincoat.

"You're taking a chance, aren't you, Tony," Kenyon said. "Knocking me off in front of witnesses. Not your style at all."

Tony Vallenta smiled, and took his hands from his pockets. He spread them. They were empty.

"Not me, Sid," he said. "I felt a need to be on the spot, that's all. Besides, what's all this about being knocked off? You're just going to disappear, that's all."

"Like the Colonel," Kenyon said. "He wouldn't play ball, would he. So he 'disappeared' and you put the bite on Ashby. Persuaded him to front for you."

"My dear Sid," Tony Vallenta said. "I don't know what you're talking about. I was inside at the time, if you recall."

"You mean it's really all down to Angela," Kenyon said.

"You're talking to try and gain time," Tony Vallenta said, correctly. "Don't waste your breath."

Where the hell was Nick?

"You set me up," Kenyon said, steadily. "And now I've returned the compliment. This is a setup, Tony, and you've walked right into it. You, and your two apes, and your tame bulldozer driver. You don't think I'd feed you a message, and then come here on my own, do you?" He gestured into the surrounding mist. "There are police out there, moving in even now. You've had it, Tony. So have the rest of you," he told them. The two apes did not even blink. Kenyon glanced over his shoulder. Holmes still had the gun leveled at him. "You'd better put that down before you get into real trouble," Kenyon told him. Holmes smiled politely, but did nothing of the kind.

"If you're talking about your friend in the Volvo," Tony Vallenta said, "he's been involved in a road accident. Some idiot rammed him, I believe."

It dawned on Kenyon then. Too late. Much too late. Vallenta's chauffeur-driven cars were all fitted with two-way radio. They had not needed a backup car. All they needed was to make quite sure where he was going. Then all they had to do was to wait for him. Vallenta had out-thought him all along the line.

Tony Vallenta moved closer to Kenyon, and stared into his eyes. Kenyon willed him to keep coming. Just a little closer . . . so that he could grab Tony and swing him round in the fraction of a second before Holmes fired . . . but Tony stopped. Close enough so that his soft voice would only reach Kenyon's ears, but out of Kenyon's reach.

"The reason I'm here, Sid," he whispered, "is that this is a personal matter. The worst thing about being inside, was not being with Angela. But you went with her, Sid, when I was locked up in a cell. I don't like that. And I don't like you."

"It takes two," Kenyon said.

"I'm aware of that," Tony Vallenta whispered. "But I love my wife. Her, I can forgive. You, no."

"You're not a fool, Tony," Kenyon said. "You must know how it was. Angela wasn't just looking after the shop for you. She was opening new branches. I told her about Archie Macintyre, more fool me, and she knew I must have seen the hundred dollar bills he'd nicked from the Blue Otter. She wasn't taking any chances. She took me to bed, and made sure you got to know about it. You did exactly what she wanted. You fed moody information to get me suspended for starters, and when I didn't lay off, she'd given you a personal motive for taking care of me.

You've just been a puppet, Tony. You've done exactly what she wanted, and you're doing it now."

Tony Vallenta's smile was icy. "I know my wife, Sid," he said. "I know her weaknesses. But she's still my wife, for better or worse. That's what it's all about."

"Did she tell you she screwed around with Clifford Warren as well?" Kenyon asked. "Perhaps that was on business, but I'll bet she enjoyed it. She enjoyed it with me, I can tell you that."

Vallenta's eyes burned with vindictive, jealous hate. Hit me, Tony, Kenyon willed him, silently. Come on, hit me. Get really mad, damn you. Take just one step forward.

"She's still the best whore in London, Tony," Kenyon said. Tony Vallenta clenched his fists. His body swayed, as he made to take that one, necessary pace forward. Kenyon tensed, ready. But Tony Vallenta regained control of himself. He unclenched his fists, and pushed his hands into his raincoat pockets.

"Not bad, Sid," he said. "You nearly got through to me there." He took a step backwards. "Do you know what to do, Jack?" he called.

"Yes, Mr. Vallenta," Holmes said.

"You're not going to have it easy, Sid," Vallenta said. "You don't deserve that. A bullet in the heart . . . oh, no. Nothing like that. Low down. Where it hurts. I want you to know what's happening, for a while. It'll seem like a long time to you, I expect. Lying in that hole. Waiting to be covered up. Time to think, Sid. Time to be sorry you ever touched the wife of Tony Vallenta."

He turned his back on Kenyon, and held out his hand. "Give me a cigarette," he said. One of the apes obliged, and lit it for him. "Thanks," he said. He inhaled with deep contentment. "OK, Jack," he said.

Kenyon dived sideways into the hole in the ground in the fraction of a second before the shot from behind him rang out. An act of mere despair, staving off the agony for a few seconds perhaps. And maybe it would fluster Holmes. Maybe he would automatically shoot to kill next time . . .

Kenyon hit the side of the waterlogged pit, rolling as he went. He grabbed a chunk of rock, twisted and turned to throw it, knowing that there was no chance, that Holmes would fire again before he even had time to aim his pitiful piece of stone.

But there was no second shot. Instead, there was the awful sound of someone screaming, the terrible noise of an animal in intolerable, impossible agony.

Holmes was not even looking at Kenyon. He was white faced and shaking, and his gun hand hung at his side, as he stared at something on the ground.

Kenyon pulled himself out of the hole. Tony Vallenta was lying in the mud, his head raised, teeth bared as he screamed and screamed and screamed. His fingers clawed at the earth. His feet were motionless.

Kenyon moved cautiously round the looming bulldozer to get on Holmes's blind side. For the moment, they seemed to have forgotten about him. They were staring at the quivering, screaming body of Tony Vallenta. The incessant, high-pitched yelling was enough to shatter the hardest, most brutal of men. No living thing should suffer like that.

None of them spoke. The two apes were the first to crack. They edged backwards, away from the screaming man, and then they turned and ran, blundering off into the mist.

Kenyon was behind Holmes now. Holmes seemed to remember about him, looked round panic stricken, failed to see him, crouched behind the bulldozer, and decided he too should get away, as fast as he could.

Kenyon went after him. He wanted Holmes. Holmes realized what was happening, stopped in his tracks, turned, and raised the gun. Kenyon flung himself forward in a rugby tackle, and brought the man down. Holmes retained his grip on the gun, and tried to bring it to bear. Kenyon gripped his gun hand, rolled over on top of him, and brought the right leverage to bear. Holmes cried out.

"Just relax, unless you want to break your own arm," Kenyon said. Holmes did as he was told. Kenyon took the gun from him, and jerked him to his feet. "I need you, chum," Kenyon said. "I think you might know where we should look for the Colonel."

Tony Vallenta was still screaming monotonously. There was another sound now, the wail of an approaching police siren. Kenyon saw headlights, and a revolving blue light through the mist. The siren died, doors slammed. A running figure materialized into Nick Vardin.

"Christ," Nick said, looking towards the source of the screaming, "what the hell's that unholy racket?"

"Tony Vallenta," Kenyon said. "He needs an ambulance, fast."

Nick called towards the police car, and Kenyon heard the crackle of the radio.

"You took your bloody time," Kenyon said.

"Some joker in a van rammed me at a crossroads," Nick said. "It was stolen. The driver got out and ran away."

"I could have been killed," Kenyon said resentfully.

"You should see your Volvo," Nick mourned. "There must be five or six hundred quid's worth of damage. I was lucky to walk away from it."

"That's the point of driving a Volvo," Kenyon said. "And it's not mine, it's yours."

"You wouldn't like it back, I suppose?" Nick asked, hopefully.

"No," Kenyon said. "This clown is Jack Holmes. Possession of firearms, discharging a deadly weapon, and suspicion of being an accessory to murder. That'll do for starters. And there are two more not far away . . ."

Kenyon rode in the ambulance to the hospital. Tony Vallenta stopped screaming soon after they gave him morphine. Instead, he started quietly hallucinating. Kenyon bent close to try and hear what he was saying. Something was going on inside Tony Vallenta's head all right, but the phrases were disjointed, and out of sequence.

". . . retire . . ." he mumbled. "I've had a good run . . . did you sleep with him? . . . I want the truth . . . so everyone's been ripping me off . . . so what? . . . I've still got plenty . . . you bitch, you whoring cow . . . all right, all right, how much? . . . a million? . . . did you say a million? . . . that bastard . . . I don't give a shit what he knows, I can fix him . . . I'd made up my mind . . . get out now and take it easy . . . I think I'd rather die than go to prison again . . . the most beautiful wife in the world . . . Angela, I could kill you, but you know I'll take it, don't you? . . . you know I love you more than anything on God's earth, don't you, you bitch . . . but after that, I'm going to quit, I'm telling you, that's me finished . . . God, you can always twist me round your little finger . . . I love you, Angela, I love you so much . . ."

The morphine began to wear off, and Tony Vallenta started groaning as well as raving. They hurried him into the hospital. Kenyon bought a packet of cigarettes and sat in the canteen, smoking, and drinking tea. Nick found him there, and said, "The guv'nor wants to know if you'd like to come along for the ride."

"Hang on five minutes," Kenyon said. "I want to talk to someone first."

He talked to the senior registrar who would assist the consultant.

"We're operating to remove the bullet," the registrar said. "It's lodged in the spine, against the spinal cord."

"Will he live?" Kenyon asked.

"Oh, yes, he'll live," the registrar said. "But there's irreparable nerve damage. He'll be a paraplegic for the rest of his life."

Kenyon did not get home until three o'clock in the morning. By then, he was exhausted, and he decided to leave it to fresher men. He was still officially suspended, but colleagues shook his hand, and smiled, and congratulated him.

"Welcome back, Sid," Detective Sergeant Len Malory said. "I always knew you were in the clear."

"Thanks, Len," Kenyon said. You blazing hypocrite, he thought.

Search warrants were obtained, and teams of men moved into action. A prosperous London solicitor was invited to assist the police with their inquiries. Clifford Warren, about to board a plane for New York at London Airport, received a similar invitation, which he declined. It then transpired that there was some query about his passport. He would be obliged to remain in the United Kingdom until it was sorted out. He complained and demanded access to his embassy, which was immediately granted. The official who came to talk to him was from the FBI.

Detective Chief Superintendent Bernard Chandler turned up at the Blue Otter, and stood at Kenyon's elbow watching, as stacks of one hundred dollar bills were removed from the strong room. Samuel Ashby was agitatedly denying any knowledge of them, and demanding to see his solicitor.

"Mind you, Inspector Kenyon," Chandler said, "I don't go along with all this stuff about a Mafia involvement." He burped gently. "That's all bullshit."

Kenyon was not inclined to argue the point. He knew that the Yard preferred to maintain, at least for public consumption, that all attempts by the Mafia to move into London had been effectively dealt with.

Men carried cardboard boxes of documents from Tony Vallenta's house for meticulous examination elsewhere.

"Angela's flown the nest though," Detective Superintendent Pindar said. "Pity. Still, it'll be good to have you back, Sid."

"Thank you, sir," Kenyon said.

Forty-three known associates of Tony Vallenta were arrested in swoops all over London between the hours of nine p.m. and two a.m. Some, after questioning, would be cleared and released. The remainder would be charged in due course. The operation was now under the control of a Commander from Scotland Yard.

"Now the brass have taken over, we can sleep easy, Nick," Kenyon said. "How about taking me home?"

The patrol car dropped Kenyon outside his flat.

"A quiet word with you, Nick," Kenyon said.

The two men moved along the pavement, away from the listening ears of the patrol car crew.

"Len Malory's a good detective," Kenyon said, "but when it counted, he wasn't there. You may be an avaricious bastard, and as bent as a hairpin, but just the same, you're my kind of copper. Suppose I have a word with your DI, and you come and work with me?"

Detective Sergeant Nick Vardin shook his head. "No thanks, Mr. Kenyon, sir," he said. "I don't think I'd like that. Life on your team would be altogether too much like hard work."

Kenyon nodded. He opened his street door, waved good night, and went downstairs. Bed, he thought, longingly. Bed, and about twelve hours blissful, undisturbed sleep.

He was flicking the light switch down when he caught a

whiff of expensive perfume, and knew he should not. By then, it was too late. He grabbed for the gun on the breakfast bar. It had gone.

"I've got it, Sid," Angela said. She was sitting in an armchair, facing him, huddled deep into the upturned collar of her coat. She must have got cold, sitting there, waiting for him, Kenyon thought. The gun she was holding was aimed steadily at his stomach.

"I need a holiday," Kenyon said. "I'd forgotten you had my keys copied that night."

"You snore," Angela said. "In between times."

"I should have made sure there was no one else in the house," Kenyon said.

"You're an arrogant bastard," Angela said. "You think you're God's gift. The idea didn't occur to you."

"Who was it?" Kenyon asked.

"It doesn't matter," Angela said.

"He might not have been arrested yet," Kenyon explained.

"You don't have to worry about that anymore, Sid," Angela said. "You don't have to worry about anything." She stood up. "Tony got it in the spine, didn't he," she said.

"Not from me," Kenyon said.

"It was your fault," Angela said. "If it hadn't been for you, it wouldn't have happened."

"You had something to do with it too," Kenyon said. "Tony wanted to get out. You should have let him. Instead, you agreed to the deal. A million dollars, your share for laundering three million dollars ransom money. Not even that. Blood money, since they'd killed the child. You've got enough. What the hell did you need with more?"

"Money had nothing to do with it," Angela said.

"He'd decided to quit," Kenyon said. "You should have let him."

"He was too big to quit," Angela said, proudly.

"So you persuaded him," Kenyon said. "No, you did more. You forced him into it."

"There was no reason for him to step down," Angela said. "Tony Vallenta was still the biggest man in London."

"Not anymore," Kenyon said.

"No," Angela said. "Now he's a cripple, and that's down to you, Sid. I can't do to you what you've done to him, but I can do some of it." Her finger curled over the trigger.

"Angela," Kenyon said, "it would be pretty hard to make it worse for yourself, but you're doing your best. You're going to lose your looks in prison anyway, so put the gun down, and stop being stupid."

"You don't believe I'll pull this trigger," Angela said. "That's what it is. Well, you're wrong, Sid. You're so wrong." She slowly extended her arm full length. Her hand was rock steady.

"I believe you," Kenyon said. "But don't, for your own sake."

"I don't care what happens to me," Angela said.

"Just give it to me, there's a good girl," Kenyon said. He took a slow pace forward. "Now. Come on."

"Yes, now," Angela breathed.

She pulled the trigger.

The gun emitted a kind of tired "phut."

Kenyon took another pace forward.

Angela frowned at the gun, and pulled the trigger twice more. The gun produced two more "phuts."

Kenyon took the gun from her, and threw it on a chair.

"A practical joker, who wished me no good at all," he said, "removed most of the charge from the cartridges before delivery."

Angela's lovely face twisted into an ugly mask of fury. She snatched a tiny, delicate little automatic from her handbag.

In one swift movement, Kenyon grabbed her wrist, twisted it brutally, and hit her, open handed, across the side of her face.

She spun across the room, and collapsed face down on the settee. Her fingers clawed at the upholstery, and she raised her head in inner agony. Kenyon was reminded of Tony Vallenta as he lay screaming in the mud.

"Now you've added attempted murder to conspiracy and being an accessory," he said.

"He's the only man I've ever cared about," she moaned. "The only one. And now he's paralyzed from the waist down. He'll never walk again. He'll be in a wheelchair for the rest of his life."

"He'll spend most of that in prison anyway," Kenyon remarked. "He'll be looked after."

He slid the safety catch of the little automatic on, and slipped it into his pocket. When he dialed Bayswater Police Station, he noticed that the tap was off his phone. He told them to send a car and a couple of policewomen to take Angela away.

"And get a move on," he said. "I want to get some sleep."

He looked at Angela, who had sunk into a heap. She was rocking to and fro, moaning gently.

What people called love was a funny kind of thing, Kenyon thought.

CHAPTER TWELVE

Kenyon tapped on the door. When she said "Come in," he turned the handle, and went inside.

"You can take the luggage down now," Sarah said. There were suitcases lined up, waiting. Her back was to him. She was stubbing out a partially smoked cigarette.

"Not me," Kenyon said. He pushed the door closed. Sarah paused, carefully screwed the cigarette into the ashtray, and turned to face him.

"I thought you were staying for a few days' shopping," Kenyon said.

"I've changed my mind," Sarah said. "I'd rather be at home."

"Has Harry changed his plans?" Kenyon asked.

"No," Sarah said. "But it's still home."

Kenyon nodded. "You might like to know that I'm off the hook," he said.

"There was something on the radio about a lot of arrests," Sarah said. "I wondered if it was anything to do with you."

"Sort of," Kenyon said.

"Well, I'm glad everything's all right," Sarah said.

"Is everything all right with you?" Kenyon asked.

"Yes," Sarah said. "Everything's fine."

"Harry Coleman is a very nice man," Kenyon said. "It's hard not to like him. You made a wise choice."

"Yes, I did," Sarah said. "He's considerate, he's kind, and he cares about me quite a lot."

"He worships the ground you walk on, as they say," Kenyon said. "It must be very heaven."

"I'm not going to rise to that," Sarah said. "I don't want to quarrel with you."

"Just once more," Kenyon suggested, "for old times' sake."

"It's not quite heaven," Sarah said. "Nothing's perfect in this life. Harry gets depressed sometimes, mostly about his children . . . I have to try and see him through it."

"You should have children of your own," Kenyon said.

"I expect we shall," Sarah said.

"I'd take a bet that Harry wants kids," Kenyon said. "So why haven't you started?"

"I don't think that's any of your business," Sarah said.

"I don't think you love him," Kenyon said. "Not really."

"Love isn't a word you use very much, as I recall," Sarah said.

"Fine words butter no parsnips, as my grandfather used to say," Kenyon said. "Actions count. They mean something. People use words when they lie."

"I need the words as well," Sarah said. "Most women do."

"Yes, I learned that," Kenyon said.

"You prefer to be on your own, in the end," Sarah said. "You don't want any real commitment. Perhaps it frightens you. I don't know."

"You wouldn't have liked it on a policeman's pay," Kenyon said. "No copper ever stayed at Claridges, as far as I know."

"That's pretty cheap," Sarah said. "You should know me better than that."

"Yes, I do," Kenyon said. "Sorry. I expect that's the first time you've ever heard me apologize."

Sarah smiled for the first time since he had walked in. "Yes," she said. "Wonders will never cease."

"If you give it a little time," Kenyon said, "you never know what other marvels you may hear."

"It's too late, Sid," Sarah said.

Kenyon was not sure that it was. Suppose he were to say something like, "All right, I'll tell you the truth. When it first happened, I didn't think about so-called love. I've seen too many people hurt each other in the name of love. I've seen too many crimes committed in the name of love, including murder. It's used all too often to excuse anything you like. Perhaps that's why I'm wary of it. Perhaps that's why I let you go without saying it. I think if I'd said it then, you wouldn't have gone to Harry Coleman. But when you'd gone, I knew that I felt something for you I'd felt for no other woman. Not just in bed. But talking to you, knowing I could see you every day, just being with you, and if that's love, yes, I loved you then, without knowing it. Now I do know it. Stay in London. It's never too late for anything. It'll be harder now, but we could still make it."

All he had to do was to say some of the things he had so often thought. She would stay then. He was sure of it. She was running away because she was afraid. She was afraid because she wanted him.

There was a tap at the door.

"Come in," Sarah said.

A porter came in. He saw Kenyon. "Sorry, madam," he said. "I'll come back later." He was about to retreat and close the door. Sarah blinked uncertainly, and fumbled for a cigarette.

"No, you can take Mrs. Coleman's luggage down now," Kenyon said. "I was just leaving." The porter held the door open for him. "Give my regards to your husband," Kenyon said to Sarah. "Say I'll write and tell him how grateful I am."

Kenyon kept the self-drive car for the time being. The five thousand pounds planted in his bank account had been handed over to the police. He was distinctly short of ready cash.

He drove to Saffron Walden, got the house ready for his father, and went to bring him home on the appointed day.

His father settled into his favorite armchair with a sigh of relief. "Well, I've cheated the old man with the scythe yet again," he said, with satisfaction.

"Don't push your luck," Kenyon said.

"Are you staying long?" his father asked.

"Until the weekend," Kenyon said. "Just to make sure you're all right."

"I'll be all right," his father said. "You don't have to worry about me, you know."

"Perhaps not," Kenyon said. "But even a cat's only supposed to have nine lives, and you're no cat."

His father chuckled. "What have you been doing with yourself?" he asked.

"Nothing much," Kenyon said.

"Time you got yourself married," his father said.

"The right one got away," Kenyon said lightly. "Oh, one piece of news. I think I shall be made up to Chief Inspector pretty soon."

"About bloody time too," his father said.